PAPER CUT

By

Matt Shultz

Editors

MATT SHULTZ
BIANCA KAHMANN
EMMA LENNINGS

Published By

JADE8 BOOKS

First Printing: 2023
ISBN
978-1-4478-4589-8

JADE8 BOOKS
Ordering Information:
Special discounts are available on quantity purchases.
AUS, NZ & U.S. trade bookstores and wholesalers:
Please contact: Jade8 Books via the Email below,
Email address: jade8books@yahoo.com

<u>Dedications</u>

To those who have supported me throughout this crazy endeavour, thank you. Some of you have left this world while others have simply left the path that I'm still traveling on, but from the bottom of my heart, thank you.

To my beautiful little family that have seen little more than the back of my head and the front of the computer screen on many occasions - you guys mean the world to me.

PROLOGUE

A hand opened a laptop and waited for it to boot up. After entering the password, an infinity symbol appeared on the computer's home screen.

In the top right corner, there were only two icons: The Tor icon, used to access the dark web, and the standard Internet Explorer icon.

The cursor slid over to the Tor icon and activated the application.

In a matter of seconds, the user was logged onto the dark net.

The website WWW.JOE.COM was typed into the search bar and then the user pressed enter.

The WWW.JOE.COM webpage quickly loaded and displayed the same infinity logo as the computer's home screen, only it was red.

Upon moving the cursor to the small Infinity logo in the top left corner of the screen, a roll-down menu appeared featuring a tab that read "Sign In."

Using the username, Joe.Jadestown, quick fingers punched in an unknown ten-digit password before hitting the enter key.

Once logged into the website, a list of sub-menus appeared on the left of the screen:

Inbox
Compose
The Original 8
Active assignments
Past assignments
Past players

The user scrolled to the inbox button clicked it, and then opened the newest message, titled,
CONGRATULATIONS
The message read as follows:

Joe,
We would like to congratulate you on successfully completing your fifteenth and final assignment. Much the same as your previous fourteen assignments, your final was passed with a hundred percent pass mark; therefore, we three of The Original 8 unanimously agree that you are ready to be activated.

As a result of carefully evaluating your proposed target, the newly promoted and very competent Captain Nicholas Dikes, as well as your recommended tactics and methods, your match has been approved.

A considerable amount of thought, time and effort has
been spent on finding your initial contact piece.
And so, it is with much pride that we can finally
announce its location to you.

Morgan Visinlary Art Exhibition
Helen Rown-Thrope building
Room 3, Chamber 2, Piece 7

Make them conscious
Make them witness
Make them fear
Make them suffer

Regards,
The original 8

The cursor moved down to the message's attachment
and clicked on the attached PDF file.
As the PDF file opened, it revealed that it was a digital
ticket for the exclusive Morgan Visionary Art Exhibition,
which was invite-only from the mayor's office.
While the user contemplated, his index finger tapped on
the side of the keyboard.
"That is interesting," a quiet voice stated in a very
gentle tone.
After that, the PDF and Tor windows were closed, and
the laptop was turned off.

CHAPTER ONE

PRESENT DAY

The air was stiflingly humid and still, the street eerily quiet in the sweltering midday heat. Steam rose from the weathered asphalt of the deserted warehouse district opposite Jadestown City.

The sky was an unbroken, cloudless blue, a reminder of the earlier downpour that had become a frequent occurrence at this time of year.

The only sounds were from the gentle sighing of the wind between the old warehouses and buildings and the rhythmic tapping of loose sheets of metal roofing; these hypnotic and calming sounds were gradually drowned out by the roaring engine of an approaching vehicle.

The thunderous roar of the engine and screeching of tyres echoed through the densely packed metal and wooden warehouses as the car wound its way through the deserted streets, becoming louder and louder as it drew nearer to its destination.

Suddenly an unmarked police car, a gold-coloured Holden commodore, skidded around the corner, tyres screeching as they struggled for grip against the slick asphalt. It veered out of control for a moment, but its driver quickly regained control and accelerated towards the warehouse at the end of the cul-de-sac.

Gathered around the warehouse, scores of uniformed police officers from the Jadestown Police Department (JAPD), plain-clothed detectives, Special Weapons And Tactics (SWAT) officers, and emergency service personnel stood in small groups, conversing when the sound of screeching tyres and revving engine quickly drew their attention to see the gold sedan sliding sideways into the street.

"Jesus!" Officer Pike exclaimed as he and the other officer pushed off the bonnets of their squad cars, having been instructed to park their vehicles nose-to-nose to block the street from any incoming traffic.
The driver of the speeding unmarked police car slammed on the brakes, bringing it skidding to a halt just inches from Officer Pike's squad car.

"Oh shit, it's Dikes!" He muttered under his breath when he spotted Detective Dikes through the front windshield.

"That's Jack's car, isn't it?" the other officer whispered as he moved to the front of the now stationary gold sedan, which was making a metallic creaking sound due to the overheating engine.

"Makes sense, though, doesn't it?" Pike whispered his reply.
Before Pike could say anything else, Detective Nicholas Dikes, a man in his late thirties, threw open the car door and climbed out. His wet, blood-covered and raggedy

clothes and his bloodied and bruised physical appearance made it clear he had been brutally beaten.

Dike's face was a mess.

Along with the blood, bruises, cuts and scrapes on his left cheek, he had a deep laceration across the bridge of his nose, which appeared to be broken.

Unfazed by any of this, Dikes marched forward with a slight limp towards Officer Pike.

"Where is he?" Dikes asked bitterly.

"Sir, the chief would like to brief you before–"

"Where is he?" Dikes roared without breaking stride.

Chief Bryant appeared at the warehouse's office door. Seeing Dikes so severely battered, Chief Bryant wasn't able to mask his concern for his lead detective and friend.

"He's in here, Nick." Chief Bryant said gently.

Dikes pushed past Pike and stormed across the open concrete pad, which led to the warehouses front stairs. Bryant stepped aside to let him in, looking him over in the process.

"Jesus, son, what did he do to-"

"The son of a bitch has Jack!" Dikes interrupted. "He had a gun to my fucking head and–" Dikes stopped short, noting the lack of surprise on the chief's face.

"What?" Dikes asked as he stepped inside and surveyed the dozen or so officers and detectives present. All conversations had stopped as soon as Dikes had entered, which both worried and angered him. Then, taking a deep breath to calm himself, he turned back to Chief Bryant.

"We know he has Jack," Bryant said.

Smith and Tran exchanged uneasy glances, their discomfort not going unnoticed by Dikes.

As he became aware of every eye upon him, a wave of nervousness swept over him, it was then he realised something was terribly wrong.

Chief Bryant, understanding the gravity of the situation, requested that everyone leave the room.

Officers and detectives filed out immediately, leaving Dikes, Chief Bryant, Smith, Tran, and four heavily-armed SWAT officers.

Two of the SWAT officers were posted at the foot of the stairs, and the other two were halfway up to the half-landing.

Bryant gestured for Captain Hale, the commander of the SWAT team, to approach.

As soon as Smith noticed her opportunity to speak to Dikes, she stepped closer.

With her intense focus and dedication to her work, Detective Smith, one of the few female detectives in the ranks, was viewed as being just as tough as her male counterparts, only a hell of a lot smarter than most of them. She had a special talent for seeing things from a different perspective than most people; this was something she recognized in Dikes, her recruiter, and the other five detectives that made up her squad. Working together, they formed a highly effective team unlike any other squad she had ever been a part of.

"What happened out there, boss?" she asked quietly as she examined his face.

Tran, an attractive and intelligent man renowned for his bravery, was chosen two years ago by Detective Dikes to join his task force. Recently, he showcased his mettle with an impressive feat - successfully solving an arson investigation and rescuing twelve people from a burning building, all within the same hour.
He had walked across and was now accompanying Detective Smith and Chief Bryant.
Dikes was about to respond to Smith, but he closed his mouth and shook his head when Captain Hale approached.

"Captain," Hale said, nodding at Dikes while pointedly avoiding looking at and not mentioning his bruised and battered face.
Dikes gave an almost imperceptible nod.

"How's the perimeter looking, Captain?" Chief Bryant asked, briefly glancing at Dikes.

"We're ready to go, sir. I've got three men on the far side of the adjacent stairwell, two on the roof and two sections along the streets surrounding the warehouse," Hale informed him. "This prick isn't going anywhere."

"He chose this place for a reason," Dikes remarked, looking around the room. "He didn't just stumble upon it. There'll be some kind of exit strategy you haven't considered yet. There's no way he's boxed himself in like this without an escape plan," an irritated Dikes explained.

Captain Hale gave Dikes a stern look but chose to let Dikes' comment slide and remained silent, understanding the stress and hardship Dikes had been experiencing in the past weeks and would soon face.

"We've done a recon of the entire warehouse, Detective. We were also able to find an old set of blueprints online. From them, we've managed to locate a hidden door on the upper level, two on the ground and one that opens directly into the warehouse adjacent to this one. All of these exits are covered either by my men, yours or the water rats. And, in the unlikely event he uses the hatch on the roof, I have a man positioned up there, plus a sniper that can be moved to cover that position." Bryant patted Captain Hale on the shoulder before Dikes could respond.

"Very good, thank you, Captain." Chief Bryant gave Hale a thankful nod. He then placed a hand on each of Dikes' shoulders.

"We need to talk about what happens from here," he said in a reserved tone as he ushered Dikes to a table in the corner of the room. The table was bare except for a mobile monitor that displayed only black-and-white static. Bryant looked into Dikes' bloodshot and exhausted eyes because he needed to gauge his state of mind. He was about to explain the rules of engagement laid out for him to follow by the country's most deceptive and violent serial killer.

"Joe said you and you alone are to head up to the second floor. He said he'll be waiting for you in one of the rooms there." Chief Bryant took a breath. "Now, he didn't say which one, but–" the rest of whatever Chief Bryant had to say dissolved in his throat. All he could do was hold Dikes by the shoulders and look sadly into his eyes.

Smith and Tran stood silently, their faces full of empathy, as they watched Chief Bryant struggle to deliver the devastating news he wasn't able to avoid.

Dikes gnashed his teeth and shook his head, growing more agitated by the second. "What's going on?" he asked as his gaze shifted between Smith and Tran before settling back on Chief Bryant. "I got the same look from them out there as you three are giving me now in here." He thundered as he pointed toward the door. "So, if you got something to say, Chief, just fuckin'-"

"He has Sarah and Marilyn too!" the chief stated forcefully, a lump forming in his throat.

Dikes felt a wave of nausea wash over him as Chief Bryant said Sarah's name; instantly, his mind raced as he tried to process this news.

"What? How? She was being watched by-" he stammered, attempting to comprehend the situation as he freed himself from the chief's grasp.

Smith dabbed tears from her eyes, "He killed them."

"No! Nooo!" Dikes bellowed, imagining the worst. Desperate to find a way to help, he frantically tried to consider his options, but his thoughts were filled with visions of Sarah suffering at the hands of the psychopath.

Dikes' lungs constricted as he struggled to process the unbearable knowledge. His muscles tightened to the point that he thought he was going to have a heart attack.

"He can't have her!" he shouted, his voice filled with anguish.

"I'm so sorry, son." Chief Bryant said quietly as he watched Dikes with a look of utter despair.
Letting out a painful scream, Dikes felt the reality of what was happening crash into his mind.

"Goddamn it!" he yelled, his hands curling into tight fists as he paced along the wall. "Goddamn it! That son of a bitch!" he shouted, throwing his fist through the nearest wall.
Those left in the room could do nothing but watch helplessly as Dikes suddenly charged toward the stairs like a raging bull.

"Just remember his rules, Nick! It might help save them up there," Bryant shouted after him.

"I don't give a shit about his rules anymore!" Dikes replied without turning. "I'm done playing this game! It ends today!"
Just as Dikes was about to bulldoze his way through the SWAT officers at the bottom of the stairs, Captain Hale grabbed him by the upper arm, holding him firmly in place while shoving a bulletproof vest into his chest.

"I know you're raging in there right now; I really do!" Hale said sympathetically as he tapped the side of Dikes' head, "But you need to keep it calm up there," he jerked his chin to the ceiling and then retrieved his personal sidearm, a Glock, and pushed it into Dikes' hand. "Now, I know he said no weapons... but, fuck him!" Hale said softly. "Just watch your spray, control your breathing… and take his fuckin' head off."

With a look that said more than words ever could, Dikes nodded, then tucked the Glock into the back of his trousers. He paused, groaning from the pain as he put on the bulletproof vest over his bloodied shirt, then bounded up the stairs.

Donning his bulletproof vest, Dikes drew the pistol as he ascended the staircase.

Once he was at the top of the staircase, he was presented with two hallways.

He followed his instincts and, for whatever reason, took the right-hand hall, pausing at each door to listen for any sign of his wife or partner. Finally, behind the fourth door, he thought he heard the sound of muffled voices. This instantly made his chest tighten and his heart pound – he'd found them!

Dikes took a moment, listening intently.

Then, after a few seconds of silence, he raised his pistol, stepped back and then kicked open the door.

Joe's eyes narrowed briefly as he watched Dikes storm in, pistol raised.

Knowing the frame of mind Dikes would be in, Joe made sure to stay directly behind Sarah for protection.

Inside the room, Dikes saw Sarah and Marilyn forced into a kneeling position at the back of the room, bound and gagged. Both had their hands tied in their laps with wide, silver duct tape and had homemade grenade-covered suicide vests locked onto them by two heavy-duty padlocks, one under each armpit.

Zip-tied to the middle of Sarah's vest was a timer counting down from five minutes and thirty-seven seconds.

To Dikes' left, his lifelong friend and police partner, Jack, was slumped against a wall. A blood-soaked pillowcase covered his head, and his white long-sleeve business shirt was stained with blood around a bullet wound in the top of his left shoulder.

A sword, still in its sheath, was laid neatly at his feet. The sight of his loved ones in such a terrible predicament made Dikes' brain lock up momentarily in shock.

It took another second for him to regain control and the first thing he did, which was something taught at the academy, was to scan the room.

In the brief time he had, he took in as many details of Joe's carefully designed scene as he could. Then, his gaze fell upon the reason they were all there - Joe. He was skulking behind the two women, using them as shields while hiding his face behind Sarah's long blonde hair. The only thing Dikes could see of Joe was the sleeves of his black trench coat as he moved his arms about.

Seeing Sarah this way made his heart sink and his stomach plummet.

Dikes noticed that her eyes were red from crying, but they were now dry. In other words, she had mentally prepared herself to face whatever Joe had planned for her head-on.

Looking at each other, Dikes noticed that she managed to flick him an eyebrow raise in greeting.

Jesus, I love you, he said to himself when he thought of her bravery.

Dikes snapped himself back to the present situation and noticed that all the pins on the vest-mounted grenades were connected by thin wires that led back to Joe. Looking around the room, he realized the building must have once been a meat packing plant. Dikes was certain that the room was not chosen randomly; he was convinced there was a purpose behind it, and he was determined to uncover the reason before Joe could execute whatever he had planned.

As Dikes' eyes took in the room, he saw that it still had several old metal hooks mounted along a rusted metal railing.

"So glad you could join us, Nicholas," Joe said calmly. "I hope I did not mess up that face of yours too much."

The rage within Dikes was palpable as Joe's words and voice dripped with cruel sarcasm. Dikes continually looked for a clear shot, desperately trying to ignore Joe's taunts.

"Careful now, Detective. You'd hate to put a bullet through this pretty little face, wouldn't you?" Joe teased as he stroked Sarah's hair.

Dikes' blood boiled at the sight of Joe touching Sarah. He narrowed his eyes, searching for any part of Joe's head that he could get a shot at, confident in his ability to hit a small target if given a chance.

"As I told them downstairs, you needn't bother with your weapon Nicholas. It will prove quite useless in here. So, place it at your feet and kick it away, please," Joe chided.

"I'll put it down when your brains hit the fucking floor!" Dikes snarled back.

"Nicholas, my boy, you disappoint me. We have discussed this many times before, have we not? Profanity really is unnecessary. All it proves is your lack of self-control and that your brain has barely developed past that of one of your Neolithic forebears."

"Let them go. I'm here now. You don't need them anymore," Dikes declared firmly as his gaze darted between Sarah and Jack.

"Yes, you are here now," Joe said with a chill in his voice, "but no one is leaving yet. We have not finished this round."
Jack groaned and stirred, lifting his head briefly before it fell back down. This caught Marilyn and Dikes' attention. Marilyn started to yell something, but it was completely muffled by the thick gag.

"He is still very much alive, if that is what you are wondering? But for how long and in what condition will be very much up to you."

Dikes' fingers tightened around the grip of his pistol as he asked, "What have you done to him?"

"Behind you is a table," Joe directed, his tone emotionless. "On that table is a camera with a flashing red button. Press it, and I will tell you."

Dikes was reluctant to look away because he didn't trust Joe, but despite this, he forced himself to glance back to identify the red button that Joe was talking about. In the split second it took him to look, Dikes saw a table with a camera perched atop a short tripod.

Dikes glanced at Sarah, mulling over the situation. Then, Joe's voice, disinterested, broke through his thoughts: "Jack does not have all day, Nicholas."

So, without taking his eyes off Joe, Dikes hesitantly stepped back, feeling for the small tripod-mounted camera with its flashing red button. He found it and pressed the button.

* * *

Down in the front office area of the warehouse, police and detectives had begun to file back in.

Chief Bryant, Smith, and Tran were discussing "what if" scenarios while SWAT waited at the bottom of the stairs talking tactics.

Suddenly, Tran noticed the monitor had turned on, and his voice cut through the room: "Hey! Hey! Hey! It's on! The screen's on!"

Everyone hurried over to the monitor.

Video from the upstairs room flashed onto the screen. Chief Bryant, Smith, and Captain Hale rushed over to the monitor.

They were able to witness Dikes on the monitor with his pistol pointed at the left of his fiancée's head. This was the first time they had seen what had become of Sarah, Jack, and Marilyn.

Smith gasped and covered her mouth.

"That fucking asshole," Tran muttered barely above a whisper as he shook his head.

Chief Bryant was unable to contain his emotions; tears formed in his eyes, and his heart was pounding as he watched on, unable to help.

He had been in the force for more than half his life and had seen all kinds of unpleasant scenes, yet none were as reprehensible and diabolical as what Joe had been putting Dikes and his squad through. This past two weeks had the chief questioning his faith, a remarkable feat for a man like Trevor Bryant.

Captain Hale was the only one who could somewhat contain his emotions. After seeing the screen, he stepped away to quietly report the developing situation to his team over their neck-mounted coms gear.

Tran was first to notice Jack and leaned in close to the screen to get a better look. "What's with Jack? And what's over his head?" he asked.

Hearing this, Captain Hale quickly moved back to take a closer look at the screen.

He and everyone else observing leaned in to try and figure out what it was on Jack's head.

Hale took in as many technical and weaponry details as possible, then stepped away to relay the information to his team again.

* * *

Dikes stepped back towards the trio, only stopping when Joe told him to.

"I pressed the button; now answer the question! What have you done to Jack? And why is that over his head?" Dikes asked, jerking his chin at the blood-soaked pillowcase.

Joe remained silent for a long while, so long that Dikes was ready to ask the question again, but this time a little more forcefully.

Then he finally spoke, "Your partner has been given a small amount of morphine and is currently under a general anesthetic. An anesthetic from which he will soon be waking. He was given the anesthetic to counteract the severe pain he would currently be feeling," Joe explained plainly, glancing down at his watch.

"Why?" Dikes asked as he stole a glance at Marilyn.

"Why what, Nicholas? Be more specific, please," Joe admonished him.

"Why would he be in pain? Are you talking about his shoulder?" Dikes asked. Even as the words left his mouth, Dikes knew it had nothing to do with Jack's shoulder. He was just hoping.

He had noticed that whenever Jack was mentioned or whenever he moved, Marilyn would strain against her bonds and gag as her pleading eyes, red and puffy, tried to tell him something.

Dikes could only shake his head apologetically for not understanding what she was trying to convey and for dragging them into this mess.

Joe snorted. "No Detective, not from the nine-millimetre minor flesh wound to his left shoulder." At that moment, Jack's head lifted and then flopped forward again, eliciting more painful groans.

Screaming beneath her gag, Marilyn leaned forward as if to stand but was forcefully pulled back to her knees by Joe.

"Stay where you are!" he growled, then added, "or else."

Trembling, Marilyn stayed in her place, too fearful of the consequences of any further movement.

Dikes had had enough of this. "Stop stalling, Joe; what did you do to him?" Dikes asked in as calm a tone as he could muster.

"You want to know why he's pumped full of painkillers?" Joe asked. "It's because peeling a man's face off without employing anaesthetic would be considered inhumane, wouldn't you agree, Detective?" Joe explained, his voice scathing. Upon delivering the astonishing news, Joe stuck his head out from behind Sarah, wearing Jack's face as a mask.

At that moment, it felt like the room had caved in around him.

Dikes was overwhelmed with a myriad of emotions yet felt none of them. His mind was in a state of chaos.

In the wake of this horrific sight, Dikes hesitated and failed to take the shot. By the time he finally lifted his weapon, Joe had already tucked his head back behind Sarah's, and it was too late.

Dikes was shocked to the core, and he could only stare in horror at Jack's stirring body, especially the bloodied and dripping pillowcase and then at Marilyn, who was shaking her head, screaming and crying.

Slowly, Dikes lowered his weapon, helpless to do anything else.

* * *

The room downstairs was filled with a range of emotions, from grief-stricken cries to simmering anger, but everyone was united in their sorrow for all involved upstairs.

Not a single person had the capacity to take action, their only sound being that of heavy breaths and muffled sobs.

Tran had to step away from the monitor, and as he pushed his way through the silent group, tears streamed down his face. Upon reaching the front door, he had to lean forward onto his knees and take deep breaths to stop himself from being sick.

Smith, overwhelmed with emotion, placed her hands atop her head and had to turn away, tears streaming down her face.

Chief Bryant was in shock and could see that his fellow officers were too. He felt helpless and confused, unable to think of anything to say or do.

Finally, Captain Hale had reached his breaking point. He turned away from the monitor and met the gaze of his SWAT team, discernible rage radiating from each of their faces. Some of them nodded in silent agreement, expressing their readiness to take whatever action was necessary.

* * *

"Who do you think the face looks better on, Nicholas? Me or old faceless Jack over there?" Joe provoked, his voice dripping with mocking laughter.

Marilyn screamed what Dikes assumed was a plethora of expletives while violently shaking with the force of her anger and fear.

Dikes felt like he was on a carnival ride combined with the world's worst hangover. His head was spinning before abruptly coming to a sudden stop at the sound of Marilyn's haunting screams.

Gritting his teeth, Dikes almost lost control as he stepped forward, ready to take a shot. "You motherfu-" he growled, but Joe silenced him by jerking Sarah's head back and pressing a large hunting knife to her throat.

"Careful there, Detective," Joe said calmly, keeping Sarah's head between himself and Dikes' weapon. "You could really hurt someone with that," he taunted.

Dikes shifted his weight, glancing left and right in a desperate attempt to get a shot off, but Joe was just as quick in finding cover.

"Well, this is fun," Joe teased.

Realizing he wasn't going to get a shot off, Dikes stepped back half a step and lowered his pistol slightly, pleading, "Just let them go! This is between you and me – it has nothing to do with them!" he implored desperately, his words laced with a hint of aggression,

"Ahhh, but they do, Nicholas. And unfortunately for them, it was your inability to follow simple procedures that has brought this upon them, and like all penalties, there is a time limit. And, as you can see," Joe tapped the timer on Sarah's chest with the tip of the knife. "You are running out of it."

Dikes' gaze darted between Sarah, Marilyn, and the timer as Jack suddenly stirred again.

There was now less than three minutes remaining.

"Everyone you hold dear is in need of your urgent attention. So, make your choice, Detective, and make it quick."

Dikes shook his head, despairing at the impossible situation he found himself in. No matter which way he looked at it, he knew one of the people he loved was going to suffer.

"You do not have the time to hesitate, Nicholas," Joe said, pressing the blade closer to Sarah's throat. "Must I use her to force your hand? And trust me, I will not be as gentle with her as I was with you earlier." His cold tone made it clear he meant every word.

Desperate to save his loved ones, Dikes considered shooting Joe through Sarah, but he knew he could never bring himself to do it, so unless he was able to think of something else, they were trapped.

Joe slowly shook his head, disappointment evident in his voice.

"This situation is out of your control. The illusion of control you think you have and the bright idea you think is just a thought away— it is all a mirage Detective. You cannot do anything other than decide between the two choices I have laid at your feet; you are a bystander with a minor role to play in all of this. So, play your part."

Dikes shook his head in defiance. "Bullshit!" he snarled as his eyes flicked to Sarah.

Joe sighed. "I am afraid you are going to force my hand. And as such, I will have no choice but to remove the one thing that is distracting you," he threatened, his voice taut with tension. "I will say it again. Put your weapon on the floor and kick it aside."

Dikes remained silent, shaking his head, hoping to get that one last opportunity to take Joe's head off.

"Look around you, Nicholas – right here, right now. You have everything to gain and everything to lose. So, for the last time, put… your… weapon… down." Joe drawled to emphasise the gravity of the situation.

Dikes resolutely refused to relinquish his pistol, his only means of defending his loved ones against Joe or finding a way out of this predicament.

Joe had run out of patience. So, to prove his dominance over both the situation and Dikes, he quickly plunged the hunting knife deep into Sarah's thigh.

Sarah screamed and collapsed forward in agony, but Joe quickly grabbed a fistful of her hair and yanked her head back.

Horrified, Dikes shouted and lunged forward, ready to shoot Joe in the head. "Argh, God damn you!" he yelled.

"Careful now; we do not want to end this party before it really gets going, do we?" Joe jeered, still holding the knife in Sarah's thigh.

"You're dead! You're a fucking dead man!" Dikes screamed as he struggled to contain his rage.

His anger was so great that it took all his self-restraint not to rush forward and attack Joe with the stock of his pistol. Joe tilted his head and then slowly twisted the knife, eliciting an even louder scream from Sarah. Her terrible, pain-induced scream reverberated around the room.

"You are still holding your weapon, Detective." Joe reminded Dikes evenly.

"Stop! Fucking stop! Take it out of her leg!" Dikes pleaded, stepping forward once more but holding the pistol in a non-threatening manner.

"Uh uh uh, that is close enough," Joe said firmly. "Now back up, Detective," he barked.

Though Dikes raised his pistol once more in anger, he was well aware that Joe had the upper hand. Glancing briefly at Jack, who was helpless, and Sarah, who was agonised with the hunting knife still buried in her thigh, he reluctantly lowered his weapon.

"Fuuuck!" Dikes yelled in utter frustration.

"That's a good boy. Now place it on the floor and kick it away," Joe commanded.

Dikes complied, placing the pistol on the floor and kicking it away to his right.

Joe yanked the knife from Sarah's leg, and she quickly clasped her bound hands over the gushing wound, stifling a scream of pain.

"Let them go—please," Dikes pleaded, his hands raised in surrender.

"It is a bit too late for manners, Nicholas. So, no, I will not be letting them go. Not only are they here as a penalty, but they will be lucky enough to witness your transformation."

Joe could see from the confusion on Dikes' face that the detective had no idea what he was talking about, so, seeing that he had the time, he explained.

"Nothing you do from this day forward will ever be taken for granted again. You will see the world in a new light—your eyes will be opened, and in a sense, you will be reborn."

As Jack's moans and movements grew louder and more frequent, Dikes' gaze flitted back and forth between him and Sarah's bleeding leg.

Joe noticed that Dikes had almost ceased paying attention to him, his focus squarely on Jack.

"Curious, aren't you? You are curious to see if I am telling the truth. Well, there is only one way to find out. Go over, remove his cover and look at his mutilated face. See what I have done to him, what he has become because of you and the choices that you made."

Dikes glanced at the pillowcase, which was now completely stained with Jack's blood as his leg twitched, and his hand flinched.

Dikes ran his hand over his face, his gaze now shifting between Marilyn, who was fiercely pleading with him beneath her gag, and Sarah, who was weeping and clutching her badly bleeding leg.

Then, knowing he had to see with his own eyes, Dikes heaved a sigh and moved toward Jack, kneeling in front of him.

"One day, you will thank me for opening your eyes to this prodigious new world, Nicholas; you really will," Joe assured Dikes while watching him closely.

Reluctantly, Dikes stepped forward, clenching his eyes shut to drown out Joe's taunting voice.

"Ooh, what a quandary! Do you use the sword to end your best friend's lifetime of agony, despair, and deformity, or do you let him live and forever have the blood of your wife on your hands?" Joe said excitedly as he savoured every moment of Dikes' suffering.

Dikes' head was spinning, and he couldn't comprehend the prospect of him having to take part in such a horrendous no-win situation.

"If you think about it, I have made the decision almost too easy for you. You have to admit, your options are now rather one-sided, are they not? You should be grateful, Detective," Joe said.

* * *

Outside the warehouse, the sound of an approaching motorbike brought a welcome interruption to the tense atmosphere.

Officer Pike and his offsider stepped forward as a yellow Suzuki raced around the same corner that Jack's golden sedan had skidded around only moments before.

Officer Pike raised his hand in a signal for the rider to stop.

The dirt bike skidded to a stop in front of them. The two officers moved in, one on either side of the bike.

"Sir, you can't proceed any further," Pike instructed. "This area has been cordoned off as part of an active crime scene," he explained.

The rider leaned aside, trying to get a better look at the commotion ahead.

"Oh, shit! Really? What's happening?"

"I can't discuss the details of this ongoing investigation at this time," Pike replied.

He had said this line so often throughout his career that he was sure it would be the only thing he'd remember if he ever developed dementia.

"So, what are you doing down here, kid?" Pike asked the rider.

"I'm delivering a letter to Chief P. Bryant," the rider said distractedly, his eyes still drawn to the commotion ahead at the warehouse.

Pike clicked his fingers in front of the young man's helmet, which brought his attention back to Pike.

The rider took off his backpack and riffled through it with shaking hands until he pulled out an a4-sized envelope.

"It's for a Chief P. Bryant, see," he read from the front of the envelope.

Pike gave the other officer a bewildered look. Then he asked the rider again, "Are you sure it's for Chief Inspector Bryant?"

"Yeah, I guess so," the rider replied with a shrug, handing the envelope to Pike.

* * *

Beneath his mask of flesh, Joe's eyes widened with excitement as Marilyn's muffled yelling filled the room. As Dikes slowly knelt in front of his oldest and best friend, he had to continue drawing deep, steady breaths to attempt to remain composed.

Knowing what he was about to see, Dikes had to mentally mute Marilyn's pleading if he stood any chance of helping Jack out of this. Then, with shaking hands, Dikes slowly lifted the bottom of the bloodied pillowcase, only briefly pausing to gather himself before revealing whatever was under there.

Joe narrowed his eyes but kept silent, not wanting to disrupt Dikes' focus.

Dikes drew another steadying breath and then continued to slowly lift the pillowcase until he saw the exposed flesh of Jack's chin and bottom lip. Blood had begun to harden and coagulate in patches while teardrops of blood hung delicately from the bottom of the exposed fleshy chin.

Suddenly, Jack's head jerked upwards, flinging the drops of blood free.

Startled by the horrific sight before him, Dikes dropped the pillowcase and stumbled back, coughing and retching uncontrollably.

With Marilyn's muffled screams echoing inside his skull, Dikes was in debilitating shock as he stared dazedly at the pillowcase, the image of Jack's mutilated face beneath it forever seared into his psyche.

Again, Jack stirred and moaned painfully.

"You now have less than two minutes, Nicholas. Decision time. Would you drive the sword into his heart to free him from a life of knowing his face was peeled from his skull, or do you say goodbye to the girl? Tick, tock, tick, tock!" Joe goaded, revelling in Dikes' agony.

Joe felt a sense of overwhelming pride as he watched Detective Nicholas Dikes' torment, for he had spent years meticulously planning, initiating, constructing, and setting in motion all of the events that would lead the detective to be in this room, at this time and being forced into making an impossible decision.

Joe was proud of what he had accomplished and a smile formed under his fleshy mask.

This was new! He'd never known pride before!

Knowing what was ahead for Jack, Dikes examined the sword at Jack's feet for the first time, its image blurred by the tears welling in his eyes.

Forcing Dikes to make a quicker decision, Joe waved the bloodied knife in front of Sarah's face and drawled out his name sardonically. "Nicholas."

Dikes gritted his teeth, turning his full attention back to Jack and the sword: Could he really do this? Could Jack live without a face?

Burn victims have their skin practically melted off and still survive, he reasoned. He'd be in immense pain but alive. But Sarah would be dead. He thought as he closed his eyes. Dikes had made his decision.

And so it was; with shaking hands, he slowly reached for Jack's top button. Trembling, Dikes released the first button as Marilyn's muffled shouts filled the room. He attempted to ignore Sarah and Marilyn's cries as he unfastened the second and third buttons, one after the other. Just as he had undone the top three buttons, Jack's hand jolted, startling him.

"Shit... shit!" Dikes shouted in alarm, his heart pounding so loud it seemed to echo in his ears. "Fuck this..." he whispered to himself.

Dikes hesitated for a moment but then went ahead and did one more button.

Marilyn had stopped screaming for the moment and could only shake her head pleadingly as she watched Dikes' every move.

The sudden silence in the room was palpable, with all eyes fixated on him, intensifying his anxiety. Meanwhile, Sarah whimpered softly as she watched on, cradling her stab wound.

As Dikes gazed upon Jack's shrouded head, he attempted to push aside the knowledge of what lay hidden beneath the pillowcase.

What he had noticed now that Jack's shirt was half undone was a black dot had been drawn on his chest.

"I've taken the guesswork out of it for you. His heart is directly below that dot," Joe explained quietly in a tone that Dikes thought had sincerity.

"I can't... I just can't do this," Dikes stammered.

Joe slid the knife under Sarah's chin once again, pressing it just firm enough to break the skin.

"And that's your choice, Detective? If so, I can end this all right now."

"No!" Dikes barked as he threw a hand up in the stop gesture. "I'm thinking aloud, asshole!"

"Make no mistake, if you continue to be so indecisive, I will be forced to push this blade up through the top of her skull!" Joe challenged.

Dikes looked around the room, his heart thumping heavily in his chest. Finally, his gaze rested back on Jack and then the sword.

Shakily, he picked up the sword and removed it from its sheath.

"The sword is sharp; I sharpened it myself," Joe explained.

"Shut up! Just shut the fuck up!" Dikes yelled as he glared at Joe, rage flaring in his eyes as he raised the blade threateningly towards Jack's chest.

A sobbing Marilyn shook her head desperately, trying to dissuade Dikes from following through with it.

Dikes slowly and shakily raised the tip of the blade until it came to rest on the black dot on Jack's chest, though not firmly enough to draw blood.

Joe's eyes drank in the scene beneath the fleshy mask, savouring every second of it as Marilyn's horrified screams provided its soundtrack.

* * *

Downstairs in the front office area, Chief Bryant sought out Captain Hale, his voice shaking with emotion.

"Captain, is there any way we can get a shot at Joe from under the room?"

Hale shook his head. "No can do, Chief. There are way too many industrial pipes blocking our access to that area of the warehouse. To take a shot like that with no prep time and no eyes in the room, there's no way we wouldn't miss the women. I assume that's why he specifically chose that room." The speed of Hale's reply indicated that he and his team had already run this scenario through to its inevitable conclusion. "Sorry, Chief." He said as he patted Chief Bryant on the shoulder and then walked back to his team.

Overhearing the conversation, a disappointed Tran turned his gaze to the monitor as Officer Pike ran into the room, handing Chief Bryant an envelope.

"This was just delivered for you, sir."

Bryant took the envelope, read his name on the front, and flipped it over. "It's from him," he muttered, seeing the neatly written name, Joe, on the top-left corner.

This got everyone's attention, and the room quickly fell quiet.

Tran and Smith rushed over to examine what was in the envelope.

Bryant swiftly opened the envelope and retrieved two photographs, causing murmurs of astonishment to ripple throughout the room.

"My God!" Smith exclaimed.

"Jesus," Chief Bryant breathed.

Seeing the photographs, Tran immediately recognised the urgency of the situation and pushed his way through the crowd and ran towards the stairs, yelling, "Dikes, no! Don't do it! Don't do it!"

"Let him through!" Chief Bryant yelled to the SWAT team on the stairs.

Chief Bryant and Smith quickly raced back through the throng of people to view the monitor.

Captain Hale, stepping aside as Tran passed, ran over to the screen and asked Chief Bryant, "What's going on? What was in the envelope?"

Bryant handed him the envelope and the two photographs.

"Oh shit," was all that Hale could say.

* * *

Joe checked his watch before tugging on a cable that was hidden behind him. The small red light on the camera faded, and the device shut off.

* * *

The monitor downstairs flickered to static. "No! Damn it!" Smith's helpless shouts echoed throughout the warehouse office.

They were now blind to what was about to happen upstairs.

* * *

Crying, Dikes turned to Marilyn, "I'm so sorry, Mare," he apologised. His words sounded hollow in his ears, and he could only imagine how empty they must have sounded to Marilyn.

Despite the gag, she still tried desperately to communicate with him as tears streamed down her cheeks.

If I'm going to do this, I have to make it quick, for Jack's sake, Dikes thought to himself as he closed his eyes and turned back to face Jack.

Drawing a deep breath, he opened his eyes and tightened his grip on the sword's hilt.

* * *

Tran rushed up the stairs, his pistol drawn. "Dikes, stop! Don't do it!" he yelled.

* * *

"I'm sorry, my friend," Dikes whispered, tears flowing freely. Then, with one long breath, he...

CHAPTER TWO

THREE WEEKS AGO

"Hey, Jonesy," Jack called from the table he and the squad shared. "Don't worry about Nick's Pepsi for this round." He jerked a thumb toward the restaurant's front door.

Detective Jones glanced through the crowded restaurant and spotted his captain getting his photo taken with two giddy, middle-aged ladies.

Outside, a small group of people had gathered, eagerly awaiting a chance to take a selfie or get an autograph from former movie star and current Detective Nicholas Dikes.

The Maître D' noticed the commotion and quickly moved to free his high-profile customer. However, before he had a chance to ask them to back away, Dikes held up a hand to signal his approval. He then flashed his signature 'wedding smile' for a photo, a preloaded facial expression he'd perfected for weddings, newspaper articles, selfies, and other photo shoots that he occasionally agreed to do.

Between having his picture taken with fans, Dikes had found his table and held up a hand, mouthing, "I'll be five minutes," to Jack.

Jack replied with a thumbs up, then turned to everyone at the table as Jones placed the tray of drinks on the table.

"He'll be with us in about twenty minutes," Jack informed the group.

Smith frowned upon seeing Dikes mouth the words "five minutes" to Jack whilst holding up five fingers.

As the newest members of the squad, Smith and Tran had yet to figure out all of their high-profile superior officer's intricacies.

"When the boss says he'll be a fan's five, that's a minimum of twenty to twenty-five minutes," Bradshaw explained.

"A fan five?" Tran asked, exchanging a puzzled glance with Smith.

"Oh, yeah," Jones chimed in as he settled into his seat. "The boss has a few variations of five minutes. First, there's the fan five, which you'll see through to its conclusion in about nineteen-ish minutes. Then there's his 'I've just had my ass handed to me, and it's going to roll downhill, so everyone in the conference room in five minutes' five."

"How long is that five minutes?" Smith asked.

"If you get to the room in two minutes," Jack answered with raised eyebrows, "and he's already there, then you're already five minutes late."

"Ahhh, but don't worry about that one; it's an easy one to tell. It's all in his tone," Jones said with a wink and a tilt of his glass. Then, halfway through a sip, he abruptly knocked his knuckles on the table, remembering another one. "Then there's his driving fives."

Tran and Smith shared a baffled look as Jack and Bradshaw laughed. "Oh yeah," they said, still snickering.

"Now, these are tricky because they don't go by distance or time. They go by mood. Sometimes he'll have to be across town, which is an easy twenty-five to thirty-minute drive, and he'll message you just after he leaves the precinct to tell you he's five out. Other times he's literally around the corner when-" Bradshaw placed his hands over his mouth to imitate a CB radio: "Yeah, Central, this is unit 8-12. Tell the squad I'm five out from the scene." "No sooner has Central clicked off than he's stepping under the bloody yellow tape."

Jack, Bradshaw, and Jones all laughed and nodded in agreement. "I've been caught out by that one a few times," Jones admitted.

Judging by the other's expressions, they'd been victims of the same trick.

They'd called these weekly squad dinners 'squeeklys'. And it was at the squeeklys that Tran and Smith came by this type of menial but informative information about their fellow detectives, both professionally and personally.

Dikes and Jack started the squeeklys back in their early days as detectives. They did so to foster closer connections with their squad mates. Over time, their weekly dinners grew so popular that they occasionally extended invitations to other police officers, detectives, politicians, and even reporters with whom the squad had good relationships. For those not in Dikes' inner circle and not invited to a dinner, this was sometimes a source of disappointment and created chatter and jealousy within the ranks, something Dikes and Jack never tolerated. At their very first squeekly, Dikes had told Tran and Smith the one and only rule: when you're at a squeekly, you're just one of six or seven friends coming together to talk, joke around, and have a good meal. There is no rank when you're sitting at the table.

As Bradshaw had predicted, it was twenty-one minutes before Dikes finally arrived and joined them at the table. In his left hand, he had a large, black plastic bag.

"Evening all, sorry about that," Dikes apologised as he shook everyone's hand around the table—except for Smith, whom he kissed on the cheek.

"All good, mate. The same thing happened to Jack and me when we arrived," Bradshaw joked as he pushed the new round of drinks to the appropriate people. Everyone laughed.

"I don't know how you do it all the time; I couldn't do it," Jones admitted, looking around the restaurant at all the people who were staring at Dikes and then whispering.

"Do what?" Dikes asked.

"All this," Jones gestured vaguely to everyone inside the restaurant. "People always stopping you everywhere you go, asking for photos, watching you eat."

As if on cue, a mobile phone's camera clicked away. Dikes' entire table turned to the table across from theirs and stared. The guilty party was a young man and his girlfriend. Copping the full weight of the stares from Dikes' table, they both sheepishly smiled and then hurried to put their phones away.

"That shit!" Jones exclaimed, pointing at the young couple in irritation.

"You're a hell of a lot more generous with your time than I would be," Bradshaw declared.
Jack leaned back, getting comfortable. "I remember before you made those movies," he said to Dikes with a smile. "Before the dark times," he joked.
Dikes and the table got a laugh out of that.

"It was overnight, wasn't it? One day, we were just two normal cops, and then boom! We were one normal cop and one superstar cop. It was literally the day after Metal Universe One came out, and it was like this," he said, gesturing around the restaurant.

"Yeah, it was a bit like that. But it's okay. It's all part and parcel of it, really," Dikes said indifferently.
He clicked his fingers, glad to be able to change the topic. "Speaking of Metal Universe," he said, reaching for the black plastic bag with a smile on his face.
Jack remembered that smile. It had been a while since he had seen it, and he was happy to see it again, with his friend in such a cheerful mood.
Dikes pulled out an action figure from the bag and handed it to Jack, eliciting an immediate laugh.

"No fucking way!" Jack exclaimed, lowering his voice to almost a whisper at the curse word.

It was an unreleased action figure of Dikes himself – one of him as the character he played in Metal Universe 1 & 2, and the other was him in police tactical gear, complete with a selection of weapons.

"Holy hell! This is awesome!" Tran said excitedly. "I know exactly where this is going."

Those in earshot of the table strained to see what the commotion was all about.

"To the wall of fame," the table chorused, followed by laughter.

"Hey, mock me all you want, but owning some of the world's rarest action figures, unopened, I might add, will be my retirement nest egg." Tran defended.

Dikes reached into the bag and handed Tran the other action figure. "And that's why I got you one of each, buddy."

Tran jumped out of his seat, taking the second action figure. "This is mad!" he exclaimed as he held the boxes side by side, shaking his head with an unwavering smile. Tran carefully placed the action figures down, walked around the table, and embraced Dikes in a hug.

"Thanks, boss man. Thanks so much, these are just... so frickin' cool!"

Dikes smiled, feeling proud of the enthusiasm on Tran's face. He hugged him back and patted him on the back. "You're very welcome, buddy."

Tran returned to his side of the table and picked up his action figures, but instead of sitting, he headed towards the front door. "I'll be right back," he said, gazing down at the action figures.

"Where are you going?" Smith asked, her brow furrowed.

"I'm putting mine in my car. There's no way I'm leaving them here with you lot. You'd probably end up spilling something all over them."

Jack laughed and shook his head, taking one last look at his action figure before setting it down. At that moment, he felt a sense of nostalgia, realizing that he was slowly losing connection with his younger self and could no longer relate to the youth of today.
Tran noticed this and quickly raced back to the table and attempted to snatch the toy up.

"If you're not going to keep it-"
Jack snatched his action figure box off the table and held it to his chest before Tran could grab it.

"Keep your bloody hands off this one; you have two of your own!" He waved Tran away and watched him race outside.
Jack tossed the box back onto the table with a laugh.

"About time they came out," he said. "You happy with them, Nick? I remember something about the heads being wrong at one point."

"Yeah, I am," Dikes replied proudly. "Yeah, they had the wrong heads on the wrong toy for a few batches, but they got there in the end. I think they turned out pretty cool."

Jack gave Dikes a genuine smile. "I'm really proud of you, kid." He raised his glass.

Jones started to laugh.

"What?" Bradshaw asked.

"I was just thinking," Jones chuckled. "The next time someone tells the boss to go fuck himself, he can just pull out two of these and say, 'Okay.'"

The table erupted in laughter.

Forty minutes later, everyone had nearly finished their main courses when the waiter approached.

"And how did we find tonight's meals and service, Detectives?"

"Brilliant as always; thank you, Franklin. Very good." Jack commended him.

Before Franklin could ask about desserts, both Tran and Smith's phones beeped and vibrated as they received texts simultaneously.

"Wait up; this could mean two less for dessert," Bradshaw said as he waited for confirmation. Tran and Smith read their messages, tossed their napkins onto the tables, and rose to their feet.

"Yep, some of us have to go to work tonight," Smith jibbed and shot him a wink.

Bradshaw smiled and wasted no time leaning across the table, grabbed both Smith and Tran's glasses, and poured their drinks into his.

"You are such a tight ass," Smith said, shaking her head in disbelief.

"You don't know the half of it," Jones chimed in. Bradshaw feigned hurt for an instant before shrugging his shoulders and taking a sip of his now-filled glass of mixed drinks.

Tran leaned forward and whispered in a hushed tone to the table, "Central's got a body at an abandoned house near the water."

Dikes stood and shook Tran's hand, then pecked Smith on the cheek. "Good luck out there tonight, you two," he said as he watched them leave.

"Be safe," Jack added. As the duo departed. Dikes made his way to the bathroom, and on his way back to the table, he was asked for more autographs and selfies. Upon his return, Jones and Bradshaw's phones beeped, prompting a confused expression on Dikes' face as he watched them read their messages.

"What the hell?" Jones muttered as he looked across at Bradshaw and then Dikes.

Dikes' frown tightened as he stared down at the table, deep in thought.

Jack had been watching Dikes' expression and knew something was bothering him. As if to confirm his suspicion, Dikes glanced at his watch and then flashed Bradshaw and Jones a wedding smile as they said their goodbyes and quickly left the restaurant.

"Be safe out there, boys," Jack said after them, but he was looking at Dikes, who was absentmindedly tapping the table with his thumb. "What is it?" Jack asked him quietly.

"Both jobs were exactly ten minutes apart," Dikes said, reaching for his phone in his pocket.

"You thinking that we'll be getting a text in nine and a half minutes too?" Jack asked.

Dikes barely nodded as he searched his messages for a particular text he'd received earlier this morning. Once he'd found it, he handed his phone to Jack.

The text read:

From:

UNKNOWN NUMBER:

Good afternoon, Nicholas; Today is the first day of the rest of your life. Enjoy your dinner tonight, and we'll begin our game after the main course has settled. Like a starter's gun, you will be given a READY, SET, and then on the final set of beeps, you GO!

Jack handed Dikes back his phone, both men exchanging a sceptical glance.

"More than a coincidence you getting that text, and then our entire squad being called out," Jack commented.

"Something doesn't seem right, does it?"

They sat in relative silence, sipping their drinks and awaiting the ten-minute mark when their phones both received a text from the central command.

The message instructed them to go to the waterfront, to a building site that was still under construction. They were then instructed to go up to the roof where a body had been found.

Jack made a motion to pay, but as usual, Dikes wouldn't let him. So, while Dikes took care of the bill, Jack re-read the text.

Once they were outside, Dikes looked for Jack's car. Whoever's car was closest, they were going to take.

"Where'd you park?" Dikes asked.
Jack pointed to the Centre Point car park building across the street.

"Okay, we'll take mine. I'm just over here," Dikes said, pointing directly across the street to his black Ford Raptor 4x4.

"What the hell is that text about? What game?" Jack asked as he climbed into the passenger seat.

"I have no idea," Dikes replied as he started the engine. "I guess we'll find out in about five minutes."
Jack looked at him sideways with a smirk.

CHAPTER THREE

Tran and Smith arrived at the address they had been given and parked out front.

It was an old two-story colonial building sandwiched between two modern high-rise apartment buildings.

The building's windows and the front door had been boarded up, with remnants of police tape still hanging from the two rotten porch posts.

Wrapped around the entire building was government-branded demolition tape, with a large red and white demolition sticker plastered across the door. Next to it was a notice of intent to demolish the house, with the date set for the following day.

Turning in his seat, Tran looked back down the empty street before looking ahead. "That's strange," he said.

"The fact that there's no one here to meet us? Yeah, I thought the same thing," Smith agreed as she scanned the streets ahead and then the house.

Smith got out of the car, taking in the old building in front of her. She noticed one of the windows on the ground floor had been smashed and was being partly held together by a ripped explosive sticker. Peering through it, she could only see blackness. Using her phone, Smith used the torch app to get a better look. The light was adequate but only allowed her to see a metre in front of her. "Hey, can you grab a couple of flashlights, please?

And ask Central where the hell is everyone?" Smith asked Tran.

Tran waved his phone as he moved to the trunk of his car.

"Already on it," he said, pulling out two sets of gloves and two flashlights from his immaculately packed crime scene kit.

After reading the information on the demolition sticker, Smith noticed that the front door was slightly ajar. She cautiously used the corner of her phone to push open the door, which creaked slowly until it was wide open, revealing the desolate, dilapidated front rooms.

Tran handed Smith a set of gloves and a long, black flashlight.

"Cheers," she said, tucking the torch under her arm and putting on the black latex gloves.

* * *

Bradshaw and Jones had arrived at the address given to them by Central Command; however, there weren't any other police on the scene.

The abandoned train yard was eerily still, the only movement coming from the murky grey canvas sheets that were flapping in the wind, tied to the rust-covered chain-link fence enclosures in the yard's centre.

"You sure we're at the right address?" Jones asked as he looked around.

Bradshaw double-checked his text message, then held up his phone for Jones to read. Seeing the message was from Central, they knew they had the correct location.

The left-hand side of the train yards was filled with forty-foot shipping containers stacked two high.

Between them and the line of decommissioned trains were twenty dog pens that had once been used by the military for bomb detection dogs during the Commonwealth Games. In the years since the pens had fallen into disrepair, half of them either rusted or knocked down by rambunctious teenagers and drunks or taken and used to make shelters for the street people.

Before falling into disrepair, the pens used to measure four meters wide and twelve meters long, made with chain link fencing covered in sheets of grey canvas. This prevented the dogs from seeing one another.

Unfortunately, the canvas had now become unusable, fading, ripping, and filled with holes due to its age.

As Jones stepped out of the car and took in the eerie train yard, he heard Bradshaw talking on his phone.

"Hey Sheila, it's Andy Bradshaw and Jonesy on job number," he held his phone out to read the job number from the text, "65375. Just wondering where the blue shirts and witnesses are for this job? There's nobody here."

Bradshaw sat and listened while Sheila explained that the job number he'd given her didn't exist and that Central hadn't sent either of them a text.

Hearing Sheila on the other end, Jones glanced at Bradshaw suspiciously, then looked back at the train yards with an uneasy feeling.

"Okay, roger that Central. While we're here, we might as well have a look around." Bradshaw said before sighing off.

Jones took out two pairs of latex gloves and two flashlights. Bradshaw slid the torch under his armpit and put his gloves on while Jones did the same.

"What do you think is going on here, partner?" Bradshaw asked Jones.

Jones shook his head, biting his bottom lip. "I have no idea," he replied, turning his flashlight towards the open gates of the train yard. A large industrial-sized padlock hung from the chain, its metal cut through.

"But I reckon someone wants us to head in that way," Jones said, nodding towards the beam of his flashlight.

* * *

Smith ducked under the demolition tape and swung her torch around the dilapidated first room.

The floor was covered in decades of dust, flaked-off paint, degraded plasterboard, and tons of general rubbish from the homeless and drug users who had frequented the house over the years it had been vacant. The internal walls and ceilings were riddled with large sections missing or having fallen and lay scattered on the floor. What still stood had been vandalised or smashed up.

Smith's boots crunched as she made her way into the next room, which she quickly realised was once the kitchen. Little was left to identify it as such, as the house had been stripped of anything of value years ago.

Her flashlight illuminated a section of the remaining backsplash tiles that had been wiped clear of dust, forming an arrow.

Following its direction with her flashlight, Smith turned her beam to a set of dilapidated and worn stairs.

The centre of each step had been worn down to half its original depth, and the step below the half-landing was missing completely.

As Smith moved carefully towards the stairs, Tran's footsteps echoed to her from the entry room.

"Hey, Smith?" he called.

"In the kitch- the next room," she corrected herself. Tran entered the kitchen as Smith placed her foot on the bottom step, which made it creak.

"Central didn't call this in," he said in a questioning tone. "Sheila said they never texted us anything."

Smith detected the nervousness in his voice and knew she felt the same way.

Who had sent them here, pretending to be police Central Command? she thought.

"Who did then?" she asked. "Who the hell can pretend to-" suddenly, a loud thump startled them, followed by something moving across the wooden floor directly above them.

"What the hell was that?" Smith hissed as she and Tran drew their weapons and pointed them towards the stairs leading to the second floor.

Tran gave her a questioning look as he joined her at the edge of the staircase, nodding to indicate they were ready to proceed.

Taking the lead, Smith cautiously ascended the creaky stairs, trying to remain as quiet as possible.

"That's not even the weird part," Tran whispered, carefully stepping over the missing step.

"What is then?" Smith asked tensely, not bothering to look back at Tran, who was covering their rear.

"Bradshaw and Jones were sent to a job ten minutes after us," he replied.

"Let me guess, Central didn't call that one in either?" Smith whispered.

"Nope," Tran answered quietly as they reached the top of the stairs.

* * *

Jones and Bradshaw ventured into the old train yard, which was close to the water, where the wind was a constant. They carefully maneuvered around the edge of the labyrinth of shipping containers, the maze of old dog pens with their ghostly flapping canvas capes, and the row of old trains.

When Bradshaw shone his flashlight towards the dog pens, he instantly noticed a white square-shaped board hanging on one of the fences. It was the same material real estate companies used for the for-sale signs, and it had a hand-painted number eight on it.

Holding his bright beam on the number, Bradshaw walked up to it. "Hey, Jonesy!" he called, leaning forward to examine it and getting a whiff of fresh paint.

"Yo," Jones replied as he jogged over. He pointed his light at the white sign and asked, "What's that?"

"I don't know," Bradshaw replied, stepping aside. "It's the number eight, I guess. It's still fresh."

Jones stepped in for a closer look, also catching the scent of fresh paint. He stepped back, scanning the rest of the yard. "Hmm," he said thoughtfully. "Bit strange."

"What's the number eight got to do with anything out here, you reckon?" Bradshaw asked, shrugging his shoulders.

Jones flicked his light around the maze of metal fencing and flapping canvas, then back at the painted board. It was then he noticed a second hole punched into the bottom of the whiteboard. He pointed his light down at the ground around their feet and quickly spotted what he suspected. Half buried under Bradshaw's boot was a zip tie.

Jones picked it up and then handed it to Bradshaw.

"What's this for?" Bradshaw asked, watching as Jones lifted the side of the white plastic with the tip of his finger, transforming the figure eight into an infinity symbol. "It's not an eight," Jones replied, stepping aside for Bradshaw to see the symbol for himself.

Bradshaw furrowed his brow in confusion as he tried to make sense of the symbol. "What is it?" he inquired.

"It's the infinity symbol," Jones replied.

"But what does it mean?" Bradshaw asked, not having a clue what an infinity symbol was.

"Well," Jones began, his eyes scanning the area with unease, "I think it's supposed to represent eternal life or never-ending or something like that."
Bradshaw stepped away to look for any other clues, firstly shifting his flashlight to the line of old trains.
He moved his beam over the cab of the closest train, then ran it along the length of the engine, passing it slowly over the maze of rusted wire fencing that had been leaned against it. Just as he was about to tell Jones he had no idea what it all meant, he heard a sound. It was the sound of gravel crunching beneath a foot. Bradshaw quickly spun his flashlight around and caught a pair of legs disappearing behind a flapping piece of canvas that leaned against one of the shipping containers.

"Hey, you!" Bradshaw yelled as he drew his pistol. Jones spun around and saw Bradshaw sprinting around the flapping sheet of old canvas in a wide arc, his gun pointed forward.

"Shit!" Jones said when a bright flash of light temporarily blinded him while he was still holding the plastic board. "What the hell!" he yelled as he let go of the board, letting it swing back to display a number eight, while shielding his eyes.

"Oh, sorry, Detective," a man's voice said. "I did not mean to startle you."

"What the hell are you doing out here?" Jones asked, trying to shake the bright spots from his vision.

"I'm from the Carrier Mail Gazette. The boss sent me down here to see what you might uncover. What did you find, Detective?" the reporter asked.

Bradshaw sprinted back to where he had started, panting with exertion.

"Has anyone come back this way, Jonesy?" he asked, shining his flashlight and brandishing his pistol. He had seen a flash of light in his peripheral while running but couldn't tell who Jones was talking to. Whoever it was, it wasn't the suspect he had been chasing, as they had gone in the opposite direction.

"No!" Jones yelled. "Well, not that I saw."

"Who's that?" Bradshaw shouted, his voice carrying over the flapping canvas as he searched the area for his target.

"Just a damn reporter," Jones replied.

"Ouch, thanks," the reporter said in a dejected tone.

"Tell him to fuck off, now! We've got an active scene here with a suspect on the loose," Bradshaw commanded, then shifted his flashlight and pistol to the shipping containers ahead.

"You've got to leave now!" Jones ordered, stepping towards the photographer and straining to make out the reporter's face through the dancing spots still in his vision.

"Okay, okay, I am leaving, Detective," the reporter grumbled as he stepped back as Jones hurriedly moved past him.

"But before I go. Do you think that it is the infinity symbol or the number eight? Or perhaps both have meaning, yes? And do you think it has anything to do with the killer or the bodies in the area?"

Jones hesitated, not quite hearing what the reporter had said over the flapping sheets of canvas. He shook his head while rubbing one eye with his free hand to try and clear the dots that still danced in his vision.

"Did you say something about a killer or bodies?"

The reporter shook his head and smirked. "No, Detective. I did not. Perhaps you-"

"Jonesy!" Bradshaw yelled.

Jones sensed a strangeness about the reporter, but with Bradshaw's yelling, he had no time to investigate further.

"Just stay out of here and wait next to our car out there! It's the black commodore. I want to ask you some questions," Jones demanded of him before taking off towards the sounds of Bradshaw yelling.

Blindly chasing Bradshaw's voice, Jones stopped at the edge of the shipping containers, frustrated that he couldn't hear over the flapping canvas tied to the fencing beside him. Quickly, he holstered his weapon and tore down the nearest two sheets. Instantly better. Now that he could hear better, he faintly heard Bradshaw yelling again, and it seemed he was heading back this way.

Jones rushed ahead to the next row of containers and, learning from before, quickly tore the sheets of flapping canvas from the wire fences next to him so he could better hear. Within seconds he could make out two distinct sets of feet running towards him.

Jones timed his appearance for when he thought Bradshaw and whoever he was chasing were about five meters away.

He stepped out from around the container, "Police! Put your hands up!" he yelled, pointing his pistol a little too high. To his surprise, his partner was chasing a small, grubby ten-year-old boy.

The kid skidded to a halt, quickly raising his hands. Bradshaw jogged up to him, out of breath. "Bloody hell, kid," he gasped, swallowing hard. "When you hear a policeman yelling at you to stop running - stop friggin running, okay?" He stood tall and sucked in several deep breaths, then placed his hands over his head.

The boy was also puffing as he looked between the two detectives.

Jones fished his badge from his pocket and held it out for the boy to take.

The boy looked at it but never showed any sign of wanting to touch it or take it.

"See? Real cops," Jones said, clipping his badge onto his belt.

The boy looked from the badge up to Jones, then across to Bradshaw, but said nothing.

"What are you doing out here at this time of night, kid?" Bradshaw asked, his breath regained enough to ask the question without pausing. "What do your parents think of you being out here this late? It's not safe out here, you know. Lots of weirdos, you know," Bradshaw said.

The kid stared at him for a long moment, then slowly raised his arm and pointed past Jones towards a line of cages covered in flapping canvas.

Bradshaw and Jones shared a confused look, then shifted their attention back to the boy.

"What are you pointing at? There's nothing there," Bradshaw asked, his voice tinged with frustration.

Again, the boy pointed at the line of fences, this time jerking his index finger three times.

Bradshaw and Jones swung their beams in the direction indicated, though all they could see were sheets of fluttering canvas. Just then, a single gust of wind peeled away all of the sheets, revealing a bloodied body tied to one of the fences.

"Shit!" Bradshaw exclaimed, quickly reaching for his weapon.

"Was that?" Jones had seen it too. "With an arm cut off?"

"I fuckin didn't see that part!" Bradshaw said, wide-eyed.

Jones and Bradshaw stepped forward with their weapons raised.

Bradshaw stopped to allow Jones to continue on his wide arc, ducking and weaving around the nearest sheet of torn, flapping canvas, trying to get a clearer view.

"I can't see shit," Jones grumbled.

Still watching Jones' light, Bradshaw followed him for several steps before turning to warn the boy.

"Hey kid, just go back to the-" Bradshaw stopped talking when he realised the boy was gone. "What the hell?" he asked, quickly flashing his flashlight around the immediate area.

"What is it?" Jones asked without turning back.

"The bloody kid ran off," Bradshaw replied, still flashing his light around the shipping containers. "Fast little bugger," he mumbled to himself.

Jones glanced around the area but couldn't see the boy, so he focused ahead. "We'll catch him later," he said, his light moving over the maze of fencing and flapping canvas.

The former military dog pens had been reshaped and rebuilt into makeshift human shelters over the years, making the area look more like a creepy maze at a country fair ghost ride than former military dog runs.

* * *

Smith had reached the second floor and spotted something unusual stuck to the shattered window at the end of the hall.

"I might have something," she said quietly to Tran, who moved up beside her.

"What do you think it is?" Smith asked, tilting her head.

"Looks like an infinity symbol?" Tran guessed. "I'll check it out," he offered, stepping over several rotted floorboards.

To their left, all of the internal walls had been removed or knocked down, giving the detectives clear visual access to the entire left side of the house.

Smith had taken a step down the hall when she thought she heard something behind the door to her right. She glanced at Tran at the far end of the hall; he was just about to check the last room on his right, so she decided to investigate the noise and clear the room herself.

"Clear," Tran whispered from the doorway at the end of the hall, then turned his attention to the hand-drawn infinity symbol.

Seeing that the door was already ajar, Smith carefully nudged it open with the toe of her boot, which allowed her to keep both hands on her weapon. It wasn't until the door was half open that something barreled at her head, making a terrible sound. Smith ducked out of the way, screaming while almost squeezing off a shot as she fell onto the dirty floor.

Hearing both Smith and something else hit the floor, Tran spun around, ready to fire, but quickly raised his weapon.

"Holy shit!" Tran exclaimed as a large feral cat scampered down the stairs, making a ruckus across the bottom floor until it was out of the house.

"Fucking cat!" Smith snarled.

"Gave me a damn heart attack," Tran said, flashing Smith a nervous smile.

"Gave you a heart attack?" Smith asked incredulously.

Tran skipped over the holes in the floor and offered Smith his hand. She took it, getting to her feet and dusting herself off as she regained her breath. She could only look at Tran, shaking her head and repeating, "Fucking cat," with the slightest hint of a smile as she placed her hand over her thumping heart.

Tran shook his head and then nodded back at the room Smith had yet to clear.

"You want me to?" he asked, jerking his chin at the room.

Smith shook her head as she drew a breath. "Nah, I got it." She stepped forward and nudged the bottom of the door with the toe of her boot again, this time bracing herself for anything.

Rather than follow Smith, Tran turned back to what had initially caught their attention. He moved carefully back to the infinity symbol, quickly noticing the black ink glistened when introduced to light. Tran leaned in to inspect it closer. "Smells fresh," he said to himself, then looked around for evidence of who'd painted it.

"Traaan!" came Smith's shaky voice from the other room and what sounded like a scuffle. It was a tone he had seldom heard, but he knew it meant trouble. Without hesitation, Tran raced back down the hall, jumping the holes in the floor and rushed into the room with his weapon drawn.

Once in the room, his light quickly found Smith, who turned her face away from the bright beam of light. "Oh, sorry," Tran apologised as he lowered his flashlight. With the flashlight lowered, he noticed a dark green velvet sheet or cover piled at Smith's feet. She'd obviously dropped it after scurrying back to this end of the room, Tran thought. But what was it from?

Tran looked back at Smith's face; her pale complexion and fearful expression spoke volumes. Without a word, she nodded towards the window on her left.

The window at the far end of the room was once painted black but was now cracked and badly scratched, but as Tran swung his flashlight around, he realised it wasn't the window she was pointing out. Tran's flashlight illuminated a red pole supporting what looked like a mannequin bust. For a moment, his brain struggled to process the reality that this was not a plastic figure but the torso of a real human being.

"What the f-" he exclaimed, raising his pistol instinctively. His eyes darted around the room as his brain worked overtime trying to piece this unimaginable scene together. "Was that covering..." Tran stuttered, lost for words, as he pointed his weapon at the green velvet, then at the torso. "That?" His voice quavered.

"Yeah," Smith answered softly, her voice also trembling. "I touched it," she mumbled as she drew a shuddering breath. "I thought it was a plastic one."
Gathering himself, Tran stepped closer to the body. The torso had been fashioned into a mannequin, devoid of arms, legs, or head, and had been impaled onto the pole through the anus. From what remained of the genitals, Tran could tell that the victim was male.
Across the chest was a deep incision spelling out the word READY.
As the realization of the scene before him dawned, Tran's stomach churned. "What the hell!" he exclaimed.

Without taking his light off the corpse, Tran turned to Smith, and the two shared a horrified and confused gaze.

"I fucking touched it!" she said squeamishly.
Tran forced himself to look back at the body, trying to take in as much detail as he could despite the shock and revulsion coursing through him.

* * *

With their hearts pounding, Bradshaw and Jones navigated their way through the canvas sheets and fallen fences until they only had one last sheet blocking their view.

Bradshaw gave silent instructions that he would step forward and pull the sheet aside while Jones was to cover them.

Jones agreed, then took up position and aimed his pistol. Bradshaw stepped forward and held up three fingers. He paused, then lowered a finger per second until his third finger closed, and then he pulled the sheet aside. Jones stepped forward, surveying the area with his weapon, ready to fire. But instead of a killer, what was revealed was the limbless, naked female torso that had been secured to the chain link fence through its back skin.

"Jesus Christ, Jonesy!" Bradshaw yelled as he quickly pointed his weapon around, looking for any sign of the killer or anyone watching them.

"What the fuck!" Jones said slowly as he straightened, unable to take his eyes off the corpse. The victim's arms, legs, and head had been removed from the body with precision cuts.

Carved deeply across her chest, just above her breasts, was the word, SET.

Bradshaw tore away the canvas and gaped in shock at the mutilated torso.

"What the hell is going on out here, Andy?" Jones exclaimed, aghast at the gruesome sight strung up in front of them.

Bradshaw lowered his pistol and shone his light onto the body. "I don't know. I really don't know," he said softly, but to no one in particular.

Then, suddenly, Bradshaw's phone rang, making them both jump. "Jesus!" Bradshaw cursed, shaking his head before checking the caller and answering.

"Damn it, Tran! You scared the shit out of us! Listen, I can't talk right now; we're—"

As Jones watched, Tran appeared to have cut Bradshaw off, for the latter fell silent as he listened intently; a frown creasing his brow as he glanced downwards. Eventually, his gaze lifted, sweeping the area of the old train yards before settling upon a window on the top floor of an old house situated between two high rises on the other side.

"Alright, have you called yours in yet?" he paused to listen. "Okay, let me call the boss, and I'll call you right back." Bradshaw hung up and took a moment to himself before turning to his partner. "The young guns just found a body identical to this; theirs has been skewered onto a mannequin stand with the word READY carved across its chest."

Jones mouthed the words, ready and set.

"I assume the boss and Jack would have been sent to a fake job that's not so fake, and they'll find a victim with the word GO carved into their goddamn chest," he said angrily. "What the hell is going on out here? I don't get it!"

Bradshaw sympathized with his partner's frustration but refrained from acting on it. Instead, he shook his head and lifted his phone to call Dikes.

* * *

Dikes' 4x4 pulled up at the address they'd been given. It was an unfinished restoration job that would eventually become a tower of waterfront apartments. Jack and Dikes stepped out and surveyed the area.

"There's nobody here," Dikes noted, as he hopped onto his Ford Raptor's side rail to get a better view.

"That's strange," Jack agreed as he, too, looked about. "But everything about this so far has been strange."

Dikes jumped down and strode toward the building's front double doors. "Looks like the party is up there," he said, gesturing to the roof.

From where they were on the ground, all Jack could see was a bright, white glow coming from the rooftop. *It gave the top of the building an ethereal look,* Jack thought to himself. This thought made him smile with a tinge of pride. He had used the word ethereal in its proper context, something he hadn't always been good at doing. In fact, until a few years ago, Jack had thought the word 'penultimate' meant 'the best'. No one had ever corrected him on it, leaving Jack to wonder if they were all as thick as him or if they just wanted to avoid embarrassing him.

With his flashlight tucked under one arm, Dikes pulled on his black latex gloves. As they approached the building, they noticed one of the doors had a square, white plastic board stuck to it with a red, hand-painted infinity symbol. The other door had been left slightly open, something Jack knew was never done on a closed worksite.

"That shouldn't be open," Jack pointed out, with Dikes merely nodding in response, busy studying the red symbol. He stopped directly in front of the doors and remarked, "This looks like it's still wet." He quickly recoiled while instinctively reaching for his weapon. Jack, not knowing what was going on, also jumped back while reaching for his pistol.

"What? What's going on?" Jack asked, looking around the building site.

"It's blood," Dikes said slowly as he searched the street for any onlookers. They shared a tense glance and then looked back at the hand-painted infinity symbol.

"Right, I'm going to get some backup out here, I think." Jack said as he unclipped his handheld and said, "Central, this is 8-11; I need you to send out four units to cordon off the Shaffer building on Julia avenue and have the forensics team come down here, please."

"Roger that 8-11." Came the woman's reply from central. Jack clipped his handheld onto his belt and then looked around the side of the building as Dikes, using the door without the symbol, cautiously entered the building. The building was still in the tear-down stage, which meant it only had the original external walls, roof and internal staircase remaining. Scattered around the ground floor were piles of rubble, some from the roof, others from the walls that had been knocked down.

There were also items that were too large to transport to and from the worksite daily—generators, pallets of plasterboard, and long piles of wood used to construct the internal walls.

After quickly surveying the bottom floor, Dikes and Jack set their sights on the internal staircase.

"Well, the text did say the roof. And that's where the lights are, so let's get climbing," Dikes said, flashing Jack an 'oh great, stairs' look.

As they ascended the staircase, Dikes' phone started vibrating. Because he was on point and didn't want to take his hand from his pistol or his eyes from his front, he whispered to Jack, "It's in my left pocket."

Jack quickly reached in and took the phone, and read the name. "It's Bradshaw," he whispered.

Dikes wrestled with the idea of not answering but thought it must be important if Bradshaw was calling so quickly after attending a job. "Shit," he hissed. "Yeah, better answer it," he whispered as he continued climbing and clearing floor after empty floor.

Jack answered and then listened for a moment before he whispered, "Yeah, we are—" but Bradshaw cut him off. Dikes could feel his heart racing as he glanced back and saw Jack's worried expression become a constant frown.

"And you couldn't find any other body parts anywhere?" Jack asked barely above a whisper.

Dikes' concern intensified, so he stopped in the middle of the staircase between the fourth and fifth floors. Jack flashed him an apprehensive stare as he listened to

Bradshaw and slowly shook his head. "Okay, well, this will come as no surprise, but we were called out to a job as well, and we're still in the middle of it, so I'll call you when we're finished. But yeah, you're right; something strange is definitely going on. Talk after we've finished here." Jack hung up and slipped the phone back into Dikes' pocket. "Well, we're right in the middle of it, buddy boy. Smith and Bradshaw's teams are down the street a bit, and they've both found bodies—or rather, parts of bodies," Jack said, struggling to find the right words. "They've had their arms, legs, and heads cut off." Dikes could feel his eyes widen, and his mouth drop open as Jack described the situation. He was at a loss for words.

"Smith and Tran's had READY carved into theirs while Bradshaw and Jones had SET carved into theirs. No guesses for what ours has written across it," Jack whispered.

"Them," was all Dikes could think to say as he stared distractedly at the wall.

"Hey?" Jack flashed him a questioning frown.

"You said it, Jack. They're bodies of people," he gently corrected his best friend. "Them, not it."
Jack wholeheartedly agreed and quickly corrected his mistake. "Them."
Dikes and Jack shared another nervous look, neither knowing what to say since they'd never been in a situation like this before.

"Come on," Dikes whispered. "Let's get to the roof and see what we find."

As they kept climbing the stairs, Dikes couldn't help but feel like they had stumbled into a book or movie. When he mentioned it to Jack, Jack could only laugh because he was literally thinking the same thing. With a shake of the head, Dikes knew the best thing to do right now was to stop thinking of possibilities and just focus on moving up to the roof as quickly possible.

As they climbed the final flight of stairs, they found the door leading to the roof shut. A bright white beam of light poured out from underneath the door. Hearing nothing, Dikes asked Jack to look away to ensure that at least one of them would still have unaffected vision until Dikes could detect the light source. Once Jack had tucked his head inside his jacket, Dikes took a deep breath to steady himself before slowly opening the door. The sudden brightness of the white light hit him like a wall.

"Bloody hell!" Dikes exclaimed while shielding his squinting eyes with his forearm.

"Jesus! It's so bright, and I'm facing the opposite way with my bloody eyes closed!" Jack shouted. Dikes quickly spotted the source of the bright light: a set of floodlights positioned on a stand that faced directly at the door, blinding anyone who opened it. Shielding his eyes, he leaned out of the doorway and followed the power cable to the switch, which he managed to turn off.

Once off, Dikes carefully moved down two steps to allow Jack to race up and clear the rooftop.

Dikes waited for him to call out, 'clear,' but only silence greeted him. Frowning, Dikes wondered what had happened.

"My God," Jack finally said, barely above a whisper. Dikes waited for a couple more seconds. "Jack? You okay?" he whispered but still got no reply. He didn't like this one bit. "Jack!" he hissed.

"I... I," was all Dikes heard Jack stammer.

Facing down the darkened staircase, Dikes repeatedly opened and closed his eyes. "Jack, what the hell is going on?"

"I..." Jack stammered again. "You're going to have to see this for yourself, Nick," he said in a strained voice. His throat had constricted as bile reached his mouth. Finally, Dikes was able to open his eyes and not just see fluorescent white. He could now see his beam of light shining on the wall down on the next flight. Feeling that his eyes were considerably clearer, he spun around and raced up the two stairs that led to the roof.

He, like Jack, halted abruptly on the other side of the door.

Jack had stepped outside to give Dikes room to move through, but both men could only stand motionless in the doorway, staring at the grotesque 'thing' ahead of them.

Ahead of them on a metre-high black display box, illuminated with soft lighting to a museum standard, stood a six-legged human-hybrid scorpion-type creature. The creature was a human hybrid because it was composed of the body parts of three different human beings.

Its body had been made from an upturned male human torso that had been gutted and the ribcage cracked wide open, exposing an empty cavity that was now filled with the hair of the three victims.
The ribs had been pulled open, individually separated, and set at two different angles per side to make them appear as rows of spikes that ran along the creature's back.

The three victim's heads were now indistinguishable from that of a human. All three had been peeled, cut and their skulls reshaped before being painstakingly merged to form a large, grotesque insectoid/mutant head that had been wired to the shoulders of the upturned body.
The ninety-three original teeth from the three victims had been replanted upside down in the creature's newly shaped gaping maw, exposing their fleshy, jagged and pointed roots to give the impression that the creature had recently feasted on raw flesh.

Six legs supported the sculpture, the rear set being two human male legs bent at a one-hundred-and-twenty-degree angle. In the centre were two female legs, similarly positioned, while two female arms formed the front legs. The hands were laid flat with the fingers splayed wide.

The creature's claws or pincers were formed from a set of muscular male arms that were expertly sewn to the torso using a shiny bronze-coloured wire, almost where the original arms once were.

Its tail was composed of the remaining male arms and legs, which were artistically wired together to form one seamless piece. To create the desired curve of the tail, the knees and elbows were bent at a forty-five-degree angle so the tip of the tail hung just above the creature's bulbous head.

The tail was wired to the torso directly over the creature's genitals. The hands at the end of the tail had been wired together in a cupped praying gesture, with the index fingers poking out a little further and joined at the tips to create the stinger.

"Jesus Christ, Nick," he whispered. "What the hell are we up against here?"

"I don't know," Dikes replied slowly.

Dikes didn't have an answer and could only manage a single head shake. He closed his eyes and focused on shutting everything out so that he could think.

It took him about ten seconds, and then his police brain began to operate. First, they would have to devise a way to temporarily preserve all three crime scenes.

Opening his eyes, he held a hand out towards Jack. "Hey, can I have your handheld, please?"

Jack quickly handed it over.

"Central, this is 8-12, over."

"8-12, this is Central; go ahead."

"Yeah, Central..." Dikes suddenly drew a blank as to who to get down here. He turned to Jack, who simply shook his head and shrugged, not knowing who to get either.

"Everyone, I guess," Jack suggested, bemused. Dikes continued. "Yeah, Central. Send every available unit down to the address Jack mentioned. We'll need everyone. And wake up whoever's not on duty in forensics. We'll need them all down here."

There was a noticeable pause before Central replied. "Just to confirm, 8-12. You are requesting all available on-duty units to your location asap? Along with all three forensics teams, correct?"

"Correct. If you need approval for any of this, call Chief inspector Bryant. I'll be calling him as soon as I'm finished with you. Oh, and let all incoming units know there are three crime scenes within a one-block radius, so they'll be told where to go once they're on scene."

"Roger that 8-12. sending all available units to your location. Be safe out there," Central said with concern evident in her voice.

"Will do Central," Dikes said, then handed Jack the handheld.

Dikes drew in a steadying breath before stepping onto the roof to get a closer look at the sculpture.

Jack was appalled as he circled it, exclaiming, "Just look at this thing!"

Dikes leaned in to inspect the horrifically terrifying head.

"I've never seen or heard of anything so…" Dikes thought for a moment. "I don't even know how to describe it, Jack."

As they tried to take in the meticulous details of the creation, of which there were many, sirens began to wail from all over the city.

"Here comes the cavalry," Jack said softly.

Dikes and Jack circled the sculpture twice before coming to a stop at the front left corner.

Dikes was captivated by the killer's use of six-millimetre thick copper wire to skillfully thread through the body parts and connect them to the torso, while having it serve as a sort of external exoskeleton to hold the body parts in the desired shape.

Remarkably, the copper wiring had been weaved and stitched through every piece of flesh without tearing or ruining the flesh in any way, whilst not detracting from the sculpture's overall look.

"How would you even practice making a piece like this? I mean, you'd have to-" Jack's words trailed off.

Hearing Jack's question suddenly sparked a thought for Dikes.

There was something very familiar about this sculpture, but he couldn't think of why. He puzzled over the question as he stepped around it, trying to recall its origin, but the memory eluded him.

As he thought, Dikes' index finger tapped away on the barrel of his Glock.

Not receiving a reply, Jack looked at his partner and quickly noticed his distant expression and that he was tapping the side of his Glock. The tapping was something Jack had seen Dikes do on quite a few occasions. It was something he did whenever his brain was onto something.

"What is it?" Jack asked.

Dikes didn't say anything at first; he just stood gazing at the disgusting sculpture ahead of them, tapping his pistol.

"Nick!" Jack said a little louder this time. "What is it?"

Dikes' head snapped around as if noticing Jack for the first time.

Nodding at Dikes' gun hand, "You only do that damn tapping thing when you're onto something," he said.

"I've seen this before," Dikes said, staring at the creature's head.

"What? This thing? You've seen this thing before?" Jack exclaimed, as he jerked his pistol at it.

He was horrified that there was another one of these things in existence and that his partner had seen it.

"Not this exact one, no," Dikes said, then he noticed Jack's expression and had to elaborate. "Not a real one, a sculpture. A Marquette," he explained.

Hearing that Dikes was only referring to a sculpture, Jack instantly relaxed, until he looked ahead at the real-life version and then instantly felt queasy again.

"Whoever made this used the clay model or the painting I saw as his inspiration."

Jack's expression was one of disgust as he looked over the human body parts sculpture while waiting for Dikes to explain further.

"There was this art thing that Sarah and I were invited to a while back."

CHAPTER FOUR

FOUR MONTHS AGO

Dressed in his finest tuxedo, Dikes stepped out of the limousine to a barrage of reporters and photographers calling his name. Before giving one of his patented wedding smiles or a wave, he offered Sarah his hand. Taking her husband's hand, Sarah stepped out of the limousine, looking stunning. She was wearing her favourite sparkling sapphire blue, backless dress.

Dikes tried to avoid the small but tightly packed red carpet; however, Sarah had different plans and took the opportunity to have some fun with him, pulling him in for a posed picture.

She placed one hand on her hip and the other around Dikes.

As they posed for the camera, Sarah murmured quietly, "consider this a complimentary photo shoot."

"Might not be costing you anything, darling," he emphasised the word 'darling'. "But I'll be paying dearly for it at work in the morning," he told her, behind his wedding smile that was tinged with a hint of regret.

"Aww, poor baby," she said as she squeezed his backside.

Dikes took Sarah's hand as they posed and then, after a few seconds more of photos, whisked her inside.

As soon as they were inside the museum, Dikes immediately felt out of place. That's why he always invited Jack to as many of these types of events as possible. But because this was an art exhibition, Dikes had zero chance of getting Jack to join him.

Dikes had even tried to bribe both Jack and Marilyn to the event by making the evening a double date, preceded by dinner at the restaurant of their choice, plus he'd put them up in any hotel in the city for the weekend, plus anything they wanted to do the following day. But true to form, these bribes were nowhere near enough to get either of them to come.

Dikes smiled, thinking of how much Jack hated the 'artsy fartsy' crowds, as he called them. And as he looked around the room at who was here, Jack had hit the nail on the head. It was exclusively artsy fartsy people.

As he and Sarah made their way through the main chamber, chambers being the name of the individual rooms for this exhibition, he could sense the eyes of the room upon him. Although he was accustomed to people continually gazing at him, they were not observing him tonight for the same reasons as everyone else usually did.

To them, he was the uncultured everyman masquerading as 'one of them'. Even the way he was dressed, which was very stylish and not inexpensive, didn't hold up to the stares of the high society artsy types who always gave off that always fashionable, alternative, arty vibe.

Glad to be away from the main crowd, Dikes had unknowingly wandered into the disturbing, 'apocalyptic realism chamber' while he was waiting for Sarah to get back from the ladies' room.

He'd stopped in front of four disgusting sculptures that sat in front of a massive painting that depicted a ruined city.

The piece was titled 'Post-apocalyptic children'. Unable to mask his distaste towards this style of art, Dikes shook his head and was about to move on when a group approached him dressed in what Jack would have called 'overpriced rags bought from an op-shop'. They wanted to get his opinion on the four pieces.

It had taken Dikes just under twenty seconds to inadvertently insult all four artists and their equally offended friends.

He'd realized he had outstayed his welcome when the barrage of insults, originally aimed at his ignorance regarding art, had shifted to personal attacks on both his acting and the overall mainstream design of the two films he had acted in, which grew steadily louder. Then, under his retreat of a wedding smile and a thumbs up, Dikes was told, in no uncertain terms, just how uneducated, narrow-minded and ignorant he was for not understanding or being able to see true genius, even when it was on display right in front of him.

Leaving the 'apocalyptic realism chamber' under such a storm of verbal abuse, Dikes was glad when he entered the next chamber, which was dead quiet and only had one piece on display. Glancing back to see if any of his new art friends had followed him, Dikes stopped to stare at a gigantic floor-to-ceiling painting that depicted a grotesque scorpion-type creature made entirely from human body parts.

CHAPTER FIVE

Within an hour of Dikes' squad discovering the three bodies, the buildings along the old train yard were awash with the flashing red and blue lights of over twenty police cars.

The JAPD had blocked all access to the entire city block. All three crime scenes had been locked down and had their own forensics teams working on evidence collection.

The police chopper was a constant presence as it hovered around the block, keeping the news choppers and drones out of the area until the roof team had erected a large tent over the entire rooftop.

Individuals had floated between the three crime scenes throughout the night, but the real prize was the 'sculpture' crime scene up on the roof.

Those coming down from the rooftop described it to their squad mates waiting to go up as the most disturbing and stomach-churning thing they'd ever seen.

It wasn't until three hours later and after their scenes had been completely locked down and signed over to forensics, that Tran, Smith, Bradshaw and Jones were able to join Jack and Dikes up on the roof.

The four of them were stopped by two uniformed officers from High Command as they stepped onto the roof.

The officers were positioned to stand guard at the entrance of a large black military-style tent that took up most of the roof, and their job was to inform all visitors to the crime scene of the rules.

"Sorry, sirs, ma'am, but we're checking everybody. Those orders have come from up high. As you can appreciate, this is a very sensitive crime scene."
The four detectives exchanged amused looks.

"Jesus, you gotta be a VIP to get up, hey?" Bradshaw asked, half joking. "It's like one of the boss's parties."

"You're not far off, sir," the officer said dryly, jerking a thumb towards the tent behind him.
Bradshaw raised an eyebrow. "Really? I was only joking," he said with a smirk.

"Believe it or not, the mayor and half her staff have already been through this place tonight. We've even caught two reporters and some members of a religious group, all posing as part of the Coroner's team, trying to get a look in here."
After showing the officers their credentials and having their names marked off the list of who was permitted inside, the first officer stood before them and drew a deep breath, like he was a little nervous.

"Okay, watch your footing while you're up here," he cautioned them. "Between the sandbags, tent ropes and these pipes right here, there's a lot to trip over," he explained as he and the other officer gestured to three ribbed pipes. "Once you enter the first tent, which is this black one directly in front of you, you will be asked to put on a hazmat suit, boot coverings and a mask. Then, once you're fully sealed up, you'll be let into the white tent. Both tents are air-conditioned, hence the pipes," he said, gesturing to the ribbed pipes again.

"But, because of what… the 'sculpture' is made from, the inner tent is set at about four degrees Celsius, so it can get quite cool in there over a prolonged period of time."

"Is all that necessary?" Bradshaw asked.

"That answer is way above my pay grade, sir. People much smarter than me have said it is, so it is," he said, with an added smile. "What I do know, though, is that if any of you have eaten recently or have weak stomachs, I strongly recommend you stay out here with us. There's no shame in that - you really don't want the image of what's behind that flap burned into your brain if you don't need to, okay?" he said sincerely, his expression serious.

Smith and Tran exchanged worried glances.

The crews working our crime scene are serious about their jobs, but everyone up here is next level, Tran thought.

"Are you all ready?" the officer asked them.

The four exchanged glances, apprehension in their eyes as they prepared to witness something they knew was going to be horrific. Finally, they all nodded in agreement.

The officer parted the heavy, black canvas flap, revealing a space that was four metres deep and ten metres wide.

Against the left wall were shelves of neatly folded white and yellow hazmat suits, alongside masks and boot covers.

To the right of the entrance, there were rows of bench seating where those exiting the crime scene could sit to remove their masks and hazmat suits. Five plastic bins were provided to store the used suits and masks. Additionally, a shelf nearby contained vomit bags, similar to those given on aeroplanes.

Several high-ranking city officials were hurriedly removing their hazmat suits while another raced out, vomiting into his bag.

As the tent flap was pushed aside, Smith caught a glimpse of what was inside. Her stomach sank, and a wave of nausea swept over her. Her heart raced faster than ever before, and her body filled with a strange restlessness. She quickly donned her mask, concealing the need to take deep, cleansing breaths.

When the rest of the squad was fully dressed, they moved to the entrance of the white tent, where an officer wearing a hazmat suit had appeared to let them in.

As soon as he opened the tent, Bradshaw stopped in his tracks at the sight before him. He was directly in front of the sculpture/creature and suddenly had no control over his lower limbs.

An odd, high-pitched sound escaped his throat as he remained rooted to the spot, transfixed by the sight.

"Jesus Christ!" Jones shuttered as he ducked around Bradshaw and came into full view of the sculpture. "Jesus

Christ!" he repeated softly, his gaze fixed on the deformed sculpture made of human body parts.

"Sir." The officer at the entrance gently encouraged Bradshaw to move further into the large, brightly lit, cold room.

Smith's attention never wavered, while Tran, who had steeled himself outside, stayed silent, his eyes unblinking.

"What the actual fuck!" Bradshaw finally exclaimed. It was as if his brain had shut down and rebooted.

Tran went to say something, but the words died before they left his mouth. Perhaps he wasn't as mentally prepared as he thought he was.

The four of them stood in disgusted awe as they gazed at the sculpture.

From the far end of the room, a man in a group of three with an iPad noticed the newcomers and shouted, "Hey, you four!"

After getting no response, he tucked the iPad under his arm and clapped his hands to get their attention.

Jones and Tran were the first to turn their heads towards the man.

"Who's that dispshit?" Jones asked Tran.

Tran shrugged.

"Hey, so, do you four need to be here? It's not a show-and-tell segment. If you're just here for a peek, wait to see the slides in tomorrow's briefing."

Dikes and Jack, accompanied by Detective Callaway, the longest-serving and most decorated forensic pathologist in the city, were studying the female's left arm, which was acting as the sculpture's middle left leg. They focused particularly on the back of the hand, which featured a tattoo of a white lotus flower.

Dikes stared intently at the lotus tattoo, trying to recall why there was something so familiar about it when he glanced up to see who the other investigator was speaking to.

He couldn't make out their faces due to the masks, but upon noticing the heights of the four newcomers, he realised they were his squad and quickly motioned for the detective in the corner.

"They're with me, Murry," Dikes explained, then waved for his squad to join him. "Guys, over here."

Staying well away from the sculpture, they moved to the corner where Dikes and Jack were.

Smith asked, her voice tinged with nerves, "What the hell is going on, boss?"

Jack gave her a gentle pat on the back and agreed, "An excellent question, Smithy."

Dikes stared into the eyes of each of his squad, seeing the same horror that he had felt when he first laid eyes on the horrendous sculpture.

He pointed to it and quietly said, "This is what we're up against. Whoever did this is unlike anyone we have ever encountered before."

He then retrieved his phone and showed them the text from the unknown number.

Tran read it first, then passed it to Smith, who read and passed it to Jones and finally Bradshaw.

As Bradshaw read the text, he shook his head in disbelief. "That explains the words across the chests," he said, handing the phone back to Dikes.

"Did the killer put the word GO on your..." Smith asked, nodding at the sculpture, not knowing how to refer to it.

Dikes gave a single nod as Jack stepped across and pointed to the underside of the scorpion creature with a pen. "It's carved under here."

The squad gathered around and knelt to have a look. Peering underneath the scorpion, they noticed the word GO carved deeply into the back of this victim.

This torso also differed from the other two in that it was covered from top to bottom with hundreds of cuts of varying sizes, creating a patchwork-like pattern.

"What's with all of the cuts on this body?" Tran asked.

"We're not sure yet. They think the cuts were all made in a way that closely replicates a paper cut. We assume it was to inflict the most amount of pain to the victim while he was alive."

At the news, Tran, Smith and Bradshaw all looked a little concerned. Jones just looked pissed off.

"Fucking paper cuts," Bradshaw muttered, shaking his head. "Who the hell is this freak?"

Callaway responded, standing up from behind the sculpture. "He or she is far from a freak, Detective. The intricate manner in which these bodies were cut, reassembled, stored and displayed in their respective locations points to a knowledge and skill base of an expert in at least six fields," Callaway said, shaking his head as if to emphasise this point. "It's imperative we don't underestimate this individual or individuals. The time, effort, methods, and money needed to hunt down, capture, and keep these three victims alive during the cutting sessions and amputations—which, from what I can tell so far, were done hours, if not days apart—are evidence of their methodical intelligence and what must be a near-limitless pool of resources."

The room fell silent as everyone took in the new terrifying information they'd just received and the reality of who and what they were up against.

Bradshaw unintentionally broke the silence with a whispered thought he wasn't aware he'd vocalised.

"We're up against evil bloody batman."

The squad turned as one as they stared at him, and judging by some of the moving shoulders, a couple of them were silently laughing.

Eventually, Bradshaw noticed everyone's masks fixed on him. "What?" he asked innocently. Jones shook his head. "You really are something, Andy." Still in the dark about what had happened, Bradshaw simply accepted the compliment with a shrug.

Still shaking his head at his partner's idiotic remark, Jones turned to Dikes. "When did you receive that text?"

"I got it this morning," Dikes replied. "It's so similar to some of the other strange messages I receive that I simply dismissed it."

Dikes then went on to show Jones some of the strange messages he had received in the past, which caused Jones to understand why Dikes hadn't taken this one seriously either.

"Take one last look at this... thing," Dikes said as he gestured to the human sculpture. "Let it sink in that this killer or killers are not playing. They're out to cause real havoc." Dikes stared intently at the sculpture before turning to his squad.

"Okay, time to head back to the office for a debrief," he said. "It's been a long day for all of us."

The squad followed him out of the white tent and into the outer change area, where they casually removed their hazmat suits.

"Is it a cold room to preserve the... that thing for good, or just for the investigation?" Jones inquired.

Dikes paused before answering, not wanting to give the answer he was about to give. "If it were up to me, it'd be for the length of the investigation," he said.

Jones shook his head. "Ignoring the moral dilemma associated with all that, which we won't get into, why does it need to be so cold in there?"

Jack pulled off his shoe covers. "I actually know this one. I heard the techs talking. It's to preserve the glues the killer used so that they can try and identify the manufacturer and where it's sold," he explained. "Plus, it keeps the body parts from decomposing quickly, thus losing any prints the killer or killers may have left behind," Jack took a bow and then shook his head at the oddity of the situation.

"We have prints from all three victims, and we're running them through the country's database as possible perps and missing persons," Dikes explained, tossing his hazmat suit into the used suit bin. "Finger crossed, hey."

CHAPTER SIX

After a brief debriefing session, in which the squad discussed each of the crime scenes and their plans of action for the morning, Dikes instructed them to go home and get some rest so they could return fresh in about five hours.

* * *

Dikes pulled his 4x4 into the parking space and took a moment to pause. His mind was racing with the events of the night, and he had just leaned his head against the steering wheel when a knock on the window startled him. His left hand quickly moved to his pistol, which was still in its holster on the passenger seat.
Seeing the shock on her husband's face, Sarah frowned. Dikes sighed heavily as he exhaled a big breath, then took hold of his holstered weapon and badge before exiting the car.

"Little jumpy, aren't we?" Sarah joked.
Dikes managed a half-hearted smile then gave her a kiss.

"It's been one of those days, then some," he said, exhausted. He reached back into the car to collect his iPad and phone, then locked it before taking Sarah's hand and walking towards the elevator.

Dikes stood in his shower with his head against the wall as the hot water splashed off his back. He was completely zoned out and hadn't realised Sarah had joined him until he felt her press up against him.

"It was that bad, hey?" she asked gently as she rested her head on his back.

Not getting any sort of reply, she looked up at him with concern. "Sweetheart?"

Snapping out of his daze, Dikes turned and looked down at her, flashing a weak 'wedding smile'. "Sorry," he said, kissing her lovingly on the forehead. "I missed that; what did you say?"

Sarah ran her hands through his dripping hair. "If you're giving me the wedding smile, it must be a bad one."

Dikes nodded absently, inhaling deeply as if about to speak yet remaining silent.

"I wish you could talk to me about these things. We're in this together, remember."

Dikes swallowed hard and then looked deeply into her eyes. Sarah couldn't tell whether it was the water running down his face or if he had been crying, but in this moment, he was a shattered man.

"I don't want you to know about the kind of things I deal with. Especially not this one. I can't be the reason why you'd carry something like this with you. It wouldn't be fair."

Sarah stared at the man she had loved and adored for the past twelve years, and for the first time, she saw that he was scared. The look on his face shook her. If this murder scene had rocked him this badly, then it must have been terrible.

"Okay, I won't ask anything more about it, but you have to promise me something."

It took Dikes a second to blink and register what she'd said before he gave a shallow nod.

"You must promise me that you will talk to someone when you get a spare hour. Or," knowing Dikes was about to interject, she placed her finger over his opening lips. "Or," she continued. "If I see that it's really affecting you mentally, I make the call, and you go see someone?" She stepped back and held her hand out for him to shake. Dikes looked down at her hand and sighed. He knew his wife's stubbornness and knew that in matters such as this, not only was she right, but she was never going to let it go until he went. So, he gently shook her hand and then pulled her in tight.

Sarah rested her head against his chest again, but she was seriously worried.

CHAPTER SEVEN

Dikes entered the precinct holding two cups of coffee and some case files he'd picked up from his meeting downstairs in the morgue.

Jack saw Dikes exit the elevator and met him halfway across the bullpen.

"Well? What was it you had to tell me?" Jack asked with a hint of concern as he waved his mobile phone.

Dikes shook his head, still having trouble digesting what he'd just learnt downstairs. "Wait til we get over," Dikes jerked his chin toward their desks, then handed Jack one of the cups of coffee.

Dikes gave Bradshaw and Jones a nod. "Morning boys."

"Morning boss / Morning," came their replies.

As they walked to their desks, Jack noticed the distracted expression plastered across Dikes' face.

"Where're the young guns?" Dikes asked, noticing their empty desks.

"They said they had to pick up something from their crime scene or get a photo of something or something," Bradshaw said with a shrug.

Jack shot Dikes a smile.

Jones could only shake his head as he leaned back in his chair. "Great detective work," Jones joked.

Bradshaw threw his hands in the air playfully.

"So, what is it?" Jack asked, lowering his voice.

Dikes looked around to ensure no one was within earshot, then waited for his squad to lean in to listen before replying, "My fucking initials and badge number were carved into the sixth rib of... of the sculpture," Dikes whispered.

"You're shitting me!" Jones's eyes widened in disbelief.

"This guy is pulling out all the stops. He wants your bloody attention, doesn't he?" Jack stated.

Dikes leaned in a little further. "He used one of those trophy engravers to do it."

Everyone was at a loss as they sat back, shaking their heads.

"It's like one of those movies where the killer just keeps fucking with the cops," Bradshaw said. "Sends him cryptic clues and shit." he clicked his fingers. "Maybe we should spend the day watching old cop movies... oh, I mean, researching." He used air quotes for the word researching.

"Who else knows?" Jack asked.

"Calloway and his socially awkward offsider, the Chief, me and now you lot."

"Let's tell the young guns when they get here, but apart from them, let's keep it between us," Jack urged, then leaned back, shaking his head.

"That young guy from the morgue isn't just socially awkward; he's a fucking nutter. I wouldn't be surprised if he did it all himself," Bradshaw added.

Dikes smothered a smile. "I wouldn't go that far, but yeah, he's um; he's just..." Dikes couldn't think of a polite way to describe the man. "A little off. I'm guessing he doesn't get many people to talk to down there."

"I'm tellin' ya, just keep an eye on him is all I'm saying," Bradshaw stated as he took a sip of coffee from his favourite cup.

Bradshaw's coffee cup was an oversized black cup with a gold JAPD detective shield stencilled on it with the words WORLDS BEST DIC written around the top and bottom of the shield in bold, silver lettering.

"You still claiming that?" Jack asked, nodding at the cup.

"If it's true, then it's true, brother," Bradshaw replied with a wide smile. "Besides, never had a complaint." He left a pregnant pause. "About my work."

"The lawyers would label that as misleading, I reckon," Jones chimed in, pointing to his cup.

Everyone, including Bradshaw, got a laugh out of that.

"Anyway," Dikes drew that word out to give everyone time to compose themselves. "Any luck with getting footage from the museum?" Dikes asked Jack directly.

Jack shook his head as he ran a hand over his unshaven face. "I rang the curator on the way over; he was pretty sure they only keep footage for seven days and then recycle the storage. He said he'd let me know either way."

Dikes then turned to Bradshaw, "Were you able to get the footage from any of the traffic cams or the St Regents across the street from the museum?"

This time it was Bradshaw's turn to shake his head. "No good boss. Apparently, every camera for a two-block radius went down a few hours on either side of the exhibition start time." He gave Dikes and Jack a curious look as he raised his eyebrows. "Then, the same thing happened again last night at all of our crime scenes. Every camera for two blocks shut down six hours before we got there and are still off this morning.

"Jeez, coincidence?" Jack said sarcastically."

"Yeah, bullshit," Jones added, running his fingers over his smooth chin. "I'm wondering how you can get so many different types of cameras turned off or taken down in such a large area, all at the same time?"

"Shit!" Dikes said as he put his elbows on the table and rested his head in his hands.

"What?" Jack asked.

"I've been trying to remember what this guy looked like, but I can't."

"Who?" Bradshaw asked.

"The museum guy," Jack replied before Dikes had a chance.

"What museum guy?" Jones inquired.

Jack glanced at Dikes. "Oh, you haven't told them? I thought they knew because you have them trying to find footage from the museum," he said with a frown.

Dikes shook his head, his face still in his hands. "I explained that the painting and mini sculpture were there, but I hadn't gotten around to mentioning him."

Jack nodded. "Nick thinks he met someone at the gallery who might know something about the..." Jack paused, trying to think of how to word it better. "The sculpture," he finished.

"I just can't remember what his damn face looked like. All I remember is those stupid rose-coloured glasses, that shitty little moustache and the beret. But not his actual face," Dikes vented.

"Sounds like Jack's type, alright," Bradshaw joked, raising his giant cup.

Jack nodded seriously, playing along with the joke. "Like you said, when you're right, you're right."

"Then his disguise worked a treat then," Jones said, appreciating the disguise as he leaned back and shot some scrunched-up paper into the rubbish can next to Bradshaw's desk, but Bradshaw knocked it away.

"Rejected," he quipped as he raised his hands in victory.

"If it's our guy, that's a ballsy move," Bradshaw said. "Think about it. Turning up to the same event and talking to the actual police detective you're about to start fucking with." Bradshaw admitted.

Everyone fell quiet for a moment.

"After seeing what we saw last night, it definitely fits our guy's MO."

"Proves he's got some cajones, that's for sure," Jack said.

Dikes continued to run the art exhibition night through in his mind, but nothing stood out, as it had been so long ago and uneventful; even his encounter with the man was not enough for him to recall the man's face or any distinctive features apart from a moustache.

"I ran into him; I remember I was escaping a bunch of... artsy types," he settled on using a name Jack had coined. "And," Dikes shook his head, "I ran into him, but I can't remember his goddamn face."

"Why do you think it's him?" Jones asked.

"Well, I don't know it's our guy, but this guy I bumped into was really, and I mean really, studying that thing hard. It just felt sort of strange at the time. And I remember thinking that then, I can't explain it."

Jack was about to take a sip of his coffee when he froze.

"This cup hasn't been downstairs in the morgue, has it?" he asked as he sniffed the lid.

"What? Of course not," Dikes replied as he discreetly shot Bradshaw and Jones a wink.

Smith approached the squad from the front of the bullpen and walked straight to her desk. "Morning, all! Morning boss."

"Morning!" they said in unison.

"Is your promotion party still on tonight?"

"You bet your ass it is," Jack replied enthusiastically, then thought about it. "Well, maybe. If it is, you need to remember to handle your drinks more responsibly this time, Detective Smith. My ass is not a squeeze toy," Jack kidded.

Smith gave Jack the finger while shaking her head, hiding a smirk. "I don't know how or why Marilyn puts up with you."

"She's the lucky one, Smith; remember that! She's the lucky one," he said, nodding confidently.

"Oh yeah, sure," she retorted.

Still racking his brain, Dikes frowned as he looked across his desk and locked eyes with Jack. Maintaining eye contact, Jack slowly raised the coffee cup to his nose and sniffed the lid. "Smells like a dead person, Dikes," he said accusingly as his stare turned to a glare.

Dikes shook his head as he took a sip of his own coffee to hide his smirk.

Jack frowned as he watched Dikes place his cup down, open the case file he'd brought in with him, and start to read it. Dikes' expression was neutral, so Jack didn't know whether to believe him or not.

"Promise me you didn't put this coffee within two metres of a headless human, or any dead person... or body part... or any internal organs, Dikes," Jack insisted with a straight face.

"Are you kidding me, Jack? I just finished telling-" Dikes leaned forward as he looked around and lowered his voice. "I just finished telling you that my name and badge number were engraved on the inside of some poor guy's ribs and all you can do is worry whether your coffee cup was in the same room as him?"

Jack leaned forward, glancing around to make sure no one else could hear, then stared at Dikes seriously and whispered, "One hundred percent, pal!"

Dikes shook his head. Inside he couldn't believe Jack didn't fall for that line. "Fine, I promise," he lied.

Dikes then went back to reading the initial coroner's reports from all three scenes.

Jack leaned back in his chair, still watching Dikes for any hint of a smile. "Well, alright then," he said, suddenly getting serious. "Let's find out why these three people were chosen. Why them? My gut feeling is that they all have something in common. I don't think these were random killings. Don't ask me why; I just don't think they were. Now, since they're from different states, it's probably not schools, but it could be sporting events or even people they all knew. We have to find out if they've holidayed at the same place or stayed in the same hotel or were members of the same Facebook group or something? These were three young people, only slightly younger than you two," he nodded at Tran and Smith.

This statement immediately stirred up a range of complex emotions in the younger detectives as they sat up a little straighter, with Tran clearing his throat quietly.

Dikes watched their reactions but remained quiet, watching to see how they dealt with such a difficult situation. The past twenty-four hours would have been extremely stressful and challenging for any detective, not to mention two who were just fresh off from being street cops.

Jack slowly looked away from them, returned his attention to the crime scene photographs on his desk, and then continued. "They all have a link to the killer somehow; I know it. I'm willing to bet Bradshaw's mug that there's a link between them."

"Hey!" Bradshaw stated as he pulled his mug close.

"We've already checked most of those suggestions and about twenty other possibilities so far this morning," Tran explained.

"Keep looking," Jack said.

"The only reason these people are dead is me," Dikes mumbled in frustration as he flicked through the folder of photographs.

Dikes' statement caught everyone off guard, causing them to exchange glances of concern. Jack looked across his desk at Dikes, feeling a little uneasy about the negative attitude he was exuding in front of the squad. Jack had seen this kind of talk ruin morale in his military days, infecting and spreading throughout the platoon like wildfire, so he was determined to nip it in the bud.

Even though Jack was twelve years older than Dikes and had been in the police force longer, there was absolutely no one he would rather serve with or under than Captain Nicholas Ryan Dikes. He loved the kid like a little brother. They'd known each other before Dikes had enlisted into the JAPD and had been best friends for well over two decades now, so it wasn't wide of the mark for Jack to think he knew just about everything about his friend.

As Jack surveyed the face of his superior officer, best friend, and brother, he was reminded of the worrisome part of Dikes' personality. He could see it on his face right now—an anxiousness that caused Jack to worry. He was familiar with the heavy burden that Dikes carried when it came to specific crime scenes, believing that he could have prevented the tragedies if he had acted differently or thought more quickly.

This mental anguish had a negative effect on those he loved, making them casualties of the cases that ultimately brought him fame and promotion. Although this quality made Dikes an excellent detective, it could also lead to burnout. Jack was determined to ensure his friend did not succumb to that fate in this case. A case that looked certain to push them all to their breaking points.

So, Jack stared at Dikes, waiting for him to look up as he cleared his throat.

"Nick," Jack said, his gaze fixed on Dikes.

Dikes looked up, instantly recognising the look in Jack's eyes. He glanced around at his squad, all of whom were watching him intently.

Realizing his mistake, Dikes set the folder aside and raised a hand.

"My bad," he said. "But it's not as mopey as I probably made it sound."

Jack raised an eyebrow.

"I'm the common link. They were killed to get my attention is what I meant," Dikes said, his voice tinged with anger.

Jack slowly sat back and crossed his arms, in agreement with Dikes' reaction. He thought that Dikes would have been more outraged, considering a psycho had killed three innocent people and then carved his name and badge number into one of their ribs.

The squad was silent as they contemplated the situation. Dikes leaned forward, fixing his gaze on Jack again; this time, he had something.

"What?" Jack asked, recognizing the look.

"It's just a guess, but was one of the victims…" Dikes paused to think for a second. Then, remembering his train of thought, he clicked his fingers and pointed at Tran and Smith, "The 'READY' body. Was he from JYC?"

Tran started sifting through the folders and papers on his desk.

Smith already had the folder open containing the files and pictures of the male's torso, and she quickly located the relevant page. "Yes. He was a second-year student reported missing a week ago," she clarified.

"And was yours," Dikes said while pointing at Bradshaw. "From either West Hampton or Livingston?" Dikes asked.

Bradshaw and Jones shuffled through their files.

"West Hampton," Jones said, raising an eyebrow. Dike continued his train of thought when he noticed Jack absentmindedly dipping a pen into his coffee cup. "And the last victim was from Livingston, a third-year student," Jack read from the reports in front of him. Suspicion crept into his voice. "Where are you going with this? How did you know?"

"Yeah, I want to know that too," Bradshaw said, tossing his folder onto his desk.

The landline phone on Dike's desk rang, but not wanting to lose his train of thought, he quickly diverted it, and Tran picked it up at his desk. "JAPD, this is Detective Tran."

"Livingston is a long way from here." Smith pointed out.

"Yeah, it is. Her family said she was on vacation down here. There's no way you could have guessed that a random student was on holiday from Livingston?" Jones said. "Have you already read the case files?" he asked.

"No, I didn't need to for that part. The universities that these three victims attended were the last three universities I lectured at."

Everyone fell silent.

"No way!" Bradshaw exclaimed.

Jack gaped at Dikes in disbelief.

Dikes nodded in affirmation.

"What was the lecture about?" Smith asked.

"Serial Killers in the 21st Century," Dikes replied warily.

The squad was silent again until Tran placed the phone down and faced Dikes. "Cap, there's a strange call for you," he said.

Dikes rolled his eyes. "Thanks."

"So, our killer is a stalker as well," Jack said as he continued to stir his coffee with a pen.

"Were your lectures for university students only?" Smith asked.

Dikes shook his head. "Free for students but open to the public."

Jack tilted the cup toward himself, inspecting its contents, swirled it, and then kept stirring.

Dikes noticed Jack's strange behaviour with the coffee but chose to ignore it.

"If he's been to all three lectures, he shouldn't be too hard to find in the surveillance videos," Smith said.

"I'll get on it."

"Thanks," Jack replied. "Can you also see if you can get the names of everyone who attended those lectures?"

Dikes picked up his phone and was about to transfer the call to his desk but hesitated. "I'm guessing he wouldn't be using his real name, and after what we saw last night, I doubt he'd overlook something so simple, but check anyway."

Dikes fell silent as he watched the flashing button, lost in thought. He was trying to put together a puzzle that still had too many missing pieces. Then, an idea came to him. He placed the receiver on his desk and took out his mobile phone, quickly scrolling through his videos.

"What have you got?" Jones asked. He then glanced at Jack, who was still stirring his coffee with a pen, and added, "We've seen that look before."

"Videos," Dikes replied, still distracted as he searched through his phone. "I record videos of the crowd as I walk out at the start of all my lectures." After a few moments, he found the video he was after and gave a satisfied nod. "Okay, here it is." Dikes turned his phone, so everyone could see. "So, I video my entry to the stage. I get them to give a little wave, we have a quick chat, which puts them and me at ease, and then I turn it off and get into it."

Bradshaw took a sip of his coffee and sat it on his desk.

"You're thinking that if our killer was at your lectures, he'd be in your videos somewhere?" Bradshaw nodded in agreement. "At least once, he will be," he added.

Jack tilted his head and asked, "Why just once?"

Dikes, Jones, Tran and Smith all wore expressions of wonderment as well.

"Well, if he's as smart as we think he is, he'll only be caught out by the boss's little intro video once. If it were me, I'd be reaching down behind someone or looking away at the start of the next two lectures."

Dikes nodded and gave Bradshaw a congratulatory smile.

"Brilliant," Jack praised Bradshaw as he pointed at him. "I didn't even think of that," he added.

Jones pointed at him too. "My partner ya'll, that's my partner right here. The single smartest man at his desk, let me tell you," he joked as he slapped Bradshaw on the back.

Dikes nodded, pleased. "Very good. So, in one of these videos, the killer won't know what's about to happen, so we need to look for anyone trying to avoid the camera or trying to hide their face the moment they find out I'm filming."

The squad all agreed as Smith stood up and packed up her case files. "I've got to go down to the lab, so I can get them to make a few copies for us if you want? Saves you sending it to us and it getting leaked via another hack," she offered.

Bradshaw and Jones groaned as they looked at Jack.

"Fucking computer nerds. That was not cool what they did." Bradshaw grumbled. "I still think it cost you your promotion."

Jack nodded in agreement, then shrugged with a hint of resignation. "What can you do?"

Dikes flashed Jack a sympathetic smile. Jack smiled and shook his head incredulously.

Turning to Smith, Dikes looked through his phone's organiser. He wrote down the four dates he had lectured on, then passed the paper and phone to Smith. "Copy across the walkouts from these dates," he said. "Just watch them and make sure they only copy the walkouts. I don't trust anyone outside of this squad with this kind of thing. I don't want to see anything of mine on TMZ."

"Roger that, sir," Smith replied firmly before heading for the elevators.

Dikes looked back down at his desk and the case file that was open with several pictures lying face up. The top picture was a close-up of the white lotus tattoo.

Dikes started gently tapping his index finger knuckle on top of the desktop. He was getting the same familiar feeling he had last night while studying it up close. But then, two things jumped to the front of his mind. One, he still had someone on hold, and two, what was with Jack's curious behaviour with the pen? It had finally piqued his interest.

"What are you doing with that pen?" Dikes asked as he placed the phone receiver to his ear.

Jack pulled the pen out, shook it, and tossed it back onto his desk.

"Just checking for fingers or other body parts," he explained as he stared at Dikes straight-faced.

Dikes couldn't help but smile. "Was the joke really worth it? That's a lot of lead-up time, and now your coffee's cold."

"Yeahhh, I think it was worth it," Jack said as he raised his cup without looking up from his paperwork.

Dikes pressed the flashing button on the desk phone.

"Dikes here."

"Hello, Detective Dikes; I believe congratulations are in order," came a measured voice.

"Ahh, okay… for what? And with who am I speaking?" Dikes asked, regarding this as just another prank call.

"With whom, Nicholas. And I have been watching you. I have been watching you bungle your way around the three crime scenes I worked extremely hard to build for you. Until you recalled your lecture introduction videos, you were making no progress whatsoever."

Dikes frowned as he listened. He thought it must be someone in the office having a laugh, so he decided to let him continue.

"Finally, you have made a connection between the "victims', as you call them," continued the voice with a hint of irritation at the word victims.

Jack had been watching Dikes on the call and mouthed,

"Who's that?"

Dikes placed his hand over the mouthpiece. "Christmas time," he whispered.

Jack threw his head back, stifling his laugh. "Another fruitcake? Nice."

Beaming, Jack picked up his phone and pressed a button to tap into the call. "Never gets old," he whispered to Dikes.

"Why is Jack now listening in?" the voice asked sternly.

Jack and Dikes both stiffened in their chairs as they stared at each other and then looked around the precinct. The calm voice returned, its tone menacing. "If you are going to listen in, Jack, then I would appreciate your full attention, please. Otherwise, I will engrave more than just initials and a badge number into the next one."

The gravity of the situation hit them like a semi-truck. Without any doubt, they knew the killer was the person on the other end of the line.

Jack felt the hairs on his arms, and the back of his neck stand on end as a wave of nervousness and fear swept over him. He swallowed hard as he searched his desk for a pen, just in case he needed to take notes, but the only one he could find was the one he'd used for his coffee joke minutes ago.

"You should listen carefully because she does not have much time remaining, detectives."

Dikes and Jack shared a worried glance.

"Jack, that pen you have in your hand will not work. That is because you stirred your coffee with it for far too long. And for a subpar joke at best."

Jack felt like a schoolboy being chastised by the teacher. Dikes' heart was thumping as his eyes scanned the room for anyone using a phone. His eyes scanned everyone around, stopping at Tran, whose head was partially covered by his computer screen. What he could see was Tran had his phone to his ear.

Simultaneously pissed off and relieved, Dikes relaxed and got Jack's attention, then jerked his chin toward Tran.

Seeing Tran smiling and on his phone enraged Jack. He tossed his phone onto his desk and stormed over to Tran. Dikes tossed his receiver onto the desk and slumped back, ready to watch Jack rip into the kid for pulling such a poorly timed practical joke. It was a great joke, just poorly timed.

"What the fuck, Tran? Do you think this is funny? You think we have time for this kind of shit?" Jack yelled.

Heads from all over the precinct turned to see what was happening.

Puzzled and a little pissed off at how he was being spoken to, Tran leaned back in his chair.

"Excuse me!" he said defensively. Jack then directed his attention back to his phone. "Ma'am, can I put you on hold for just one second, please? I'm so sorry about this; thank you," Tran said politely.

"What the fuck are you doing?" Jack snapped at Tran again.

Tran placed his hand over the bottom of his phone as he quickly stood up. "What the fuck do you think you're doing?" Tran shot back. "Can't you see I'm taking a call?"

"No, seriously, kid, what the fuck are YOU doing?" Jack marched around Tran's desk and snatched the phone out of his hands.

"Give me that, you little shithead! Hey Dikes, can you hear me?" Jack asked, exasperated.

Dikes quickly reached for his receiver and put it to his ear.

"You hear me now?" Jack asked again. But when he saw Dikes shrug and shake his head, Jack was at a loss. Even more so when he heard a female's voice on the other end asking who he was and why he was yelling at her? Jack pulled the phone away from his ear and scowled in utter confusion.

"Tell Jack to hand the phone back to Detective Tran," came the calm, measured voice on the other end of Dikes' phone. "I am sure Mrs Frankston would appreciate being able to finish filing her daughter's missing person's report. After all, Detective, it is Chloe that you will be attempting to save very shortly."

For the second time in minutes, Dikes was in genuine shock. He gestured for Jack to come back and pick up his phone.

Jack apologised, genuinely contrite. He shook his head and threw his hands up, unable to express the gravity of his regret. "I'm sorry, Tran. I'll explain everything soon," he promised, offering Tran a quick smile before returning his attention to the phone. "Are you ready now, gentlemen? Have I got your full attention yet?" asked the nameless voice.

"Who is this?" Dikes asked, not expecting an honest answer. "The name I'll give you is Joe," came the reply. "That's all you need to know about me for now, Detectives."

Dikes and Jack exchanged a knowing glance, aware that they were somehow being watched. They had to find out who it was without arousing suspicion.

Dikes quickly scanned the faces of the crowd outside, but the precinct was situated on one of the busiest intersections in the city, making it impossible to keep track of everyone.

Jack, meanwhile, discretely searched the faces of everyone inside the building.

"So," Dikes began, "tell me about Chloe. Where is she?"

"Really? That is what you have chosen to lead with, Detective? Nothing about the personalised gift I built and left for you on the rooftop last night? Not even a simple thank you?"

Jack and Dikes remained silent, not knowing how to respond to Joe's comment about the personalised gift he had left them.

"I take it from your silence that it appears you both understand the gravity of the situation," Joe said. "You'd do well to catch on quickly, Detectives—for Chloe's sake." Jack looked at Dikes with a furrowed brow and mouthed 'Who's Chloe?' But, before Dikes could wave him away or write his answer down, Joe cut in.

"Chloe, Jack, is, right now, being reported as a missing person by her mother, Mrs Rebecca Frankston. Mrs Frankston is currently on the phone filing that report with your fellow detective, Detective Tran. Mum knows she is missing because I told her she was just minutes before I rang you."

The muscles in Dikes' jaw knotted tightly. "What can I do to get her back safe?"

"Patience is a start. Although, in this particular case, it may be her undoing."

"Why doesn't she have time, Joe?" Jack asked.

"Wow, for detectives, you really do ask the wrong questions." Joe chastised. "You should be asking me a question like, where she is? Knowing her location and getting there under the time specified would negate the when, why and how."

"You're right, sir. Where is Chloe?" Dikes played along, asking politely.

"Before we get to that, I would like to apologise for my harshness at the start of our conversation. Upon reflection, I realise I was too critical of you when I said you were bumbling."

"You said bungling at the start of our conversation, not bumbling."

There was a noticeable pause before Joe spoke again, which Dikes took as a small win.

"Very good, Detective. Gold star for you," Joe toasted with a verbal nod of approval. "Oh, you were correct when thinking we had met at the exhibition those months back."

Grimacing, Dikes clenched his jaw, his intuition affirming his suspicions. He resolved to heed his instincts more often in the future, but for now, his priority was to locate Chloe and then hunt down Joe—though he struggled to recall the man's physical appearance.

Joe feigned mock pain as he said, "That's a blow to the old ego, not having a face you remember, Nicholas!"

"Honestly, Joe," Dikes said curtly, his gaze sweeping the passers-by. "Right now, I don't care about anything but getting Chloe back safely. So why don't you tell me where she is? I'll go save her, and then you can talk about yourself all you want. Where is she?"

"Okay, let us start, shall we? If this was a movie, you would not be getting this information until halfway through, maybe giving you just enough time to thwart my plans and save the girl. And who knows? Perhaps you will."

"So why tell me now?" asked Dikes, his voice strained with frustration. He felt like Joe was wasting valuable time, and it was beginning to irritate him.

"That is the Nicholas Dikes I have been waiting for," Joe stated, satisfied with Dikes' reply. "Just like you, I am out to prove myself. On one side of the coin, we have you, the superstar detective trying to be the finest in this city's history. But on the flip side of that very same coin, we have me; I am out to prove that I can bend, manipulate and break this fair city's hero in any way I desire. I will show the world that even those deemed untouchable can be broken down like a disobedient dog. So, I have chosen you, Detective, to be my dog." Joe's voice dripped with disdain.

Dikes reluctantly held his tongue, and when he saw Jack about to open his mouth, he waved him off with a shake of the head.

Jack hated staying silent but followed his friend's instructions.

"I see you are ready to write now, Jack, so listen carefully because I will only say this once."

Jack pinned the phone between his ear and shoulder as he searched for a new pen.

"Chloe Frankston. She is a straight-A student at the University of North Jadestown. Cheer captain and recently voted 'most likely to succeed' by her peers. She hoped to finish her degree and then join the Jadestown Police Academy to become a strong female detective like your very own Detective Smith here.

Jack quickly wrote down the information Joe offered, clicking his fingers to get Tran's attention. He motioned for Tran to bring the missing person's report over so he could match it with the new information.

"Her future successes now depend on you, Nicholas. Her life is quite literally in your hands. If she dies, it will be because of your inability to follow simple directions or not to have asked the correct questions."

"Where is she, and how do I get her back alive?" Dikes quickly asked. His face tightened as his patience had almost worn through.

"Jack, in your top drawer, is a phone for Detective Dikes; give it to him, please. I will call again in ten seconds." The phone went dead.

Jack opened his top drawer, spotted the never before seen phone and then tossed it across to Dikes.

"He's been in me goddamn drawers," Jack muttered angrily.

Dikes was looking at the mobile phone when it rang. The phone's ringtone was the Dexter TV show's theme song. Jack and Dikes exchanged unimpressed looks.

Dikes answered the phone as he and Jack walked to the centre of the busy bullpen.

"Before starting, we must go over some basic housekeeping. What I consider housekeeping, you must consider rules, Detective. If you ignore any of the rules I am about to explain to you, you and those close to you will incur a penalty. Do you understand?"

"Yes," Dikes replied quickly, wanting to get this out of the way.

"Number one. Under no circumstances are you allowed to quit our game. You are not to hand this case to another detective; it is yours and yours alone to complete to the very end. Do you understand?"

"Yes."

"Number two. You must play your part in this game until the very end. To clarify, to end the game, either you must die or I. Do you understand?"

"Hey! Killing these kids is not a fuckin game, you prick! You don't–" Joe cut him off with a firm yet controlled voice.

"Do not interrupt, Detective, whilst I explain the rules, or, as previously mentioned, you and those close to you will incur your first penalty. And yes, this is a game! A game where you and I are the only true players on the board. That board is this wretched city, and all who dwell in it are our pawns, to be moved and sacrificed at our discretion."

Jack moved beside Dikes and leaned in to listen.

"Three. Now listen carefully to this one because you will be dealt the most severe repercussions if you breach it. Under no circumstances are you to come knocking on my door, Detective. I stay well clear of your and Sarah's personal life, so you will pay me the same courtesy. Clear?"

"And the fourth?" responded an impatient Dikes.

"The fourth is you. You alone have twelve minutes to get to South Port Beach, or young Miss Frankston will be marked 'absent' for the remainder of her life." Joe abruptly hung up.

Dikes stared briefly at Jack, then took off running.

"Shit!" Dikes yelled as he pushed past other officers walking past.

Seeing Dikes run through the precinct had Tran, Bradshaw and Jones quickly to their feet.

Jack, unsure of what had been said, found himself at a loss for words. He initially chased after Dikes but then came to a halt, surveying his squad with confusion.

"Where's the boss going?" Bradshaw asked.

Dikes pushed through the crowd gathered near the water bubblers.

Jack was a little confused as to why Dikes was running away. So, again he started running after Dikes but stopped at the edge of the bullpen.

"Where are you going?" Jack yelled after Dikes.

"I'll text this phone's number at some point on the way," Dikes yelled back to Jack.

Smith had just exited the elevator with Dikes' mobile phone in hand as Dikes ran past her. She went to offer it to him, but he was already ten metres away, running for the front doors.

Seconds later, Jack, Tran and Jones ran by.

"What's happening?" she asked wide-eyed and ready to run, but got no reply.

Then just as she was about to sprint after them, Bradshaw casually walked by, sipping coffee from his oversized cup. He flashed her a smile, raised his mug, and then nodded toward the front desk. "You coming?"

"Where?" Smith asked, her voice rising in confusion. "What in the world is happening?" she wondered aloud as she trailed after Bradshaw.

Jack saw Dikes quickly maneuver around the crowd and sprint out of the precinct. "Argh, shit!" he cursed in frustration.

With Tran, Jones, and Smith following close behind, Jack pursued Dikes through the front of the precinct and then out into the street.

Meanwhile, Bradshaw was trailing at a more leisurely pace, still carrying his cup.

Dikes ran straight into the street, dodging pedestrians and vehicles alike. "Move! Out of the way, please!" he shouted before making a dash for his 4x4.

Jack, Smith and Tran ran into the street after him.

"Where are we going?" Jack yelled.

Dikes glanced back to see his squad running after him.

"No," he yelled over the sound of the traffic as he held up his hands in a stop gesture. "He said I have to go alone. He's watching us, Jack! Find out how and I'll get this number to you as soon as I can so we can talk."
Jack stopped running and held out his hands in the middle of the footpath to stop the rest of his squad from giving chase.

"We're not going after him?" Tran questioned.
Jack shook his head. "He said he had to do it alone," he explained. The words tasting sounded sour in his mouth. This 'game' was only minutes old, but already he hated what it was doing to his friend.

Chief Bryant marched out of the precinct and up to the squad as they watched Dikes climb into his vehicle. "What's with Dikes?" he asked with a concerned look. Dikes quickly started the vehicle, flicked on his red and blues, and then, with screeching tires, accelerated into the traffic.
Jack flashed the chief an apprehensive stare. "It's best if I explain it all back inside," he said.
Accepting this, they took one last look in the direction Dikes had driven before moving back inside.

Once they were back inside the precinct, all eyes were on them as Jack led everyone back to their desks. Then it occurred to him that Joe was watching everything they did and said, so he marched straight past their suite of desks and led everyone into the male restrooms.

"A word in your office, Chief?" Jack asked with a smile.

To Chief Bryant's credit, he didn't hesitate and walked straight into the toilets. Smith, Jones and Tran were hot on his heels, with Bradshaw bringing up the rear, letting the door swing closed behind him.

"What is going on out there?" Bryant asked Jack as he pointed to the door.

"It's the murdered college kids. We just discovered their connection with each other, and then he rang us here.

This immediately got everyone's attention.

"Who's he?" the chief asked, frowning.

"He calls himself Joe."

"And why did he call you?"

Jack shook his head. "He didn't call me, sir; he called Nick. He called him to-" Jack shrugged, not knowing how to explain it. "He called to sort of lay down the ground rules for this game he wants to play. Apparently, the… the sculpture he led us to last night was the start of the game; he said it was a gift for Nick."

"Bloody hell," the chief said.

He and the squad exchanged disturbed looks.

"I guess it's going to be a cop vs killer type of thing. Anyway, he said he's taken another girl, which we've just confirmed is a missing person because her mother just reported her missing to Tran." Jack nodded to Tran, who nodded to confirm Jack's statement.

Jack then continued. "I couldn't hear much of the last part of the conversation, but I'm pretty sure he's given Nick her location and a time limit to get there."

Chief Bryant rocked on his heels slightly as he took it all in, then jerked his chin to the door. "And why are we in here?"

Jack sighed. "Oh yeah, I forgot that part. Because the shithead has bugs and cameras out there somewhere." Jack pointed to the toilet door. "While we were on the phone with him, he was basically giving us our play-by-play, down to the pen I was using to stir my coffee with."

Chief Bryant jerked his head back, frowning. "Why were you stirring your coffee with a pen?"

Jack shook his head dismissively. "Long story, sir, it had to do with this awesome joke," he trailed off as he waved the chief away. "I'm telling you, he knew everything about this place and us. A little too much." Jack said quietly, almost mumbling, as he mulled the thought over.

Bryant's expression darkened. "What are you getting at, Jack?"

"I guess I'm saying we can't rule out that this guy could be a cop."

This got everyone looking at each other with looks ranging from concern to disbelief.

"Look, I'm not saying that this Joe character is part of this precinct or anything. But we have to be open to the possibility, don't we? He also hinted at having some knowledge of Nick's personal life. Like he might have it in for Nick. Like, maybe he's jealous of him or something. I dunno."

"You're closer to him than any of us. Have you noticed anyone acting any differently around him lately?" Tran asked.

"No, not really." Jack shook his head as he thought back over the past week. "No one really stands out." Jack suddenly clicked his fingers which got everyone's attention. He quickly realised he'd mistakenly made them think he had remembered something important and quickly shook his head as he waved his arms.

"No, it's not something I just remembered; it's something Joe did, which could also back up my 'he's a cop' theory," Jack said bitterly, which indicated how annoyed he was at this next point. "The prick had a phone planted in my top drawer."
This took everyone by surprise.

"I don't know whether he had a cop plant it or if he had the balls to do it himself, but it just goes to show how serious this guy is."

"If he did get a cop, surely no one out there would risk their job over doing something as stupid as planting a phone in one of our drawers?" Tran asked, as he pointed at the door.

"You'd be surprised, kid. There are a lot of ways to lose your money in the city. Cops are no different than your average... Joe," the chief said slowly,

"The chief's right, he could have offered them a wad of cash and told them it was a harmless joke," Jones explained with a shrug of his shoulders.

"If we go through the precinct footage and find out that it was one of our guys or girls, we'll see how harmless it is with my foot fair up their ass," Jack threatened angrily.

Dikes' story about the art exhibition suddenly popped into Jack's head. "Scratch that whole him having someone else plant it theory," Jack said as he leaned against a cubical door. "He would have planted himself."

"Why do you say that? Why would he risk being caught?" Bryant asked.

"Because that's who he is! He's got some big balls, Chief. Nick was telling us that a few months back, he was invited to some artsy fartsy crap at the museum, and get this, that...," Jack struggled for a word to describe the scorpion sculpture as he pointed at the floor, indicating the morgue. "You know, the scorpion thing, well, it was a display piece at this exhibition! And get this! Nick said he even ran into the guy, Joe, which he then admitted to just before."

The hush in the room was tangible as they grappled with the amount of new information they had just received.

"And that's just from this morning?" Bryant asked. Jack nodded and sniffed. "In the last five minutes, really."

"Jesus," Bryant said as he glanced at his watch. "And it's not even morning tea yet?"

CHAPTER EIGHT

As Dikes' 4x4 slid sideways around a corner, cutting across two lanes of traffic, he nearly collided with a truck that had just emerged from a nearby street. His driving wasn't as clean as it usually was because he was trying to text Jack a blank message from Joe's phone.

"Wo!" Dikes yelled, jerking the steering wheel hard left and narrowly avoiding a van, sending his vehicle into a sideways skid.

As his 4x4 skidded sideways, for some inexplicable reason, a memory of the art exhibition came to him.

* * *

Drawn in by the vulgarity of a painting of a scorpion composed of human body parts, Dikes didn't notice the man next to him until he collided with him. Fortunately, neither man was knocked down, nor did they spill their drinks.

"Whoa, sorry, mate," Dikes apologised as he placed his hand on the man's back to steady himself while also giving him a gentle pat.

The man looked at Dikes, then turned back to a statue before doing a double take as if recognising him. The two men smiled and exchanged a nod before turning back to the sculpture. It was a three-dimensional representation of the hideous creature from the painting Dikes had just been staring at.

"Not a problem. I've done the same thing twice tonight myself," came the man's polite response. "Some of these pieces can be... a little off-putting for some."

"Yeah, I agree. They're out there, alright! Like this one here, it's so-." Dikes quickly stopped talking. "Oh, crap," he mumbled, staring straight ahead, trying to avoid eye contact with the man he may have insulted. "You didn't make this one, did you?" Dikes asked sheepishly, pointing, with drink in hand, to the sculpture.
To Dikes' relief, the man got a laugh at this and quickly put him out of his misery. "Oh no, definitely not!"

"Oh good! Thank god," a relieved Dikes said as he audibly sighed with relief. "I thought I'd have to do another runner!"
This made both men laugh, and Dikes instantly calmed down.

"Not my medium, I'm afraid." The man explained.

"I'm Nick, by the way," Dikes said as he extended a hand.
The man shook Dikes' hand and bowed slightly.
"Joseph," he said.

"Nice to meet you, Joseph," Dikes said as he and Joseph turned back to the extraordinarily horrifying and strange piece.
Dikes was immediately struck by three things during their brief introduction. The first was his short-cropped hair that he wore under a black Kanga beret. His well-

trimmed but very thick moustache, which Dikes thought was probably fake, and his rose-tinted, octagonal glasses. A smile spread across Dikes' face as he thought of Joseph as the stereotypical art person. Even down to the name. Perhaps Jack was rubbing off on him a bit too much.

Dikes gazed at the sculpture, his disgust growing with each passing moment. He couldn't tell if the art piece's subject or the artist's painstaking attention to its vulgarity was causing his revulsion.

This sculpture was crafted to resemble a sixty-centimetre-tall clay scorpion created from the body parts of three humans. Its legs, pincers, and tail were all made from small human arms and legs, while its body was a human torso, flipped over with the ribs torn open and the stomach filled with hair. For its head, the creature had three human heads moulded and shaped together to give it an unnatural, insect-like appearance.

"So, what's your medium?" the word faded into the ether as Dikes turned to see Joseph already across the room, hands behind his back, inspecting the next piece. "Medium," Dikes finished with raised eyebrows. Sarah suddenly slid her hand into his.

"My god! What is that thing?" she asked with disgust, looking at the scorpion piece.

"Yeah," Dikes shook his head, then looked back at the sculpture. "Me and my new art friend, Joseph, couldn't figure it out either.
Sarah looked across the room as the man Dikes had called Joseph walked casually around the corner, his

hands crossed behind his back as if he was taking a leisurely Sunday stroll.

"Naww, look at you, making artsy type friends already.

Dikes pointed to the empty place beside him. "Clearly," he joked as he and Sarah had a quiet chuckle, then looked back at the artwork.

Sarah squinted, then leaned forward to read the gold nameplate.

"It's called apocalyptic future."

"Of course it is," Dikes said as he shook his head. They looked at each other with raised eyebrows.

"I have absolutely no idea about art," Dikes admitted. "But I do know that I think this is crap," he said softly, not wanting to offend anyone else. "Let's go this way and look at butterflies, rainbows, or something that's not this," he gestured around the room.

Sarah agreed, and the pair moved into the next hall.

* * *

"God damn it!" Dikes swore as he regained control seconds before jerking the wheel right and speeding down another street.

"I actually patted the prick on the back," he said to himself out loud.

Again, Dikes tried to remember what Joseph looked like, but no matter how hard he tried, all that came to mind was the beret, moustache and glasses. "Goddamn it!"

Dikes yelled as he slapped the steering wheel. "Joseph."
He repeated as he shook his head.

Pushing on his vehicle's horn, Dikes threw the steering wheel hard left and then sped into the beachside car park, screeching to a halt just inches from the bumper of a parked car.

The Dexter theme played loudly from the phone as it vibrated on the seat. Fumbling with his seatbelt, Dikes grabbed the phone and quickly answered. "I'm here. Now what?"

"On the beach, ahead of you, are two red umbrellas. Buried beneath each umbrella is a coffin. Both coffins are lined with explosives. If the lid seals remain intact after eight minutes, they will explode. Coffin one contains Miss Frankston. Coffin two contains a formerly convicted fifty-two-year-old paedophile. He was first arrested after he confessed to raping and killing six children between the ages of five and eight. Unfortunately, your justice system declared his confession forced because of a technicality. This made it inadmissible, which in turn torpedoed the entire case. He was acquitted of all charges and walked free that afternoon. You, Captain, must make a choice… the paedophile or the girl?"

Dikes shielded his eyes against the sun as he scanned the beach for the two red umbrellas.

Being a beautiful, sunny day, the beach was heavily populated with hundreds of people and at least fifty umbrellas. Unfortunately for Dikes, fifteen of them were sizeable and red.

Dikes' sighed as his shoulders and confidence plummeted.

"Seeing that this is your first outing, Detective, I will give you a hint. The girl is on the left."

Dikes hung up and threw the phone into his pocket, and raced across the car park to the beach.

Running onto the sand, Dikes quickly counted six red umbrellas to his left.

Stopping at the first red umbrella, Dikes quickly flashed his badge that he had pulled from his pocket, then apologised to the people under the red umbrella as he pushed them aside.

One of the ladies refused to move.

"Lady, get out of the way!" Dikes yelled.

"Um, no," she said in a bitchy tone, then rolled back onto her stomach.

Dikes didn't have time for this, so he grabbed the edge of her towel and pulled it out from under her. Flipping her and covering her in the sand, Dikes quickly knocked the umbrella over, forcibly helped the lady back to her feet to move her, and then threw her towel aside.

"Asshole!" she yelled as she shot daggers at him.

Dikes dropped to all fours and began sweeping the loose, dry sand aside. Finding nothing, he jumped up, checking his watch. "God damn it!"

He quickly located the next umbrella and raced across to it.

"Get off the beach now!" Dikes shouted as he skidded to a stop in the sand at another red umbrella.

He hurriedly pushed people away and yanked the umbrella out of the ground, breaking the handle off. Then, he thrust the aluminium pole into the sand. No coffin. He cursed under his breath and ran to the next red umbrella, warning everyone to evacuate the beach. Repeating the process, time was running out as he searched for the hidden coffin.

The phone in his pocket rang, and without pausing to take the call, Dikes raced ahead to the next red umbrella.

"What?"

"Tick, tock, tick, tock," Joe taunted in his annoyingly calm voice. "You're running out of time, Nicholas."

"Shut up!" Dikes shouted back, then pocketed the phone again.

Onlookers saw Dikes coming and quickly moved aside as he ripped out another red umbrella.

"You have to get off the beach," he warned.

As much as Dikes warned people, they didn't seem to be listening.

Exhausted, he thrust the pole into the sand, and to his surprise, it hit something hard. Stunned, Dikes repeated the process and again, the pole connected with something solid. He threw the pole aside and immediately started digging with his hands.

"Help me!" Dikes pleaded desperately to the crowd that was gathering instead of heeding his warning to leave.

As the onlookers increased, no one stepped forward to assist in the digging.

"Come on, help me, for Christ's sake!" Dikes implored, glancing at his watch. Suddenly, a very muscular man pushed his way through the throng and shouted, "Move! If you're not going to help the man, get out of the way!" he yelled as he picked up two small buckets. He tossed one to Dikes, and with a nod, the pair began to dig.

It wasn't long before Dikes' arms grew heavy and burned with lactic acid, but he never slowed in his frantic pace to attempt to free the teenage girl. One by one, other people moved in to help dig as the crowd of onlookers grew.

Dikes glanced up at the onlookers and saw two families with their children. "My name is Detect-"

"We know who you are, Detective," said one of the mothers, cutting him off.

"Great. I need as many of you as possible to go and get everyone away from all of the red umbrellas. One of them has explosives in it."

Thankfully, several people immediately took off, running to the other side of the beach, and were telling people to clear the area.

Relieved, Dikes took a deep breath and then continued digging as the number of people helping grew to ten.

It didn't take long for the group to clear enough of the sand away that the shape of the coffin could be seen.

A few minutes later, Dikes glanced at his watch and realized that they were quickly running out of time, so he told everyone to focus on clearing the sand around the lid of the coffin.

The diggers quickly turned their attention to clearing sand from the coffin's lid, and within seconds, the lid was almost clearly exposed.

"Good job!" he yelled, then started pushing people out of the hole. "I need all of you out! There's explosives inside, so I need you all to move back just in case!" he shouted.

The parents quickly grabbed their children and ran away while the people helping with the digging scrambled out and retreated with the rest of the crowd to what they thought was a safe distance.

"You too, big guy, you have to get out... just in case," Dikes said as he and the muscle man exchanged a nod of gratitude.

The muscle man climbed out. "You be careful, dude." He said to Dikes.

"Thanks," he yelled at the muscle man who was already running back to the wall of onlookers. "Hey, can you check that everyone is off the beach down that way, too," Dikes yelled, pointing.

Without looking back, he gave Dikes a thumbs up then yelled, "Will do."

Dikes took a knee beside the partially covered coffin and scraped the last of the sand from the lid. He felt around for the seam, found it, slid his fingers underneath and lifted, but the lid only lifted a finger's width before it got stuck. Sand had fallen back into the hole at the far end where everyone had climbed out.

"Shit," he growled as he scampered across and cleared the sand away.

Moving back to the centre of the coffin, Dikes strained and heaved as hard as he could to get the lid open. Because sand had fallen back into the hole at both ends, it made the job of lifting the lid that much harder. Then, slowly, centimetre by centimetre, the coffin lid rose, and like a practical joke on Halloween, a man shot out of the coffin, latching onto Dikes' shoulders.

The distraught man quickly tore off an oxygen mask he had been wearing and gasped for air. "Oh, thank god you got here!" cried the balding man in his mid-fifties. "I was almost out of oxygen! Thank you."

Fuck! What have I done? Wrong God damn person! Dikes silently chastised himself.

"Nooooo!! God damn it!!" Dikes screamed, his frustration getting the better of him. Distraught and exhausted, he could only shake his head and glare at the man disdainfully as he slumped against the wall of the sandy hole.

One hundred meters away, a thundering, earth-shuddering explosion rocked the beach. The blast hurled tons of sand, towels and whatever else was lying on the sand in the immediate area thirty meters skyward.

"Argh!! Damn it! Goddamn you!!" Dikes screamed as he thumped the sand and watched as debris rained over the surrounding beach.

Terrified screams were heard all over the beach as confusion and chaos erupted. Adding to the chaos were the hundreds of cars and building alarms that had been set off.

The middle-aged man clambered to his feet and attempted to crawl away, but Dikes leapt forward, grabbed him by the scruff of the neck and pulled him back into the coffin, knocking him onto his knees.

"Stay there, you sick fuck!" Dikes growled, barely able to contain his rage.

Looking up at Dikes, the paedophile was all too aware of why the policeman was glaring at him so intensely. Everyone who knew of his deeds gave him this look. Over time, he had grown to appreciate this look, having committed unthinkable acts and yet managed to get away scot-free. He had become a cult hero among his kind. As he knelt there, looking up at the policeman who radiated the desire to punch him, Malcolm smiled the widest, most obnoxious grin he could muster. "Ouch," he feigned as he reached for his right leg. "I'll have to sue the city for my injuries."

Dikes could only shake his head at the audacity of this man, then climbed out of the hole. He'd been around him for long enough. But, the truth was, he didn't trust himself not to start raining down punches on his smug-looking face.

On his feet, Dikes could only watch as smoke rose from the large crater one hundred meters down the beach. He was about to call for backup when he heard the approaching sirens.

"Hey," Dikes shouted to the muscle man, who was already jogging back over to him.

"Can you do me a favour? Can you watch that piece of shit for me?" Dikes asked, pointing at the paedophile. "Don't let him leave until another unit gets here and takes him."

Muscle man nodded and jumped into the coffin, and stood over the much smaller man.

"Oh, and don't let the lid close; it'll set it off and..." Dikes nodded at the smouldering crater.

"I got you," the muscle man said, then glared down at Malcolm.

Mentally agitated and shocked, Dikes slowly made his way to the smoking crater. Once there, he stood at the blackened lip and stared, heartbroken, at where he imagined the coffin had been sitting just minutes ago. Buried beneath the sand with a terrified young lady inside. There was nothing left of the coffin that was any bigger than the size of his pinky either inside or scattered around the crater.

The mobile phone rang, playing the eerie Dexter theme song. Dikes rolled his eyes to the sky as he took it from his pocket. Then, with the phone in hand, he stared at the name that Joe had programmed into it. JOE.

It seemed an eternity between the time it first rang and when Dikes mustered the enthusiasm to answer it.

"I never said 'your' left."

Joe hung up.

Seething, Dikes clenched his teeth and was about to throw the phone away when it hit him.

If Joe's left is the opposite of mine, then that must mean he's watching me from.... Dikes thought, then looked out to the ocean. It only took him a second to locate a boat not far offshore. It was a long, white cabin cruiser with a bright green stripe running down its side. Squinting, Dikes could make out a lone figure standing on the stern of the boat. The figure was watching him through a pair of binoculars.

"Son of a bitch!" Dikes thundered as he ran into the water, drawing his pistol.

Swimmers that were still making their way out of the water scattered before him as he took aim and fired three shots.

Dikes watched as the figure fell back out of sight. He then tilted the barrel of his pistol down, keeping an eye out for any sign of movement. Suddenly, the figure reappeared and quickly moved into the cabin of the cruiser. The boat then started and began to speed away. Dikes took aim and emptied the rest of his magazine at the retreating vessel.

"Shit!" Dikes snarled, then ran out of the water and back to his vehicle. He climbed in, grabbing the radio as he started the car's engine.

"Central, this is 8-12; come in."

"8-12, this is Central; go ahead."

"I need a full medivac team and the bomb squad to Main Beach."

"Copy that 8-12."

"And get all available water units to Abe Point. They'll be looking for a white cabin cruiser with a green stripe heading south. The driver may have a possible gunshot wound," Dikes informed them as he put his car in reverse and quickly backed up.

"Suspect should be considered armed and extremely dangerous. I repeat, suspect is extremely dangerous."

"Roger that, 8-12. Will notify Medivac, bomb squad and Water Patrol."

Dikes sped out of the car park and along the road that ran parallel to the ocean.

"There's a-" Dikes paused, knowing that the police channels were constantly monitored by certain public groups. "There's also an alleged paedophile being held by a member of the public on my order at the beach. Unknown at this time of any outstanding warrants. Please request an investigation."

"Roger that. Back-up has just arrived, 8-12. Over and out."

* * *

Two police boats were dispatched from the nearby police marina with their lights flashing and sirens blaring.

* * *

Dikes occasionally glimpsed the suspect's cruiser through the gaps in the buildings as he sped along the road.

* * *

The water police came around the spit and immediately spotted the suspect boat. One stopped directly in the path of the incoming cruiser while the other went wide to flank it. Officers aboard the stationary craft rushed to the port side, aiming their weapons at the approaching cruiser.

The captain of the stationary police boat picked up his handset and switched it to megaphone mode.

"This is the JAPD water police! Turn your engine off, bring your vessel to a halt, and put your hands on top of your head, or you will be fired upon!"

The suspect's cruiser continued its course, even increasing its speed.

"I repeat, turn your engine off, or you will be fired upon."

The suspect's cruiser maintained its stubborn course.

"Lou, fire a warning shot," the captain ordered.

Officer Lou Riley, a broad-shouldered man, steadied himself on the rolling deck of the police boat, took aim at the passenger window, and fired. It wasn't as central as Lou had liked, but the glass on the cruiser's portside window exploded, showering the suspect with glass.
The cabin cruiser banked hard left and stalled, almost throwing the suspect overboard.
The stationary police boat sped forward and then, along with the second police boat, moved into position on either side of the stalled cruiser.

"Put your hands on your head and get down on the floor!" the captain called out through the megaphone.
The suspect staggered to the back of the cruiser, placing one hand behind his head.

"Get down... I said, get down on the floor, now!" a second officer ordered as he and two others boarded the suspect's craft.

"I'm the… I'm… I'm the victim here. I was just shot at for no reason!" the suspect stammered as he was forced face-down onto the deck.

"Keep your head down. You have the right to remain silent!" the captain roared as he stepped on board.

"You're arresting me? I just told you I was the one shot at. Look at me; I'm bleeding!"

"You have the right to an attorney," the captain continued.
Once the suspect's rights were read, he was pulled to his feet.

The suspect was a thin, balding man with a tight moustache. He was wearing tan cargo shorts and a blue and white Hawaiian shirt that had a small tear and was smeared with blood on the upper left sleeve.

"So, who's going to help me with my arm? I'm bleeding," the suspect said calmly.

He now seemed almost resentful of the police and how they were treating him as he was transferred onto the police boat.

"Careful, I've been shot, you moron," the suspect yelled as an officer held him by the left arm.

"Shot?" the officer scoffed as he lifted the sleeve of the shirt and observed the minor flesh wound. "That's a scratch," he said with a smirk to his partner. "At best."

* * *

Dikes had lost sight of the cruiser behind the wall of towering holiday units but continued speeding in that direction.

"Base, this is 8-12; come in. What's happening? Have they seen the boat yet?" Dikes asked nervously.

"Wait one, 8-12," Central replied, then fell silent. It was almost a minute before Central reported back.

"8-12, they got him. They have the suspect in custody. I repeat, they have suspect in custody." Central said, unable to hide the relief in her voice.

"Yes!!" Dikes yelled as he punched the air and then slapped his steering wheel repeatedly. "Great job, guys!

Great frickin job," Dikes said excitedly as he replaced the handset.

With jubilant relief, Dikes slapped the steering wheel again and pumped his fist. "Yes! Got you!" he exclaimed as he slowed his vehicle to a safe speed.

CHAPTER NINE

In a Hotel room five stories above the city streets, a man dressed in a black suit walked past the wall-mounted flat-screen television carrying a black case. Playing on the television, a local news reporter was presenting her to-camera piece as the suited man unclipped the locks on the case and then opened it, revealing a black and gun metal grey sniper rifle. The rifle had been broken down into three pieces and came with a Vortex Viper PST x24 scope, two magazines and twelve single, brass-coloured 7.62mm rounds, all packed tightly in the rigid foam casing.

"As reported earlier this morning," the reporter in the red dress continued, "a suspect in the murders of three college students has just been apprehended after a high-speed chase involving both ground and water police. The chase was initiated after one of the city's high-profile detectives failed to save a possible fourth victim from an explosion that rocked South Port Beach shortly after nine-thirty this morning. The suspect is currently in police custody and is being brought here," she gestured to the building behind her, "to the JAPD precinct for questioning."

As the television continued playing in the background, the room's lone occupant began assembling the high-powered rifle. The time it took him to assemble the weapon demonstrated his proficiency.

The reporter continued, "Reports of a middle-aged man being pulled from a coffin buried approximately 100 metres away from the explosion at South Port Beach have emerged. He is reportedly part of the investigation but is not being questioned in connection with the explosion or the three murders."

The suited man carefully loaded three large calibre bullets into the rifle's magazine, slid the magazine into the rifle and cocked the weapon. He then crossed the room and placed the rifle on a desk he'd positioned in front of a window that had been cracked open just a centimetre.

Looking through the gap in the window to the street below, he watched the swarm of reporters jockey for position in front of the precinct as two police cars pulled up.

Handcuffed, the suspect from the boat was hauled out and pushed through the mass of reporters into the precinct.

The suspected paedophile was lifted from the second car and pushed behind the first suspect.

Jack, Smith, and Tran met the arresting officers in the foyer and then led them to the elevators.

"Fifth-floor interrogation rooms, please, Captain," Jack said to the arresting officer.

"You not coming up?" Smith asked.

Jack shook his head. "I'll wait down here for Dikes. He'll definitely want the guy from the boat. You and Tran head upstairs with him; you'll be in the room with us while Bradshaw and Jones take the suspected paedo."

Smith nodded then she, Tran, the suspects and the arresting officer stepped into the elevator.

Several minutes later, Dikes' car screeched to a halt just behind the police cars the suspects were delivered in. Before he could get out, cameramen, photographers, and reporters had swamped his vehicle, and cameras were shoved in his face or pointed at him through every window.

"Jesus Christ," he mumbled as reporters slapped his windows while yelling questions at him. "Fucking vultures," he continued without moving his lips. Without answering a single question and only saying, "Excuse me," Dikes made his way into the precinct, where Jack was waiting for him next to the front desk.

"Nice reception you got there," Jack said with a smile.

Dikes rolled his eyes and followed Jack into one of the waiting elevators.

"How long ago did they get here?" Dikes asked.

"Maybe five minutes ago. But because of these shitty old elevators, they're probably only just walking into the interview rooms now."

Once in the elevator, Dikes and Jack turned and faced the sea of reporters who were still yelling questions at them from the front doors, which had been blocked by three uniformed police while the suspects were taken in.

Because the elevators faced the main street, it gave the public and press easy access to film and photograph the detectives as they entered or exited.

And because the precinct building was so old, the ageing elevator doors took an age to open and close, leaving the press plenty of time to film them. It wasn't just the doors that were slow; the climb and descent between floors were just as painfully slow.

Over the years, Dikes and Jack had mastered the art of standing in the elevator smiling, discussing case details without moving their lips. Perfect for times like this.

"I'm really sorry about the girl, Nick," Jack said forlornly. "I really am."

Dikes remained silent; the only movement came from his jaw muscles as they knotted and tightened as he clenched his teeth.

"Bloody elevators," Jack said after a few seconds of silence, giving the press a half smile. "Listen, one hundred percent of people would have made the same decision you made if given the same misinformation."

Dikes opened his mouth to speak but stopped when the elevator doors began to rattle closed.

Once the doors had closed and they were alone, Dikes turned to Jack. "But it was me that got her killed, Jack," he said dejectedly. His expression hardened as he took Jack tightly by the shoulders and smiled. "But we got the fucker; we got him," he smiled behind gritted teeth.

Jack smiled. "I'm glad you got him, bud; I am," he said sincerely.

"This prick can't get off, Jack," Dikes said, releasing him.

"I was about to say the same thing. Let's make sure everything we do on our end is clean and by the books." Dikes agreed with a silent nod.

The boat suspect was forcefully shoved into a chair opposite the window, which faced the Commonwealth Hotel.
Detectives Jones, Tran, and Smith filed into the room, with Smith standing at the back, gazing out of the window.
Jack and Dikes arrived four minutes later.
Jack spoke up: "You're in a world of hurt now, arsehole."
He immediately regretted swearing, briefly flashing Dikes an apologetic look, which Dikes waved away.
The suspect shook his head, protesting, "I'm not him! It's just a coincidence!"
Dikes replied with an air of calmness, "Of course it is. Just a big coincidence that you were at the beach today when a young girl was murdered. That you were watching it all through binoculars. Just a coincidence that you took off the second you saw me looking at you."
Dikes could feel his anger rising. He had to be careful with this guy because the entire case would fall apart if he lashed out.

"I'm not that killer!" he said nervously as he placed his handcuffed hands on the table. "I heard them talking in the car on the way over here. They said I was the one that's been killing those students and joining their bodies together. It's not me. I didn't kill anyone!"

Hearing the suspect mention the killer's method of joining the body parts together got everyone's attention.

"Joined together?" Jack asked, playing dumb.

"Yeah, the scorpion thing," the suspect explained. "They said they'd been chopped up and turned into some scorpion creature. I wouldn't do that; I couldn't do that to anyone," he said.

Dikes made a mental note to have a very stern talk with the arresting officers and remind them to keep their damn mouths shut when transporting suspects. Nothing regarding the human sculpture has been released to the public yet. But that talk was for later. What he needed to do right now was get a confession.

"Who did it then, Joe?" Dikes roared. "If you're not the killer, and we have the wrong guy, then who did it?"

"I... I... don't... how am I supposed to know?" the suspect stammered as he stared fearfully at Dikes. "And my name's not Joe."

"What were you doing at the beach today? And why were you watching Detective Dikes through binoculars?" Smith asked in a soft but firm tone. She had her arms folded firmly across her chest as she remained in front of the window.

"Wha... what?"

"You heard me, sir," she said firmly.

The suspect's eyes bounced nervously around the room to each detective. Dikes slammed his hands onto the table in front of the suspect, bringing his attention back to Dikes.

"Answer her," Dikes said behind gritted teeth.

"I was… I was paid to be there," the suspect said, stumbling over his words.

"Someone paid you to go to a beach where a teenage girl was about to be murdered? They paid you to watch her murder and then flee the scene? You accepted money for this deal?" Smith asked.

The suspect nervously nodded. "You make it sound so… so creepy."

"It is, though, isn't it? Jack asked.

"He paid me two thousand dollars. For that, all I had to do was go and watch; I didn't know anything about a girl or that she was going to be blown up," he said as his eyes again bounced between detectives.

"Someone paid you two thousand dollars to watch the beach?" Dikes scoffed. He didn't believe it and was sick of his stories already. Turning up the heat somewhat, Dikes leant in close to the suspect's face.

"Why would someone pay you to watch the fucking beach?" he hissed angrily.

"I never said I was there to watch the beach," he stammered. "I was there to watch you," he said as he nodded at Dikes.

Everyone looked at Dikes.

Dikes was taken aback by this and shot Jack a questioning glance.

"Who paid you?" Jack asked, stepping in to help but in a gentler tone. With so much built-up aggression in the room, Jack thought it best to change tact for a minute.

"I don't know his name. Well, not his real name. I only know the name he uses on the PayCheque app."

"And what makes you think it's not his real name?" Tran chimed in.

"Because there was no middle or surname for that account; that's why I assumed it was an alias."

"And what was the name on the account?"

"Joe."

Dikes could feel the pent-up aggression evaporate, along with any chance of this man being the killer.

Dikes maintained his poker face as he gnashed his teeth and straightened to his full height. Jack slowly turned, shooting both Smith and Tran an apprehensive look.

"What instructions were you given?" Jack asked, getting back on track.

"I... I was told to be positioned just off the headland and wait for a police car to show up. So that's what I did. I wasn't there for long when I heard a car screech into the car park with its lights flashing. So, from then on, I did what I was paid to do; I just watched him," he nodded at Dikes. "Through my binoculars."

Dikes frowned and moved to the window beside Smith.

"And then he-" the suspect pointed his shackled hands accusingly at Dikes. "He shot me! That's why I took off," he explained. "Who in their right mind would just stand there while some lunatic shoots at them?"

Looking out across the city, it crossed Dikes' mind for the first time that maybe they were in over their heads on this one. When he turned and saw the apprehension on Jack's face, he knew his partner was coming to the same conclusion.

"I didn't kill those people, Detectives," he said. "I have a ten-year-old daughter myself."

Dikes was deflated. Just a minute ago, he was certain that this was their Joe, but regardless, he was going to push on him to see why Joe had chosen him and what, if any, further information he could get out of him.

Jack sat at the desk in front of the suspect while Dikes leaned in from the other side.

"Can we contact Joe directly using the PayCheque app?" Jack asked.

The suspect nodded, but before he could reply, a muffled bang outside the building made everyone in the room jump. Smith peered out the window, trying to identify the source of the sound. Jack maintained eye contact with the suspect and slapped his palm onto the table to get him to look at him. "Don't worry about whatever that was; just answer the question."

Before he could respond, a commotion erupted down the hall.

Dikes glanced back at Tran, about to tell him to investigate it, only to be met with a deafening thwack as the suspect's head exploded from the chin up, covering Dikes and Jack with blood, skull and brain matter.

Dikes dropped to the floor with a thud.

Jack attempted to push himself away from the desk, but his hand slipped in the slick pool of blood, causing him to stumble and crash onto the desk before finally plummeting to the floor.

Smith was showered in tiny shards of glass as she and Tran dove for cover under the window frame. Glancing at Tran, she saw a worried expression on his face.

Jack scrambled backward, cursing, his hands shaking as he tried to wipe the blood from his eyes.

Dikes crept closer to the suspect and saw that his head had been all but blasted off his neck, leaving only the lower half of his jaw dangling beneath the few scraps of his ear still attached.

Tran, who was still staring at Smith, asked, "Are you alright?"

She felt the side of her face, which had started to sting and bleed; traces of her blood were on her fingers. Nervously, she asked, "Am I okay?" Just then, she heard something from the doorway.

Bradshaw and Jones rushed to the doorway with their weapons drawn, their clothes and faces covered with blood.

"Oh shit! You too!" Bradshaw shouted.

With blood and fragments of the suspect's head dripping down his face, the Dexter theme song played from Dikes' pocket. He ignored it and then spat disgustedly as something lumpy slid into the side of his mouth.

"Ugh, that's disgusting," Smith said as she watched Jack peel a blob of fleshy remains from his forehead.

"You fuckin' think?" Jack retorted as he looked toward the shattered window and then at Smith's face. Seeing the side of her face bleeding, Jack quickly tamped his anger. "You okay, Smith?"

"I'm fine," she replied.

Dikes turned to the bloodied Bradshaw and Jones at the doorway. "What do you mean, us too?"

A secretary had heard the commotion and stepped into the doorway. Seeing the bloody carnage, her horrified screams washed over the office.

The suspect's headless body slowly slid off the table and flopped into a heap onto the floor next to Jack.

Bradshaw stepped into the room, his breathing quick from the adrenaline rush.

"That paedophile we were questioning has less of a head than your guy!" he exclaimed, gesturing to the bullet hole in the window.

Jack nodded, his eyes widening in disbelief. "That son of a bitch shot right between our heads!" he said.

Smith and Tran stared in amazement at the bullet hole.

"There couldn't have been more than five centimetres between us at the time," Jack continued. "I felt the damn bullet fly straight past my ear!"

Dikes glanced at the window to get an idea of the shots direction.

"It came from one of two buildings. The Hammerstein or the -" Dikes popped his head up to get another look. "The Commonwealth," he guessed.

"Smith, Tran, radio Captain Hale, he's training with his troops in the basement of our building today, send him across."

Smith and Tran quickly drew their radios, explaining the situation and Dikes' orders to Captain Hale. Within minutes he'd ordered both of his squads to change to live ammunition and swiftly moved from the JAPD basement to the buildings Dikes had identified as potential targets. The Dexter theme song continued to play from Dikes' pocket as the young guns continued their conversation with SWAT.

Jack spat as he asked, "You gonna get that?" About to wipe his face with the back of his hand, he realised it was covered in blood and small chunks of brain. "Oh, Jesus," he muttered, his annoyance increasing as Dikes' phone kept ringing.

Finally, Dikes pulled the phone out of his pocket. Across the screen was the name "JOE". He held it up for everyone to see and pointed at the body. In a stern tone, he proclaimed, "This is what we're up against. Never forget that. Unrelenting evil."

Tran shakily asked, "He's actually calling you right after doing... this?"

Dikes shared an uneasy glance with Tran before he pressed the answer button. "What?" Dikes answered irritably.

"Is that any way to answer the phone, Nicholas? I am only calling at this time because I know your schedule suddenly freed up."

Dikes felt something slimy slide towards his mouth, so he wiped his mouth onto his shoulder.

"What do you want?" Dikes asked firmly as he got to his feet.

"Just to chat. It doesn't look like-"

Dikes hung up the phone, his patience with Joe exhausted. He strode calmly to the window and stood in full view, no longer willing to be pushed around and humiliated.

"Get down, boss!" Smith yelled.

"He's not going to shoot me," Dikes said in a reassured tone.

Dikes scanned the wall of windows across the street. Then he saw it! The silhouette of a man standing motionless in a room directly across the street. He looked to be holding a long rifle.

Without taking his eyes from the silhouette, Dikes wiped the side of his mouth with his sleeve while talking to Tran and Smith without moving his lips. "Tell your teams he's in the room directly opposite ours, it's the one with the window slightly cracked open," Dikes explained. "It looks like he has a rifle case with him. So, approach with extreme caution!" he ordered.

Smith fed Hale the information while she and Tran peaked around the edge of the window, only game to take short glances.

As if acknowledging what Dikes had just said, the silhouette gave a nod, patted the case and then stepped away from the window.

Dikes couldn't be sure of the nod, but it sure looked like one.

"You can hop up," Dikes said calmly to everyone. "He's gone."

With deep breaths, Tran and Smith stood up beside Dikes in clear view of the window, exchanging nervous glances but ultimately trusting Dikes.

"Across the street. Same floor as us," Dikes said, then turned to Jack.

Tran received an alert on his phone. "Alpha team is in the lobby of the Commonwealth sir, it'll be secured within three minutes. If that was him at the window just now, then we have him pinned in."

Smith also explained that the second team was only minutes away from locking down the other building.

"Let's get across there and get this prick once and for all," Dikes said.

Jack was still attempting to clean his face when he and Dikes ran out of the office. Smith, Tran, Jones, and Bradshaw sprinting after them.

As they raced through the fifth-floor interrogation level of the precinct, everyone gave them a wide birth. While passing the duty officer's desk, Jack grabbed four handheld radios and tossed one to each member of the squad.

CHAPTER TEN

Chief Bryant had just stepped out of the elevator on the fifth floor when he encountered the entire floor in chaos. Then, to his horror, Dikes, Jack, Bradshaw, Jones, Smith, and Tran ran towards him, covered in blood.

"What the hell?" was all the chief could utter when Dikes yelled at him to hold the elevator doors for them. After seeing his chief's horrified expression as they piled into the elevator, Dikes quickly assured him it wasn't any of theirs.

"Then who's the hell is it?"

"The suspect and the paedo. But the suspect was innocent. Of the killings, anyway." Jack explained as a piece of jelly-like brain matter fell from his head to his shoulder

To his credit, Chief Bryant's expression didn't change, and he didn't keep questioning them. It was only after he had walked down the hall and checked in both interview rooms that everything started to make sense.

It was quiet inside the old elevator as the squad waited patiently for the doors to close. Jack swatted half-heartedly at something that had brushed against his ear and then looked to see what it was. After examining his finger, Jack stared in horror at the attached piece of brain. Hoping to keep his breakfast from paying everyone a visit in the elevator's confined space, Jack exhaled slowly between pursed lips.

To free his finger from the brain segment, Jack gently shook his hand, but it didn't come loose.

Drawing another deep breath as he stared ahead, Jack was confident that everyone was now watching him.

He was correct; everyone in the elevator and the people still in the hallway watched him until the doors slowly closed.

A glance passed between Smith and Tran, neither inclined to smile in such a bizarre situation.

Dikes considered offering advice to his friend, but Jack's slow shake of the head and a solid scowl silenced him.

Jack thought of kneeling so he could wipe the brain segment off his finger onto the floor when he noticed the handrail. As he leaned forward to wipe his finger on the handrail, he suddenly considered it unethical and decided against this idea as well. Taking an awkward stance between kneeling and leaning, Jack ended up doing the only honourable thing that came to mind. A single sniff later, he stood straight and slowly slipped his hand into his pocket to deposit the sticky brain piece.

Everyone's attention was now focused on Jack's face. The squad knew that he was probably just seconds away from some sort of monumental blow-up, so they remained silent and avoided eye contact with him as he glanced around the elevator.

With his hand still in his pocket, the expression on Jack's face did not disappoint; it was a mixture of disgust, perplexity, and anger as he continued wiping and flicking the stubborn brain segment off his finger. Several seconds later, Jack pulled his hand from his pocket, but what he saw made his shoulders drop. There was still a small piece of brain attached to his finger. Jack groaned inwardly and blinked slowly as he drew a deep, anger-building breath.

While the others looked away or pretended to check their phones, Dikes bit his top lip to stop himself from smiling.

Jack slid his hand back into his pocket; this time, he squeezed the brain segment between his other fingers, trapping it between the inner pocket material.

Dikes looked across at the rest of the squad, and even though he was covered in blood, Bradshaw nearly laughed. Dikes frowned and shook his head before looking away.

Jack retrieved his hand and breathed a sigh of relief to find it free of brains. He straightened his jacket and realised that it, too, was covered in gore. He looked at Dikes, who was similarly splattered and then at Bradshaw and Jones, who were both sprayed with a lot of blood. Smith had a few cuts on her left cheek from glass, but Tran was spotless. Without a word, Jack turned and faced the front.

As the elevator doors creaked open, the detectives were greeted by a sea of cameras, photographers and reporters that had been allowed back into the foyer area.

There was an immediate hush in the bustling foyer as everyone noticed the blood-covered detectives and inhaled sharply in shock and disgust.

Dikes and Jack stood motionless, their gazes fixed forward. Not a single reporter moved or uttered a word, creating an unsettling stillness that filled the area.

The silence was broken a few moments later when the elevator doors slowly closed. To stop the doors from closing, Jack placed a hand across one, blocking it. As a result of his action, two things happened simultaneously. It stopped the doors from closing and caused the invisible barrier between him, his colleagues, and the reporters to be broken. The reporters and cameramen suddenly rushed forward, shouting questions at the blood-spattered detectives.

Jack held out his hand to keep the crowd of reporters back. He was delighted to find that the blood covering him was effective at keeping them at bay better than usual, so he took wider and quicker steps, which allowed him to brush up against and lean on the retreating reporters and cameramen, staining their freshly pressed clothes with blood.

Smith rushed forward to help, but Jack shook his head.

"I've got this, kid," he said with a smile.

As she watched several reporters stumble back and fall, trying to avoid the blood-stained detective, Smith could only smile.

Having escaped the reporters, the six detectives sprinted across the street to the adjoining building. Ducking under the yellow and black police 'crime scene' tape that had already been put in place, they raced into the lobby, where they were met by Captain Hale.

"Captain," Dikes introduced himself.

"Detective," Hale nodded and gave a quick glance at Dikes and his squad, not mentioning the blood and gore. "Both teams have locked down the buildings you instructed. But it's this one you're more confident he's in, correct?"

"Correct, Captain. I'm sure I saw him in the window directly opposite our interrogation room seconds after the shots that…" He gestured vaguely to himself and his squad.

"Roger that. What's your call on breaching the room?" Hale asked.

"Jack and I will be taking that floor and room; if I can get your men to lock down the stairwells above and below the fifth floor while I send two of mine down to secure the basement elevators. You're welcome to join Jack and I, Captain."

Hale nodded. "Will do, sir," he said, then turned to issue orders to his team.

Dikes turned to Bradshaw and Jones. "I want you two to take the basement and car park levels. Absolutely no one in or out of this place until I give the order."

Jones and Bradshaw nodded and ran to the stairwell.

"And be careful down there," Dikes yelled after them. "I don't need to tell you how smart or vicious this guy can be. He's already planned this escape, god, knows how long ago, so look out for..." Dikes thought for a moment and shrugged. "Traps or anything, I guess." Bradshaw and Jones gave a nod and a thumbs up as they disappeared into the stairwell, followed by one of Captain Hale's SWAT officers.

Dikes then addressed the young guns. "After what we've seen, just be careful." Dikes finished.

"Yes, sir," Tran and Smith replied.

"You two take the elevators to the fourth and sixth floors, one at each end of the halls. Jack, Captain Hale, and I will take the fifth floor and the room!"

Smith and Tran nodded, and the two groups split up.

* * *

Taking a deep breath, Dikes slowly opened the door that led to the fifth-floor hallway. Seeing nothing but an empty hallway ahead and knowing the building was a T shape, Dikes gave Jack and Hale a nod and then moved into the hall with his pistol poised. He immediately turned and took a position in the left hall while Jack moved down the hallway to the right and Hale straight up the middle.

"Clear," Dikes whispered.

"Clear," Jack replied.

"Clear," said Hale, who had dropped to one knee, awaiting orders.

The trio realised that the room they sought was down the central hallway, so they proceeded cautiously down the hall Hale had cleared, examining every door they encountered.

Dikes turned to Jack and pointed to the three doors ahead on the right-hand side. He gave a shrug and mouthed, "Which one?"

Jack and Hale surveyed their location in relation to the precinct, and, to get his bearings, Jack closed his eyes. When he opened them, he nodded towards the door two doors down from where they stood. Hale concurred.

"It's one of those two," Hale whispered as he tilted his head to the left to get a better view of the numbers. "Twenty… three or twenty-four," he concluded.

The three men agreed, raised their weapons to a firing position, and then moved toward the first door.

The building's fire alarm and sprinklers suddenly ignited with an audible hiss, releasing torrents of water. In addition to the sprinklers, an alarm sounded, and blue flashing lights embedded along the ceiling lit up and led to the staircases.

"Distraction, or he's torched the room!" Jack shouted over the noise.

Hotel guests rushed out of their rooms, holding jackets, blankets, or whatever they could grab to protect themselves from the water.

Hale, Dikes and Jack exchanged annoyed glances as they navigated their way through the crowd of rushing people to room twenty-three. In spite of scrutinising every male face passing them and any luggage they carried, they had no real idea what their man looked like.

"Fuckin' Joe," Dikes shouted a little louder than he meant to.

From the corner of his eye, he saw Jack and Hale staring at him.

A subtle shake of his head was all he responded with instead of speaking.

Jack and Hale both comprehended the unspoken message. Then, with a quick, sharp whistle, Hale gestured towards the door.

"Fucker has torched the room," Hale hissed as smoke wafted from under the door.

Completely drenched now, the trio readied themselves in front of the door.

Hale allowed the last few people to run past, then moved in front of the door, ready to kick it in.

With a nod from Dikes, Hale stepped back and then kicked the door open.

The moment the door swung open, thick white smoke with an acrid smell billowed out of the room, forcing the trio back and to cover their mouths as best they could with their sleeves or the crook of their elbows.

As prepared as they could be, the trio moved into the room to clear it.

Once inside the smoke-filled room, they discovered the couch, television, and table next to the window had been doused in a flammable liquid and set ablaze.

Dikes and Jack cleared the adjoining rooms while Hale cleared the main rooms and kitchen area.

"Clear!" Jack yelled from a bedroom.

Dikes had his mouth buried in the crook of his elbow, coughing as he cleared the bathroom.

"Clear!" Dikes yelled between coughs.

"All clear!" Hale yelled, having cleared the rest of the apartment.

"Jesus, I can't breathe in here!" Jack shouted in frustration as he headed for the window.

Careful not to let his pants catch on fire, Jack pushed the burning table aside with his boot. As soon as the flaming table was no longer a threat, he quickly slid the window wide open and leaned outside, gasping for clean air. Once his vision had cleared, he was annoyed to see that all of the cameras below were pointing up at him.

"Argh bloody hell," he grumbled, not wanting to be on the five o'clock news hanging out of a burning window.

He took a deep breath and then disappeared back into the smoke-filled room.

Back inside the smoky apartment, Jack quickly covered his head with his wet, bloodied jacket, then moved out to the hallway where Dikes was leaning forward on his knees, drawing deep breaths while Hale was coughing but hadn't taken in as much smoke as Dikes.

Dikes remembered that every floor had a fire hose, so he glanced around and quickly spotted one at the end of the hall.

Still coughing, Dikes ran to the fire hose, opened and unlocked its reel and then ran it back to the doorway of the room; once there, he turned on the nozzle and began extinguishing the flames. It took Dikes less than two minutes to put out the three fires. Once they were out, Jack and Hale moved back into the room as an exhausted Dikes tossed the hose to the floor.

No sooner had he dropped the fire hose than the building's sprinklers turned off.

Upon re-entering the room, Dikes noticed a peculiar smell he couldn't identify.

Hale ran his gloved index finger along the corner of the desk, then pinched it against his thumb.

When he pulled them apart, they were connected by strands of congealed ooze. "He's used an accelerant," he explained.

"We could have gotten here twenty seconds after he left, but because he used this stuff, we still would have come away with nothing," Jack said sourly before they heard noises from the hallway.

Dikes was closest to the door, so he leant back to look. Three firefighters walked briskly towards him in full firefighting gear. He gave them a wave and then leaned back into the room. "It's the fireys," he told the others. Seconds later, the fire lieutenant entered. "Gentlemen." He gave a single nod before examining the room and spotting the hose on the floor next to Dikes. "Nice job, men. You definitely saved the room."

"All his doing." Jack pointed at Dikes.

"Well done, Captain," the fire lieutenant said. "But for now, how about you three give us five minutes to legally give this place a structural tick of approval? Then you can let forensics in."

That all made sense to Dikes, and before he could open his mouth to speak, the lieutenant cut in.

"No need to worry, Captain Dikes; we won't be touching anything. We want to see this guy put away as well," he said sternly.

Dikes was confident that the lieutenant knew the process well enough that he and Jack could get some fresh air and regroup with the rest of the squad.

"Let's get out of here for ten. Let these boys handle it," Dikes suggested to Jack, who was kneeling before the couch, staring at an area covered in the sticky goop. Jack stood, then followed Dikes and Hale out of the room while shaking his head disappointedly.

"There's no need to come back. There's nothing in here for us to find. Any DNA or prints he may have left behind are non-existent or destroyed by now. That sticky shit has destroyed any trace of it."

* * *

Dikes, Hale, and Jack descended the stairwell, their clothes drenched.

As they descended, they hugged the left side while firemen and other first responders rushed up the stairs.

The trio exited the stairwell and was greeted by a packed lobby. Everyone evacuated from the hotel was either gathered in the lobby or out front of the hotel. Officers were moving people into lines so other police officers could interview them.

When Dikes spotted Bryant in the crowd, he changed directions so he could intercept him.

In full chief mode, Bryant grabbed an officer by the arm as he passed.

"Make sure you tell Sergeant Symonds that I want every last one of them interviewed, photographed and fingerprinted before they're allowed to leave," he ordered, pointing to the mass of hotel staff and guests standing outside. "Any IDs they have on them, room keys or if they worked here, which area?"

"Yes, sir," the officer replied, then turned to find the sergeant.

Bryant was about to issue more orders to another officer when he saw Jack, Hale and Dikes approaching.

"Anything?" he asked hopefully, but the look on all three men's faces said it all.

Bryant then looked Dikes and Jack up and down.

"At least the water washed most of that crap off, you two," the chief said with no hint of a smile.

"Yeah," was all Jack could think to say as he ran his hand through his wet hair.

"So, do you think forensics will have any luck up there?" Bryant asked.

Dikes, who shared a look with Jack, shook his head.

"Nothing, boss. He covered every surface he'd touched with some sort of thick accelerant, then torched the room," Dikes explained.

"I'm pretty sure it was a mixture of lacquer and paint stripper," Hale cut in. "So even if he hadn't lit it, we wouldn't have gotten any prints off anything anyway."

"Son of a..." Bryant grumbled as he looked at the lobby full of people. "And you still can't remember what he looks like from the art event?" he asked.

Annoyed at himself, Dikes shook his head. "A very vague idea of his height, but not his face," Dikes explained, clearly frustrated.

"Speaking of which," Jack said as he spoke into his handheld. "Tran, Smith, you two got anything?"

"Nothing here," came Tran's voice. "Once the alarms went off, I just sent everyone down to the lobby," he explained. "No one had a gun, hard case or anything that even resembled one."

"Same at my end," came Smith's voice over the handheld. "No one's entered this hall or the stairwell since the initial evacuation," reported Smith.

"Jones, Bradshaw, what about you two? Has anyone tried to leave via the basement level?"

Waiting for a reply, Dikes watched as water dripped from his jacket's left cuff onto the lobby's white tiles. The pooling water was tinged with red.

Getting no answer, Dikes glanced at Jack, who was frowning as he waited impatiently for a response.

"Jones, Bradshaw, you copy?" Jack repeated.

Nothing but icy silence greeted them.

Hale immediately pressed the activator on his neck to talk to his team. "McMillan, you copy?"

Everyone remained silent as they waited for a response.

"McMillan, you copy, son?" Hale asked; a tinge of concern had crept into his voice.

"Jones, Bradshaw, you copy?" Jack asked firmly.

As they were waiting for a reply, Dikes and Bryant exchanged a concerned look.

Hale and Dikes then exchanged the same look. Dikes quickly tossed his radio to Chief Bryant, and then he, Hale, and Jack raced towards the staircase. Jack tossed his handheld to Dikes.

Captain Hale ordered three of his team to meet him down on the basement level but to enter via the street ramp.

"Smith, Tran, meet us down at the basement level; take the stairs," Dikes ordered, hoping he was successful in keeping his nervousness out of his voice.

"Roger that/yes sir," they replied.

Drawing their pistols, the trio ran back into the staircase and headed down.

Dikes, Hale and Jack descended the stairs quickly and quietly. When they reached the basement car park door, Dikes counted down from three. Once he hit zero, they burst through the door.

As Dikes cleared the left side, Jack swept the right while Hale moved forward, checking under and between the parked cars ahead of them. Once the area had been cleared, they stood quietly for a moment, just listening. Then, the phone Joe had given Dikes beeped and vibrated; it had received a text.

FROM JOE:

Two minutes too late, Nicholas. Better luck next time.

I will call again soon.

Dikes showed the other two. He was furious.

"Damn it!" Jack yelled.

"Then where are our-" Hale was asking when an elevator started moving. It was coming down to the basement from one of the floors above.

The trio exchanged solemn glances.

"You sending someone down, sir?" Dikes quickly asked Bryant.

"No." Bryant's confused voice crackled over the radio. "I thought they were shut down?"

"Smith? Tran?" Dikes questioned.

"That's a negative, sir, came Tran's voice. "We're still in the stairwell, just passing the third floor."

"We have movement in..." Dikes glanced up at the elevator number. "Elevator three," he replied, quickly attaching the radio to his belt so that he could keep a firm grip on his pistol.

The three men were poised, weapons ready, as they stared intently at the elevator doors. Jack and Dikes stood in a stance of readiness, their leading legs forward for stability, while Hale knelt and aimed through the scope of his M4 tactical machine gun.

In order to make sure they were alone in the parking lot, Jack quickly glanced around the area one last time.

There was a mechanical whir, then a click, followed by a series of clunks as the elevator doors slowly opened to reveal the bodies of Bradshaw, Jones, and McMillan.

They had been unceremoniously dumped on top of each other on the elevator floor.

Bradshaw had been shot in the cheek and right eye, while Jones and McMillan had their throats viciously slit.

In total shock, Dikes and Jack involuntarily lowered their weapons.

Dikes could only stare ahead, disbelief and horror washing over him.

Unable to comprehend the sight of his friends' blood-covered bodies, his eyes welled with tears, his mind spun, and his stomach churned, leaving him speechless and not knowing what to do.

Meanwhile, Jack stood speechless, his eyes wide with horror, his hands trembling from the shock of the scene that lay before him.

After a lengthy pause, Captain Hale rose and engaged the safety on his weapon.

Tears rolled down Jack's face as he struggled to contain his seething anger and profound grief. His jaw muscles tightened in a way that matched the storm of emotions inside him. He longed to destroy everything around him, but he knew it wouldn't do anything to alleviate his suffering. "FFUUUCKK!!" Jack screamed as he spun around, blindly punching his weapon in the air. "Fuck you, you piece of shit!" he yelled.

The only response he received was his own angry echo. Before the elevator doors could close, a teary-eyed Captain Hale stepped in, carefully avoiding the pool of blood and locked the elevator doors open.

For Hale, it was still important to check all three men for a pulse, despite knowing that none of them had one.

Hale could do nothing but gnash his teeth in frustration and anger as he slung his M4 and stared down at the deceased officers.

Jones and Bradshaw had obviously been good officers. They had to be if they were part of Dikes' extended squad. But McMillan was one of his. He'd personally chosen the young man from a pool of over two hundred applicants. They'd trained together, fought, laughed, and broke bread together. The death of Sergeant Timothy Andrew McMillan was more than just the death of a colleague; it was the death of a friend, murdered by some cold-blooded piece of shit that Hale would now do anything to get his hands on.

With a loud bang that echoed around the basement car park, the door to the stairwell opened as Tran and Smith ran out.

At first, neither of them knew what was happening. Dikes was squatting against a car with his head bowed, resting the back of his pistol against his head, while Jack paced back and forth, swearing and murmuring under his breath, tears in his eyes.

They heard the boots of Captain Hale exiting the elevator and then saw the three bodies.

"Oh my god!" Tran exclaimed.

Smith covered her mouth with her hands as tears welled up in her eyes.

It was a devastated Captain Hale who exited the elevator, gazing deeply into their eyes as he silently passed them. Smith could see the pain in his eyes as he stepped away from the elevator without saying a word to anyone. Instead, he proceeded to the far end of the basement car park on his own.

Smith watched him speak quietly into his communicator to his team. With tears in her eyes, she glanced back at the bodies. She was shaking and couldn't bear looking at her murdered friends anymore, so she moved back towards the stairwell and then broke down.

"You seem to be able to see and hear everything we do, you gutless fuck!" Jack yelled as he gave the finger using both hands to the ceiling. "Fuck you, you limp dicked mother fucker! Fuck you and your whore mother!" He continued to yell angrily while turning in a three-sixty, looking for any sign of Joe's cameras.

Dikes collapsed onto the cold concrete floor with his hands resting over his knees. Tears flowed as he stared at the bodies of his friends piled in the elevator ahead.

* * *

The moon shone high in the night sky above the city, its light barely visible through the flashing red and blue lights.

Chief Bryant stood among reporters, microphones and cameras, giving his final media briefing for the day.

A tall, pointy-nosed reporter pushed his microphone in front of the others.

"Is this the work of the same individual responsible for the South Port beach incident? Do you have any leads at this stage?"

The chief pushed his glasses closer to his face with his index finger. "We have several leads under investigation, but at this time, I am not at liberty to discuss any of the specifics," he dodged artfully.

Summers, the pretty female reporter in a striking red dress, pushed her way to the front and loudly cut in over other reporters trying to ask questions.

"Is there any truth to the rumours that the suspect brought in for questioning over the spate of recent murders was, in fact, shot while in police custody?" she asked in a terse tone.

"Yes, a male suspect was taken into custody earlier today concerning the explosion at South Port beach, but, as I explained, I cannot discuss anything further at this time. Thank you."

"And is it also true that that suspect was previously under investigation for sex crimes and suspected syndicate ties?"

This caught Bryant off guard, who looked back at his support staff for clarification, but they knew nothing about this man and could only shrug.

"Ahh, that part I wasn't aware of, Miss Summers," Bryant admitted honestly. "Where may I ask, did you get that information?"

"Am I doing your job now, Chief?" Summers half-joked.

"Wouldn't be the first time, would it?" the chief rebuked with a half-hearted smirk. Other reporters laughed with him.

"It came in as an anonymous source, along with a background report on the suspect your man chose to pull from the beach instead of the innocent seventeen-year-old school girl."

Hearing Summers word her comment this way irritated Bryant.

"That's not true or fair, Miss Summers, and you know it. So just keep your guesses and opinions to yourself in the future," Bryant snapped angrily.

Summers threw her hands up. "Excuse me, Chief. That's not one of my opinions; I'm just telling you the facts from today."

She stared defiantly at Chief Bryant and knew any heated response she'd receive would only be good for her report.

"We're all very aware of you and your opinions, Miss Summers. Now, before I give you one of mine, can I ask you a few simple questions?" Bryant asked politely.

With a pretentious nod and not bothering to hide her smirk, she said, "Fire away, Chief."

"Were you at the beach today Miss Summers?" the chief asked.

"No," Summers retorted disdainfully.

"Oh. So, when Detective Dikes was at the beach and was deliberately fed misleading information. You weren't there?"

Summers took a long moment to reply to the chief's question. "No, Chief. I wasn't."

"So, when he was put in a lose, lose situation but still risked his own life to save the young lady? You were surely there then, right?"

Summers blinked slowly. "You know I wasn't."

"You must have been there, Miss Summers? After all, you're the one criticising every move he makes and telling the world that he CHOSE to save that man instead of the young lady."

Summers didn't reply; the smirk had been firmly wiped from her face as her stare melted into a glare. She was on the receiving end and hated it.

"Just give my detectives a goddamn break! They risk their lives daily for this city, for you people, and as you've seen today," the chief pointed to the building behind him. "Sometimes, it ends up costing them their own damn lives." His voice cracked with emotion. "They don't need reporters giving out misleading information or clickbait stories that discredit their attempts at saving lives." The chief stared directly at Summers as he said this. "My detectives are going through hell right now; they-" the chief paused because his emotions had gotten the better of him again, and for the moment, he had to look away and draw a couple of deep breaths. "We just- we just lost two of our best detectives today. Two great family men, two great friends. Murdered by a gutless piece of...." Chief Bryant censored himself and stopped talking.

One of the reporters clapped slowly and loudly. "Well said, Chief. Well said."

Another cameraman leant out from behind his eyepiece. "And thank you to the three officers that gave their lives today too. Officers?" he asked, looking to Chief Bryant to provide the names of the fallen officers.

The chief gave a nod of gratitude to the cameramen. "Officer Jones, Officer Bradshaw and SWAT specialist, Mcmillian," the chief informed them.

There was a look of embarrassment on Summers' face as she lowered her head.

Seeing her like that didn't please the chief, but it calmed him enough to continue.

"My intention was not to embarrass you, Miss Summers. What I want you to know is that you, all of you," he said, gazing at the sea of faces before him, "as reporters, you have great power. Uncle Ben said it best to Peter Parker: with great power comes great responsibility. If you are given information from a private source that may help us in an active investigation, get it to us as quickly as possible; you never know, it might just save a life. This will not only make you a good reporter but a great human being. And in times like these, I think we need a lot more great human beings, don't you?" He gave Summers' shoulder a gentle squeeze.

Summers nodded. The venom in her glare had diminished, and she looked genuinely moved.

"I'll have that information to you in the next ten minutes, Chief," she said quietly.

"Thank you," Chief Bryant said as he flashed her a smile.

Chief Bryant then turned back to the crowd. "If I'm honest, we could really use your help with this one. The individual instigating this chaos is easily the most vicious and calculating murderer we've ever seen. So, my thinking is, if we all work together and quickly spread any of the newly relevant information I can get to you, we might just have a good chance at catching this... this individual, quicker than us doing it alone."

CHAPTER ELEVEN

In a narrow alley hidden from the main street, Dikes and Jack were sitting on the curb. Behind them, Smith and Tran were leaning against the wall beside an open door, Tran staring ahead while vaping and Smith going through evidence on her phone.

The door was propped open with a stack of milk crates. The corridor beyond led to a door that opened to the area behind the hotel's service counter in the main lobby.

A few metres from the four remaining squad members were the two ambulances that would be carrying the three bodies away.

Staring absently at the ambulances, Tran sucked on his vape pen as his mind wandered aimlessly, avoiding the terrible events of the past forty-eight hours. But then, his brain was drawn to the memory of when he had looked into the elevator and seen the bodies of his friends. He remembered the way Captain Hale had looked at him as he stepped past him on his way out.

Though Tran knew it had not occurred in slow motion, his mind replayed the incident in that way each time.

"Goddamn it!" he admonished himself quietly, angry at his brain for not sticking to its absentminded daydreams.

"What?" Smith asked without looking up from her screen.

Even Jack turned back to see what Tran was talking about.

Tran dismissed them with a wave of the hand and shake of the head. "Doesn't matter," he said quietly, then looked at Smith's screen as he returned to his vape.

On Smith's screen were the hotel's schematics. She was going through them for the third time. She was trying to locate any overlooked hallways, air conditioning vents, or old laundry shoots that may have been covered over in one of the building's countless renovations.

She was about to go over them again when she received an email that contained thirty-three photographs. The photographs were of bags, briefcases, backpacks and suitcases belonging to the people trying to leave the hotel during the evacuation.

Quickly flicking through them, Smith was trying to identify the type of rifle case that Dikes had seen and described to them while still thinking of how Joe had escaped and then sent the elevator down to the basement.

"He's stashed the rifle inside somewhere. I'm sure of it. And I bet there's a remote-controlled servo motor set up attached to the elevator control unit," Smith said confidently to no one in particular.

"Why? What makes you think he didn't just walk out with the weapon before we locked the place down?" Dikes asked.

"Unless he's Usain Bolt, there's no way he could have made it out of the building before SWAT got there. Hale had the front of this building locked down in under four minutes and the ramp that both the Commonwealth and Hammerstein use in five. This is why I'm certain he's also got original plans for the building and has used an old set of stairs or elevator shaft we don't know about.

"Keep looking, kid; you'll find it," Jack said gently, forcing a smile filled with sympathy. "What are you flicking through there?"

"Pictures; I asked the on-duty sergeant to send me pictures of every backpack or briefcase-type bag." She waved her phone. "I've just finished going through them, and none of them looks anything like the one the boss described," she explained. "Plus, if he'd actually left through the base..." Smith paused to get her head right because saying 'basement car park', let alone thinking about it, made her want to cry. "Through the basement level after he..."

Suddenly, the Dexter theme song played from Dikes' pocket, prompting everyone to turn to him.

Exhausted and emotionally spent, Dikes lowered his head.

Jack quickly took out his phone and was ready to record the conversation, but Dikes sat motionless without showing any sign he was going to answer the phone.

"You gonna get that, boss?" Jack asked in a hushed tone.

Dikes didn't immediately respond; instead, he just sat with his head bowed.

Jack flashed the young guns a reassuring look and then whispered. "You need to pick it up, Nick."

Reluctantly, Dikes looked up, nodding in agreement. "Yeah, I know."

When Dikes answered the phone, he put it on speaker for everyone to hear as Jack pressed record on his phone. Dikes remained silent for the first few seconds because he had decided that he was not going to speak first.

Why? Because, fuck Joe, that's why, he thought. There were a lot of sounds coming from Joe's end of the call, sounds you would expect from a bustling city street. There was a lot of traffic, an occasional beeping horn, and the sound of people simultaneously walking and talking.

"Good afternoon, Nicholas, Jack, Jasmin and Akeno. Please do not take the 'good afternoon' portion of my greeting as an insult or that I am in some way being insensitive to your current situation or state of mind. By definition, being past twelve o'clock, I am simply wishing you good fortune for the remaining hours of the day."

It was with a frowning expression that Dikes turned to Jack shaking his head at the utter stupidity of Joe's opening statement.

Hearing what Joe had just said had instantly piqued Smith's curiosity, so she quickly stepped closer to listen in.

Receiving no reply, Joe paused for a moment before continuing. "The reason for my call was to back up my earlier text message and state the obvious, which is that I left the Commonwealth Hotel some time ago and am now on my way to the next location. I was-"

Dikes had had enough and abruptly cut him off. "What do you really want? Why are you calling?" he demanded, furious.

"I want," Joe emphasised slowly, "to make sure you are mentally stable enough to continue with our game." Dikes was speechless and had nothing to say.

"Detectives Bradshaw and Jones and specialist McMillan were not part of today's play, Nicholas; they were simply in the right place at the wrong time."

"No! You murdered them!" Dikes corrected him angrily.

"I disagree. Before I was forced to take action, I gave all three men several chances, which they ignored. They would not have died today, Detective, had they not played the role of super cops and let pride dictate their actions."

"Bullshit!" Dikes yelled into the phone as he held it close to his mouth. "You murdered them in cold blood, you gutless prick! They were great cops; of course, they wouldn't let you just walk away! What good cop would?" Dikes yelled and had to restrain himself from throwing the phone against the brick wall ahead.

Again, there was a slight pause before Joe began to speak. "I expect that your emotions are quite raw at the moment and are partly to blame for your lack of command over your aggression, Detective."

"Is this a joke? You called to just talk shit at me?"

"Most definitely not!" Joe said defensively, sounding confused. "My call was certainly not intended to rile you up. On the contrary, its purpose was to save you from wasting your time and energy on pointless endeavours, such as continuing your search at a location that I am no longer in. That way, you can take a momentary pause, refresh, and be ready to begin the next round," Joe explained calmly.

"Oh, yeah, that's what we'll do, just pull everybody off this job because you said you're not in here. Sounds smart, Joe," Dikes mocked.

Again, there was a noticeable pause before Joe replied.

"You are correct, Detective," Dikes rolled his eyes and shook his head. "If you had taken my word at face value, then I would have been quite disappointed in you." The line was silent again for a long moment before Joe spoke again. "I believe this call may have been a mistake on my part. For that, I apologise." Joe then hung up. Dikes wore a frown of confusion as he stared at the phone, then turned to survey his squad's expression.

"What the hell was that?" he asked in shock. "He apologises for calling at an inopportune time, but not for killing three—no, five—nine people in two days!" Dikes exclaimed in anger.

With their faces vividly imprinted in his mind, Dikes thought about each of Joe's known victims over the past forty-eight hours. This thought really emphasised how indiscriminately callous Joe was and what he was truly up against.

Jack stopped recording and then replayed the last ten seconds to ensure he'd recorded the conversation. Smith kneeled between Dikes and Jack. Seeing their blank expressions, she felt compelled to explain what someone exhibiting these traits might appear like to the average person.

"Did you notice what happened at the end of the conversation? It seemed like he was reflecting on the reasons why he called and the timing of it. It was as if he had no idea how emotional you were going to be at a time such as this. Which is strange in itself. And when you didn't give him any response or weren't as reciprocating to his reasons for him calling, it left him completely stumped.

Jack replayed the last thirty seconds of the call.

"Apart from the obvious, I really think Joe has some major psychological problems in regard to his emotions. Or lack of," Smith assumed.

Hearing Smith's explanation, Dikes thought he understood. "It's not that I don't trust you; I can assure you I do," Dikes affirmed, then pointed at Jack's phone, "but do you think we could get this audio confirmed by someone with qualifications that would hold up in court? This would be useful in helping us obtain warrants to start searching through hospital and doctor records. If he's as detached as you say, there has to be a medical record out there somewhere from when he was younger."

Smith agreed and then turned to Jack. "If you could forward me a copy of that recording, Sarge, I could send it to some of my former professors for evaluation. They're qualified psychologists, so their diagnosis and opinions will be definitely accepted in court."

"Brilliant!" Dikes said as he exhaled loudly. *Finally, we have something to chase*, he thought.

"Okay, just sent it to you," Jack said to Smith.

"Imagine being so disconnected from feelings and emotions that you-" Tran stopped talking when he heard the sound of the approaching gurneys.

In an instant, Dikes and Jack were on their feet, and the four detectives stood rigidly at attention, saluting, honouring the memory of their three fallen colleagues as the gurneys were wheeled past them. As they held their salute, Dikes and Smith were both overcome with emotion, watching in sombre silence as the bodies were gently loaded into the back of the ambulances.

The squad held their salute until the vehicles had slowly disappeared from view.

Dikes continued to gaze ahead at the empty alley before sinking back onto the lip of the gutter.

With a stuttering breath, Tran exhaled his vape, the vapour temporarily fogging his view of the towering buildings.

Jack muttered under his breath, "Poor bastards."

Smith sighed sadly. "It doesn't seem real, does it?" she said, her voice heavy with emotion. "I understand that our job is dangerous, and I accept that. But three of us are dead now... it just feels..." She trailed off, unable to express her feelings. Jack placed a comforting hand on her shoulder, offering her silent assurance.

Everyone agreed and stayed quiet until Tran broke the silence.

"What a fucking day," he said.

"Yeah," Jack agreed as he pulled out his cigarettes. "It's like a year's worth of shit got dumped on us all at once."

Tran's gaze shifted from the high rises to Jack, who had taken out a cigarette. "Really, Sarge?" he asked, nodding towards Jack's cigarettes.

"What?" Jack asked as he lit his cigarette.

Ignoring the impending argument between Jack and Tran concerning vapes and cigarettes, Smith shook her head and busied herself by sending the audio files and a brief explanation email to her former professors.

"This guy is different," Dikes said softly. "Always two steps ahead and has his escape routes covered. He's vicious in a way we've never seen before."

Jack observed Dikes' expression carefully.

"If you three continue working with me, he'll probably kill you too," he stated flatly.

Everyone considered what Dikes had said.

"I think we'll get him," Tran said. "I honestly do. We just have to be smarter, more cunning, and we need to try and think like him, somehow."

To Dikes, it sounded like Tran was trying to convince himself more than give them a pep talk. And as much as he admired the kid for trying, he didn't want any of them near him because Joe would surely use them to get to him.

Dikes knew he had the best squad on the force; hell, they had the highest arrest rate and had solved more murder cases than any two squads combined in JAPD history. Moreover, they'd hunted down and captured some of the country's most notorious killers. But Dikes had a bad feeling about this one. This, Joe, was different.

Jack patted Tran on the back. "I think you're right; we will catch him, but until then, youngin', you just stick close to us old boys; that way, you can keep suckin' on that crap," he added with a nod at Tran's vape.

Tran smiled.

"You need anything else from these two tonight, Captain?" Jack asked Dikes as he took a drag on his cigarette.

With a heavy heart and an audible groan, Dikes stood and met the gaze of each of his squad members. Pride and sorrow filled his being as he regarded them. "I'm proud of you. All of you, okay."

The three detectives nodded.

"Go home, get washed up, hug your family tight tonight and let the names Bradshaw, James and McMillan fuel the fire we'll need to catch and kill this prick," he said as he raised his chin and looked Tran in the eyes. "You're right, Akeno; we will get this son of a bitch," Tran gave a tight-lipped smile and a nod, then replied, "I won't be having an early night, and I don't have any family in this city to hug, so I'm going to clean up and then head over to Rusty's for a drink to say goodbye to the boys if anyone wants to join me."

"I'll join you," Smith agreed. "You guys coming?" She asked Jack and Dikes.

Dikes flashed them a forced grin while Jack responded with a warm, inviting smile. "Well, we'll just have to see how late we go here, and I'll let you know, alright?" The young guns both nodded, then gave Dikes a concerned look before heading for the door.

"Oh," Dikes said loudly to catch Smith and Tran before they'd left. "I think the chief already told them, but just in case he hasn't, tell the evidence people to take shots of the crowd out there. Not only the hotel staff and guests but the crowds watching as well."

Smith nodded, gave him a thumbs up, and then she and Tran disappeared inside.

Jack waited for the young guns to leave before turning his full attention to his friend.

"I know it's a hard task, but don't let this guy get to you like this. Not in front of them. They need to know we can catch him," Jack said firmly.

"When, Jack?" Dikes asked earnestly. "And how are we going to catch this guy?" Dikes lowered his voice and then continued, "I mean, he buried two coffins on a public beach without anyone seeing, hearing, or reporting a goddam thing. Then he killed two suspects that were inside interrogation rooms on the fifth floor of a fucking police station, then killed two armed detectives and a member of the SWAT team without leaving so much as a goddamn fingerprint. We have absolutely no leads, no suspects and no idea what's next. All we think we know is he's a fucking nutter who can't process his own feelings. He's basically a ghost!"

Jack was relieved when Chief Bryant came down the hallway because he didn't have an answer and had no idea what to say in response.

"Goddamn reporters!" Bryant grumbled as he exited the corridor.

"You seemed to be doing okay out there, boss," Jack said with a half-smile. "Good to see someone finally put that nosey bitch in her place," he added.

Bryant rolled his eyes. "She's a pain in the ass, that woman."

"Did the Fire Department find anything we didn't up there?" Dikes enquired.

"Nothing," Bryant replied.

No surprise registered on Jack and Dikes' faces, as they had expected this to be the case.

"What was the name used to rent the room?" Dikes asked, hopeful.

Bryant smiled. "You're going to love this; it was Joe, but this time, he used your surname." He gestured towards Dikes.

"My surname?" Dikes said, pointing to himself and shaking his head.

"He's got some balls, this guy; I'll give him that," Jack remarked.

"Was the clerk able to give any kind of description?" Dikes asked.

"Nope," Bryant replied quickly. "It was an online booking, paid for with an Austrian card connected to an anonymous account. The room key was picked up by a messenger on a bike."

Bryant raised his hand as Dikes was about to ask a question. "And before you ask," he began, "the clerk can't remember which service it was. Unfortunately, there's no footage for us to go off of, as Joe somehow managed to knock out every camera for a two-block radius again."

Jack and Dikes were astounded.

"I know we keep saying it, but who the hell is this guy?" asked Dikes, his frown deepening.

"Can you imagine how much time and…. well, I have no idea what else you'd need to pull that off. Money, people, I guess, I really don't know," Jack admitted.

Dikes ran his fingers through his hair as he gazed up at the moon, which was gradually being obscured by dark clouds. "If I'm not taken off this case, Chief, more people will die—our people,"

"You were told you weren't allowed to be taken off this case—wasn't that one of his rules?" the chief asked.

"Stuff his rules. If you don't take me off this case, the next person in a body bag could be Jack, you or one of the young guns. Put me on traffic duty or something. Throw me behind the front desk. I really couldn't give a shit. Just get me off this goddamn case!" yelled a defeated Dikes. After staring pleadingly at the chief, Dikes stormed off with a shake of his head.

Jack was about to follow when Chief Bryant took him by the arm. "Let him go, Jack."

Jack watched helplessly as his tortured friend stormed inside.

"The techs found your cameras," Bryant said. Then seeing Jack's confusion expanded on the details. "The ones in the ceiling back at the office."

Jack nodded knowingly. "Ahh, I got you. Where were they?"

"This, Joe had them planted all over the precinct!" Bryant exclaimed, shaking his head with a mix of surprise and annoyance. "And even inside our evidence locker and ammunition bay—I'll have hell to pay for that from the higher-ups," he added with a wry smile, trying to lighten Jack's mood.

Jack's lips twitched upward in a distracted smile, but it soon faded as he shook his head. "Who is this guy?" he wondered aloud. "That's the million-dollar question," Bryant replied. "They're back at the office and already dusted for prints when you're ready." Jack raised an eyebrow, and Bryant shook his head in response. "No prints," he confirmed. Deflated, Jack nodded, then looked back into the building, where his friend had gone. He was deeply concerned.

* * *

Dikes, fresh from the shower, leaned forward onto his desk, his head buried in his hands. He had been ruminating over the events of the day, his mind racing over a myriad of 'what if' scenarios, but he soon realized this was getting him nowhere. Drawing a deep breath in through his nose, he sat upright and began sorting through the beach incident statements when suddenly, a box full of Micro-cameras and their receivers were tipped onto his desk.

Also having showered and changed, Jack sat the empty box on the edge of the table and noted that this was how Joe had been watching them.

"He had these scattered all over the precinct," he said.

Dikes picked up one of the cameras and studied it, comparing it to another one he had in hand.

"Have you checked who's been up there lately? Looked through the station logs?" he asked, pointing to the ceiling.

"We went through the building's records for the past twenty-four months but won't know anything for at least a week or two," Jack replied. "The little shit should call himself the phantom instead of Joe," he quipped.

Suddenly the image of the coffin exploding on the beach smashed into the front of Dikes' mind. It made his stomach turn. He felt horrible that he'd gotten the whole situation so wrong, and because of this, a young lady had died. Her mother would be at home right now, grieving over her lost daughter because of him.

He should have known Joe was going to pull some kind of trick, or he should have recruited more people to help dig both coffins up. But then, more could have died, he thought as his heart pounded beneath his ribcage. Dikes' mind continued running through different scenarios that may or may not have worked, but he should have tried something more than he did.

I didn't put her in the coffin, but it's my fault she wasn't pulled out, he thought to himself.

Seeing the pained expression on his friend's face, Jack knew he had to get Dikes out of this office.

"There's nothing more you can do here tonight," he said gently. "So, while we've postponed your promotion party until after the funerals, I'm sure a drink to honour our fallen friends and colleagues is the right thing to do, don't you?"

Dikes let out a deep breath as he remained silent.

"So, for now, just let this piece of shit," Jack pointed to the roof, "sit tight for the night."

Dikes tapped his desk with one hand, musing over Jack's suggestion. Spinning the camera in his other hand, he eventually concluded that it was a good idea.

"So, get up, put on your best dress and at least have one beer with your squad. Nick, the young guns are hiding it well, but they are hurting as much as you and me while they're running around the city following us," Jack explained.

Dikes tossed the camera onto the table, nodding with renewed determination.

"Good. About time you acted like a captain. Now let's send our boys off the right way tonight, hey," Jack said, clapping Dikes on the back as he helped him into his jacket.

"Where would I be without a wife like you, hey?" Dikes retorted with a smirk.

Jack smiled but ignored Dikes' comment. "Tuck your shirt in properly. You look a mess," he said.

CHAPTER TWELVE

TWELVE MONTHS AGO

The afternoon sun was setting over the city skyline, its inhabitants too focused on their screens or transport to notice the innocuous alley echoing with the yapping of two small dogs. These canines were barking in the familiar way that small dogs do when they detect a larger dog on the other side of a fence. The L-shaped alley, nestled between the city's three oldest buildings, was rarely used these days since neither of the private businesses that backed onto it had any use for it anymore. A male figure, overdressed, particularly for this alley, strode casually down its centre. His hard-soled leather shoes made clacking sounds that echoed around its high walls with each step.

One of the dog's furious yapping changed to growling, and then, after what sounded like a tussle, it began squealing and yelping horribly. Soon the squealing yelps gave way to gurgled 'arffing' sounds, and soon, only one dog could be heard, only it was no longer barking, just making a soft whining sound.

Now that the alley had fallen silent, except for the distressed whimpers of a single dog, the sound of the hard-soled shoes grew louder and louder with each step. A nine-year-old boy, his hands stained with the blood of the dog he had just killed, froze. Not knowing what to do, he feared whoever was coming might either rob and beat him, as the older street kids often did, or spot the dead dog and call the police to have him arrested. He had always despised the police; they were never kind to him. Acting quickly, the boy placed his knife down, determined to free the remaining dog and make his escape. He tugged at the leather leash, desperately trying to unknot it from the gutter pipe. However, with his tiny fingers now slick with blood, the knot seemed to grow ever tighter. With no other option, the boy grabbed the dog's collar and prepared to cut the leash with his knife. In a panic, while he looked for where he'd put his knife, the trembling animal released its bladder.

With a fright, the boy looked up to see a well-dressed man stop five metres away, staring down at him.

Startled, the boy stumbled back, eventually backing himself into the corner of the alley.

Joe's eyes drifted to the living dog, then back to the boy. The boy then remembered he'd left his knife lying beside the dead dog - the most valuable thing in the world to him. Scolding himself for his stupidity, he was unable to bear the thought of losing it, so didn't immediately run away.

Joe noticed the boy's eyes darting towards the knife. He quickly stepped forward and covered the blade with the toe of his right shoe.

The boy, frustrated that he hadn't reacted sooner, clenched his teeth but remained silent.

Joe could tell the boy was upset at having lost his knife, but by the way he kept inching further away; he also knew the boy was scared of him and wanted to avoid being apprehended.

Joe was about to ask the boy what he was doing when he noticed the clean T-cut incision on the dog's throat and stomach. He knelt down and studied the dissection, marvelling at the precision and skill the boy had used to make the clean cuts, considering he had done it with a crude pocket knife. It was obvious that the animal had been killed humanely, and yet when it was dissected, none of its internal organs had been damaged.

After hearing shuffling, Joe quickly followed the sound and spotted the boy running down the alley.

"Young man!" Joe called out in a stern but non-admonishing tone. "Come back here, please. You'll need your knife, yes?"

The boy froze mid-stride, his wide eyes darting between Joe and the dog. The boy hesitated before slowly turning back, his wide eyes darting between Joe and the dog. Fear still held him in place, but the desire to reclaim his knife kept him from running.

Seeing that the boy was not going to come any closer, Joe slowly rose, taking his foot off the knife, and held his hands up in a gesture of peace. "I am not here to hurt you. I promise. And I am not here to get you into any trouble either. May I ask you some questions? I promise it will not take long."

The boy remained silent, but he didn't flee, which Joe took as a sign that the boy might be open to hearing what he had to say.

"First thing, my name is Joe. Second, if someone asks you a question, it is considered rude not to answer them. So, let us try again. And; if you are not confident enough to talk to me yet, that is completely fine. What you can do is nod or shake your head. Then, once you become more comfortable with me, you may choose to use your words or not. The choice is completely yours. Does that make sense to you, young man?" Joe asked as neutrally as he could.

As he stared nervously at Joe, the boy drew a shaky breath.

It was then Joe noticed it; the boy was rubbing his blood-covered thumb and index fingers together as he considered his options. The action was as if he was rolling a ball of lint between the two fingers.

The small, seemingly insignificant gesture of rubbing his fingers triggered a cascade of memories within Joe, stirring up a wave of nostalgia and reminding him of his own tick.

Eventually, the boy gave Joe an almost imperceptible nod.

Joe accepted with a nod and then gestured to the dead dog. "Why did you kill this animal?"

The boy frowned and squinted simultaneously. An expression that Joe took as the boy attempting to explain his reasoning without having a vocabulary to illustrate it. As if to emphasise his point, the boy opened his mouth to speak, but couldn't articulate his thoughts, so he closed it.

"Okay. Let us start from the very beginning, shall we?" Joe verbalised this thought more for his benefit rather than the boys. After all, he'd had exactly zero positive experiences regarding children.

Joe chewed on the corner of his lip as he thought of a series of questions basic enough to start a dialogue with the boy.

"Okay, were you..." Joe stopped to correct his wording. "Did you just kill this dog?" Joe asked, pointing to the unmistakably dead dog.

The boy blinked and then nodded once.

"Okay," Joe said. "Have you done this to... any other dogs or animals before today?"

The boy cocked his head slightly and looked at Joe suspiciously, suggesting that he didn't like or trust that line of questioning.

Joe looked down at the suit he was wearing and flared the jacket. "You assume I am a police officer, don't you?" he asked mockingly in a southern drawl.

The boy nodded immediately.

"Yes, well, not that you would believe me, but that could not be farther from the truth." Joe declared with a smirk. "In the interest of full transparency, I did just fly in from a lecture titled, Serial Killers in the 21st Century, presented by the very famous, Detective Nicholas Dikes." While explaining this, Joe gave the boy the side eye to watch his expression. As expected, the boy looked even less convinced that he wasn't a policeman.

Joe was looking around the alley and along the littered ground, trying to think of how he could prove to the boy that he was not a policeman when he heard the tied-up dog whimpering. Looking down at the dog, Joe raised an eyebrow.

At first, Joe knelt down, patted the dog, and then pointed to the knife on the concrete as he turned to the boy. "May I?" he asked.

The boy was taken aback. An adult had never asked his permission for anything before. And so, it was with a momentary frown that the boy gave the nod.

"Thank you," Joe remarked as he picked up the knife. Then, in one swift motion, he grabbed the dog by the scruff of the neck and ran the blade straight up through the dog's lower jaw, through its brain and out through the top of its skull.

To his credit, the boy never flinched, never even blinked, for that matter at the killing. Something that did not escape Joe's attention.

With the dog's twitching body dangling from the blade of the knife, Joe stood up and faced the boy. "Do you still think I am the police?"

With a look of sudden excitement and enthusiasm, the boy shook his head. Then, to Joe's surprise, he spoke. "No."

Joe raised an eyebrow. Then, just as you'd flick mud from the blade of a knife, Joe flung the dog's lifeless body onto the ground, flipped the knife around in his hand, then held it, handle first toward the boy.

The boy didn't hesitate to step forward and take his knife.

With the boy now standing beside him, Joe knelt in front of the original dead dog and gestured for him to do the same. Then, like an eager student, the boy knelt and waited for Joe to ask his next question.

"Do you kill because you like hurting these animals?" The boy quickly shook his head. "No. I kill them because... Because I feel like I have to. These ones I kill quickly," he explained, pointing to the dog in front of them.

"These ones?" Joe asked.

The boy nodded. "The interesting ones. The ones I want to learn from."

Joe's frown deepened as he wracked his brain for the boy's meaning behind his wording. "Okay, so these ones." Joe pointed to both dogs. "These are the interesting ones?"

The boy nodded.

"What are the other type?" Joe asked, intrigued at the way the boy's mind worked.

The boy's face darkened. "The hurting ones. The ones that chase me or are set on me to scare me."

"The hurting ones," Joe repeated as he pondered which way to take his line of questioning in the limited time he had left.

"Okay, these hurting ones, can you tell me how you kill them differently?"

The boy nodded. "I take my time with them. I cut them where it hurts the most. I don't let them die til they've suffered."

Joe drew a sharp breath; his eyes flashed brightly for a second with the overwhelming knowledge that he'd just experienced a feeling. It was brief and had vanished as quickly as it had appeared, but he was one hundred percent sure he'd just experienced his first human emotion. His mind was racing as to why now? Why here? Was it because he had perhaps found a kindred spirit? Looking into the boy's expression, Joe could see he'd also felt the same strange and instant bond.

Joe glanced at his watch; he'd run out of time and had to leave.

"Listen, young man. I have really got to go. I have someone at home waiting for me."

In response, the boy nodded, then stood up beside Joe and shuffled some rubbish with his broken shoe.

Joe then noticed the boy's worn shoes with his toes poking through their tattered end.

"If I promise to come back tomorrow at 12pm, will you promise to be here?"

The boy nodded vigorously as he tried masking a smile.

"I would like to begin teaching you. Would you like that?"

Again, the boy nodded. He was genuinely excited.

For the first time in his life, the boy felt like someone understood him and how his mind worked. This man standing in front of him didn't look at him like he was a broken person or call him names like freak or murderer. Instead, he was nice to him. He liked the feeling of being treated nicely. He liked it a lot.

Joe rummaged through his pockets for loose change, but the thought of giving the homeless youth such a meagre sum of money was insulting. He reached for his wallet, prepared to give the boy all his money, but hesitated.

Would giving the boy free money be teaching him anything? He asked himself. Joe thought about this for a second, then peeled off a twenty-dollar note and then a ten.

The boy's eyes flashed wide.

Joe handed the boy thirty dollars and said, "Your first lesson is this: the fate of this money is in your hands, young man. You can take the thirty dollars and spend it on whatever you wish, then disappear, and we shall never see each other again. Or, you can use it to purchase new shoes and clothes and learn from me - on one condition: you must never come to a lesson dressed as you are again."

The boy remained silent as he looked at the money.

"If you turn up to your next lesson dressed suitably, I shall hire you for three days a week to deliver groceries to my door, for which I will pay you ten dollars per delivery." Joe fished into his pocket again, but this time he pulled out a small white piece of paper with his hand-written grocery list on it.

"Here's tomorrow's list." He handed it to the boy. "Purchase what is on the list just prior to our first lesson, then bring it with you." Joe peeled off another twenty dollars. "Whatever is left from the twenty dollars you may keep."

Joe left it at that and walked to the end of the alley. "I'll either see you at 12pm tomorrow, or I won't."

The boy smiled widely as he looked at the money and then at his toes, which he could see wiggling through the end of his shoes.

"If you choose to work for me, you'll have to move uptown. Think about that!" Joe said as he disappeared around the corner.

The boy looked at the empty alley, a smile forming across his thin lips.

CHAPTER THIRTEEN

PRESENT DAY

It was a miserable day for the funerals; more of a misting than rain as the three hearses, carrying Bradshaw, Jones and McMillan slowly made their way up to the steps of City Hall. As the hearses came to a halt, the funeral procession began.
The tragic deaths of the three officers, three decapitated teenagers, the two suspects shot in the head while in police custody, and the superstar detective leading the investigation had become international news.

The city of Jadestown had come to a fear-induced standstill. All schools, universities, and major sporting events had been cancelled for the rest of the week. Neighbourhood militias were formed in an effort to protect their city blocks from any suspicious individuals that they deemed to be lurking around their streets unnecessarily, further burdening the already taxed police department. People were gripped with fear and panic, dreading what the maniacal killer, known as Joe, was going to do next.

Arriving at the top step, ready to deliver his address to the bereaved families of the fallen officers, Dikes felt strangely numb.

As thousands of people gathered and millions watched online and on TV, he addressed the crowd with emotion-filled words.

He paused only once during his speech; when he had to tell Bradshaw's children what kind of man he was and what kind of friend he was.

After he'd finished his speech, Dikes saluted the three officers in their coffins and recited a poem 'Stop all the clocks' by W.H. Auden.

Dikes folded the paper on which he'd handwritten the poem and tucked it into his breast pocket. With his part of the funeral procession completed, Dikes drew several deep breaths then marched down the steps to the front of the parade where he'd be marching alongside Chief Bryant and Captain Hale.

As he marched between the ranks of fellow officers to find his mark, he spotted his squad, who made up part of the second rank of officers. He managed a forced smile which all three mirrored.

No sooner had Dikes stepped onto his mark, did the ratter tatt tatt of the military drums commence, followed by the traditional Scottish bagpipes.

Dikes relived every bloodied detail of that fateful day during the march to the cemetery and second-guessed every decision he made leading up to his two friends' deaths.

Maybe two of the three would be alive today if he'd just kept the squad together and not sent Bradshaw and

Jones down there alone. But then again, they weren't rookies; they were seasoned veterans and knew what they were doing. Dikes thought, trying to reason with his own thoughts.

He'd expressed these thoughts to Jack, who set him straight in typical Jack fashion. "If you'd have sent Smith and Tran down with them or even waited until you and I went down there, the only difference in the outcome would be the extra number of flags being placed over coffins today," Jack explained to Dikes.

While marching, Dikes had heard Smith sniffing. Without noticeably turning his head, he shot a caring glance back to Smith. For the past week, he had seen her holding her emotions in check, but the day itself and the culmination of those emotions were just too much.

"Hang in there, Smith," Dikes whispered.

"All good, boss," she replied.

And that was that. Dikes didn't hear a peep out of Detective Smith for the rest of the march.

The rest of the day flew by in a blur of salutes and handshakes for Dikes. Only as his men were being lowered into their final resting places did his mind finally give out and focus on the mundane.

Beads of rainwater forming along the brim of his peaked service hat monopolised his attention until the ten shots fired at the conclusion of every service person's funeral snapped him out of this daze, and his mind once again jumped back into the various scenarios and choices he should have made. Naturally, this annoyed the hell out of him.

CHAPTER FOURTEEN

Dikes tossed his soaking hat onto his desk, spraying droplets of water over everything; he was too drained to care at this point.

With a groan, he undid the silver buttons of his sodden dress jacket, careful not to tear off his military and police medals and hung it carefully over the back of his chair. Jack walked into the precinct two minutes later and, like Dikes, headed straight to his own chair. They exchanged looks of weariness with briefly raised eyebrows, but neither was in the mood to talk or express their thoughts on how they thought the day went. Not yet, anyway.

Jack slumped into his chair, jacket still buttoned up, and stared at the ceiling as he swung back and forth. His heavy sigh echoed throughout the empty precinct, which was unusually still today due to the funerals, few callouts and dismal weather.

Dikes folded his arms across his chest, tapped his boot against the leg of his desk and savoured the silence, using it to think.

For a while, the only noticeable sound was the creaking of their chairs whenever one of them moved.

Jack was unimpressed with the silence and let out a loud, slow drawl; "Fuck Joe."

Jack slowly spun in his chair, taking in the empty office from all angles. "I like it like this," he said to Dikes.

It took a moment for Dikes to realise he was being addressed. "Hmm? What'd you say?"

"I said, I really like the office like this," Jack replied. "It makes it feel like a real office, the kind of office where people are cracking the shits because they didn't get the specific ream of paper they ordered on time or giving the new guy a hard time for not refilling the coffee machine. You know, the real important office stuff," he finished with a chuckle as he continued to spin around. A smile spread across Dikes' face. He was about to add something of his own when the phone, set to vibrate in Dikes' top drawer, buzzed. Dikes took out the phone, glanced at the screen then hung up and tossed the phone onto his desk.

Soon, the station began to fill with the familiar sounds of police officers and civilian staff working, keyboards clacking and rubber-soled boots moving across the vinyl floor.

The phone vibrated again, catching Jack's eye this time. Dikes, however, was reluctant to answer it.

"Calling at a time like this is definitely a Joe move," Jack said, sniffing with annoyance. "What a dickhead," he said, adding a smile. "You want me to tell him that?" Jack asked seriously.

Dikes grabbed the phone as he flashed a thin-lipped smile at Jack. Dikes stared at the phone for the longest time, sighed, and then pressed the answer button.

"Good afternoon Nicholas," came Joe's calm and soft voice. His voice really aggravated Dikes on a cellular level.

Before Dikes knew what he was doing, his thumb had pressed the red end call button.

This move not only surprised Jack, who had been watching, but also himself.

"Ha ha, nice move, boss," Jack said with a wide smile as he spun in a three-sixty while giving the middle finger to the ceiling. "Fuck you, buddy," Jack said flippantly.

Dikes couldn't hide his amusement as he looked at Jack, but again the phone vibrated, displaying Joe's name. Reluctantly, Dikes again pressed the answer button.

"What?"

"Tsk tsk tsk, Nicolas. We have had the discus-" Dikes cut him off.

"What the hell do you want, Joe? What the hell do you want?" Dikes yelled, his voice cracking with emotion, which got everyone in the building looking in his direction. "I get that you get a kick out of watching us hurt, and right now we..." Dikes let his words trail off.

"You are wrong, Detective. It is not your pain that I thrive off, not entirely; I enjoy the unpredictability of attempting to predict your actions or reactions to certain events I have set in motion. It is the evolving game that drives me, Nicholas."

As Dikes stared at the ceiling, he was so full of anger that he could hardly hold back tears. He was being closely watched by everyone in the room, especially Jack, who had stopped spinning in his chair.

"This isn't a game! The fact that you think it is shows how fucked up you are. You killed innocent students, policemen and... two others; whether or not they deserved death was not a call for you to make! It's not a-" Joe cut him off.

"In light of your continued highly emotional state so early on in our game, which I absentmindedly had not accounted for, I believe that continuing the game would adversely affect your ability to compete in it at your optimal level. A good analogy would be like hunting a bore you've already shot before releasing it for the hunt. Furthermore, my reputation would be negatively impacted as a result of winning in such a way. So, to assist in the recharge of your cognitive battery, I propose a one-week respite."

Still fuming, Dikes could only shake his head in frustration.

"Whatever, Joe," a deflated Dikes said slowly.

"You are making my point with your body language and the manner in which you are articulating your words. Despite my reluctance, I will pause all future proceedings on the condition that you and your team cease their search for me. You, Jack, and I must be the only ones involved in this deal. This arrangement should not be disclosed to anyone else. Am I clear?"

Dikes forced a mumbled yes.

"So, if you have nothing to add to my offer and agree to the terms that I have set out before you, you will not be hearing from me for seven days from the second I hang up this phone."

"How do I know you'll stick to your word?" Dikes asked sceptically.

"Have I lied to you yet, Nicholas?"

Dikes turned to Jack with a troubled expression. Jack mouthed, "What's happening?" Dikes knew he and his team needed time to regroup and get into a better frame of mind, so while staring at Jack, Dikes agreed to Joe's seven-day truce.

"Very well, Detective, seven days from today, we will re-commence our rivalry. That will make it the evening of the new date that has been set for your promotion party, yes?"

Dikes was confused; he still hadn't been told when the new time and date were. Not that he gave a shit about a party.

"Check your emails, Nicholas," Joe spoke with a hint of amusement in his voice. "Judy sent everyone the new information three hours ago."

It irritated Dikes as to how much Joe knew.

"Okay." That was all Dikes could think to say.

The phone went dead; Dikes looked at the screen to ensure the call had ended, then tossed the phone back onto his desk.

"That was strange," he said as he interlaced his fingers behind his head and leaned back while turning to

Jack. "You're never going to believe what just happened."

CHAPTER FIFTEEN

It had been seven days since the JAPD had buried three of its own.

For Dikes, the week without harassing phone calls from Joe or attending his staged crime scenes was a blessing. The promise he and Jack had agreed to was to refrain from searching for Joe while he was at work, working as a detective. It was a promise that he and Jack had kept. At home, off the clock, however, things were very different. In his downtime, Dikes continued searching through videos on his phone, crime scene photos, coroner's reports, and lecture notes he had given over the past four years at the four colleges.

In the past seven days, he had been burning the candle at both ends, and he was exhausted. Tonight, however, he was allowing himself a few hours to unwind. After all, it was his promotion party.

Rusty's Bar was at capacity, which made it hard for Jack to push a fatigued Dikes towards the bar.

An officer in uniform shook Dikes' hand, "Congratulations, sir," he said enthusiastically. Dikes politely responded and smiled when the officer requested a selfie. The officer snapped several shots, quickly checked their quality, and then stepped away, thanking Dikes for his time. After only two steps towards Jack, three young officers, clearly just out of the academy, rushed forward, begging for selfies with the celebrity detective. As Dikes accommodated their request, he looked at Jack with a look that screamed, "Help me."

"That does it," Jack mumbled before whistling loudly to get everyone's attention. There was an immediate hush in the bar, followed by Jack clapping his hands twice above his head. "For those of you who want one of those selfies or autographs from the man of the hour, you have until he makes it to the bar to do so. Anyone caught asking after that will be on shit detail for the rest of the month." Laughter erupted in the bar as the volume quickly returned to its previous level.

On his way up to the bar, Dikes continued to be stopped by fellow officers and some who he recognised as reporters. He assumed they were here to glean gossip from any of the younger, loose-tongued officers who'd had one too many free drinks.

After his case had gained worldwide attention, Dikes noticed an uptake in people asking for selfies and autographs or suspiciously showing up wherever he happened to be.
Obviously, there are people who enjoy the attention that celebrities receive; Dikes was not one of them.
Finally nearing the bar, Dikes was happy to see his wife waiting for him. She was standing with Jack's wife, Marilyn.

"Congratulations, Nick," Marilyn said, giving Dikes a kiss and hug. "We're so proud of you," she continued, placing her hands on his cheeks.

"Thanks, Mare," Dikes said with a genuine smile. Sarah ran her hand affectionately through Dikes' hair.

"Hi, sweetheart. How was your day?"

"Yeah, it was fine," Dikes sounded tired as he kissed Sarah on the lips. "Just getting things ready for what we think will be a pretty hectic week," he said as he flashed Jack the side eye.

Sarah noticed her husband's sneaky glance. "Well, keep your little secrets for now, Detective Dikes," she teased and then flashed him a wink. "I know you're not in the mood for a party tonight, especially after the weeks you've had. But please try and enjoy yourself. Even if it's just for an hour. Just accept everybody's congratulations, do your speech, and then we'll get out of here."

Dikes looked lovingly at her; she'd read him like a book.

"I love you," he said, hugging her tightly.

Taking a beer from the bartender, Chief Bryant made his way over to Dikes and patted him on the back.

"Ladies" he smiled as he greeted the two women and kissed them both on the cheek. "Come on," was all he said to Dikes as he jerked his head at the small stage at the front of the room.

Dikes followed the chief through the crowded bar to a small stage at the front of the room; rather than take the stage with the chief, Dikes preferred to remain among the crowd for now.

Chief Bryant picked up a fork from a nearby table and tapped it against his glass to get everyone's attention. Within seconds the bar had fallen quiet.

"Good evening, everyone, and welcome to the night we finally get to celebrate our superstar policeman and newly promoted captain, Captain Nicholas Dikes." The chief pointed at Dikes as the room erupted with cheers and glasses being raised.

The group consisting of Jack, Sarah, Marilyn, Smith and Tran cheered loudest as they clapped, wolf-whistled and whooped.

Amid the cheers, Chief Bryant held up his hand. "Alright, settle down, you lot. I still have to finish my bloody speech," he quipped and waited for the room to quieten before he continued. "on behalf of everyone here tonight and those that couldn't make it." Chief Bryant paused, then raised his glass. "I'd just like to congratulate you on your well-earned and overdue promotion! It's a credit to you for your eight years of hard work and dedication to the Jadestown police department."

The crowd clapped and whistled.

"To conclude, I'd like to impart some wisdom on you, or as the young ones say these days: I'm gonna drop some knowledge on your ass." Everyone laughed. "Remember, some obstacles can seem insurmountable at the time, but with your tenacity, dedication to hard work and the team of special people you have around you, I am one hundred percent sure you will conquer them.

Congratulations, Captain Dikes!" he cried out triumphantly.

Dikes climbed onto the stage and was hugged by the chief.

"Well done, son; I couldn't be prouder," he whispered quietly, holding back tears of pride as he patted Dikes on the arm.

"Thanks, Chief," Dikes said, turning to survey the room of faces staring up at him. Despite his efforts to hide it, a wave of sorrow swept over him as he thought of the friends that should have been here but weren't, causing his smile to falter. Only Sarah and Jack noticed, exchanging a knowing glance.

"So, I'm not going to give a big speech tonight. I'll save it for the day we put this prick, Joe, behind bars or in the ground,"

Dikes' words were met with raucous applause and some aggressive cheers.

Raising his glass, Dikes declared determinedly, "To Jones, Bradshaw, McMillan, and the four young adults that lost their lives to this piece of shit!"

The crowd repeated the names loudly as they raised their glasses to salute their fallen friends.

Dikes stepped down from the stage and was again barraged by well wishes and patted on the back.

"I've never seen him like this before," Sarah remarked quietly to Marilyn as they moved a little further away from the bar as people swarmed it.

"Neither have I. How has he been at home?" Marilyn asked.

"This promotion was supposed to bring him home more, but I haven't seen him at all in the last two weeks. And even when he is home, he's reading through reports or studying photos of crime scenes that he's asked me never to look at."

Marilyn took Sarah's hands as she gazed at her sympathetically. "I feel for you, honey. I really do. Once they catch this weirdo, he'll be hanging around the house so much that you'll be egging him to go back to the office," she joked as she gave Sarah a tight hug.

Sarah gladly accepted the hug. "You're probably right." she said, forcing a smile.

"Of course, I am, but listen, tonight isn't about the negative, so enough of this doom and gloom and let's change the subject, hey? Just for tonight."

Sarah nodded in agreement, liking the idea.

Marilyn cocked her head, her wide grin growing wider as she leant close to Sarah's ear. "So, when are you two going to start trying?" she asked in a hushed tone, glancing around the room to make sure no one heard her.

Sarah's eyebrows flew up in surprise as she stammered, "I... I don't know. When the time is right, I guess. We haven't really spoken about it too much lately."

Marilyn wasn't deterred by Sarah's vague reply. "I know you want one sooner rather than later, yeah?"

Sarah's gaze shifted to her husband, who was looking tired as he chatted with Bryant, Smith, and Jack.

"Yeah, we're not getting any younger, but-."

"That talk might just be what he needs to get him out of this funk," Marilyn cut in, her voice laced with encouragement.

Sarah smiled absentmindedly as her eyes lingered upon her husband, the fatigue on his and his team's faces unmistakable.

Unbeknownst to Sarah, Dikes was struck by the same thought—his team was exhausted, and they needed to be rested and ready for the call he knew he'd be receiving the following day.

Suddenly, the barman's powerful voice boomed over the other conversations in the bar. "Dikes! Phone call!"

Dikes immediately glanced at Jack, who shook his head, tapped his watch and silently mouthed, "Not time yet." Hesitant to take the call, just in case it was Joe, Dikes excused himself from the group and moved to the bar, kissing Sarah on his way past.

"Use the one in the hall," the barman explained. "You'll be able to hear better,"

"Thanks, Bill," Dikes said and proceeded down the narrow hallway to the phone booth between the restrooms. He picked up the receiver.

"Dikes here."

"Have you told Mummy and Daddy Frankston how sorry you are for letting their little girl be torn apart by three pounds of C4?" Joe's taunting voice sounded down the line.

Instantly aggravated, Dikes glared at the floor.

Watching her husband from across the bar, Sarah could see that something was wrong by his sudden change in demeanour.

"I thought you didn't lie, Joe?" Dikes asked.

"I do not lie, Nicholas. Why do you ask?"

"Because you said seven days. That's tomorrow."

"Incorrect, and you have just been promoted to captain, a detective captain, yet you fail at such basic mathematics?"
Joe paused, giving his words time to sink in. "I told you I would give you seven days from the day of the funerals," he reminded him, his voice neutral. "We spoke after the funerals at 6:32pm. It is now 6:34pm—two minutes more than seven days," Joe chided.

"Her blood is on your hands, you gutless little prick!" Dikes fired back. "And you tell the ten-year-old girl at home that her father won't be at coming to another one of her birthday parties because you blew his goddamn head off. Gutless move, by the way. I thought you liked to kill up close and personal?" Dikes growled.

"Like a good artist, I was simply trying an unfamiliar medium. Though I must admit, taking a life from a hundred meters away has no poetry or elegance to it, does it? You cannot feel them taking that last, gasping breath. You are not there to taste their soul as it leaves the body and enters yours."
Marilyn noticed Sarah's concerned expression and followed her gaze. She saw Dikes talking aggressively

into the phone. She took Sarah's hand, and they looked at each other.

"Let's get Jack," Marilyn suggested.
The two women quickly made a beeline to Jack, who was deep in conversation with Tran. When he spotted them approaching, he threw his arms out wide.

"Here they are, my two favourite ladies," Jack said as he wrapped his arms around them.

"Jack," Marilyn whispered, then indicated to Sarah with her eyes.

"What is it?" Jack asked, suddenly alarmed. His jubilance instantly evaporated.

"Something's wrong," Sarah stated, then pointed at Dikes, who was still on the phone.
What Jack saw made his heart skip a beat. Dikes looked extraordinarily annoyed as he spoke on the phone.
Jack and Tran excused themselves and quickly made their way through the crowd to Dikes.

"Why are you calling me here? If you know where I am all the time, just come down, and we'll sort it out like men!" Dikes challenged.

"Your macho bravado is entertaining, Detective. You speak to me as though I am a foe. I am not your foe, Captain. A foe is, more often than not, an individual with standing and skills equivalent to one's own. You are not my equal, Nicholas. You are the joker in my deck of diamonds. So, never make the mistake of placing us on the same level again, otherwise…"

"Fuck you!!" Dikes yelled into the mouthpiece and threw the phone against the wall.

Jack and Tran rushed to Dikes' side as those within earshot stared on with apprehension and bewilderment.

"Joe?" Jack enquired.

Tran picked up the phone and listened to see if Joe was still on the other end. He wasn't, so he gently hung the phone up.

"Only that shithead can get that kind of reaction out of you," Jack concluded.

Dikes pushed his hands through his hair. "Argh!" He growled as he turned away from everyone watching.

"So, what did shit-for-brains have to say this time?" Jack asked.

Leaning against the wall, Dikes attempted to calm himself. "I don't know. A lot, a lot of... nothing. He was just baiting me, I think," Dikes stammered as he looked around the room.

Some of the people in the crowd had turned to watch him but turned away when they saw him look at them.

Jack was worried; Joe clearly had Dikes rattled.

"I thought we had seven days?" Jack asked, frowning as he thought.

"Seven days for what?" Tran asked.

Jack shook his head with a smile, then gently nodded in the party's direction. "I'll explain it all to you and Smithy later, bud," Jack gave Tran a pat on the back.

Tran realised what Jack was insinuating and went back to the party.

"We did. Seven days ended two minutes ago, apparently." Dikes checked his watch. "Five minutes ago," he corrected himself.

Jack thought about it for a moment, then agreed. "Oh yeah. He's right, you know."

Sarah came over to check on her husband. "Are you okay?" She was extremely concerned. "Was that him?" Dikes stared at Sarah and then nodded.

"Now that I'm allowed," he said, using quotation fingers, "I've got to get to the office and keep looking for him. We must have overlooked something." Dikes set his beer on the nearest table.

"What are you doing?" Jack asked with a frown.

"Heading back to the office. There's been work piling up over the past seven days I need to look into."

"Legally, I can't do anything," Jack explained as he pointed to his nearly empty bottle."

Dikes gave Jack a reassuring pat on the shoulder and smiled. "That's fine; I'm not expecting you to come with me tonight; plus, I've only had a few sips. So, you have fun for the rest of the night and come in fresh in the morning." He then turned to Sarah. "Are you going to stay, or I can drop you home on the way if you want, sweetheart?" Dikes asked, missing the troubled expression on Sarah's face.

CHAPTER SIXTEEN

The morning sun glimmered off the towers of glass and mirrored windows in the city skyline.

Jack bounded up the precinct's stairs that divided the large rounded foyer from the bullpen, with two large takeaway cups of coffee and a small yellow envelope and folded paper tucked under one arm.

The night officer greeted him as he passed with the news that Dikes had been at the precinct all night; he'd set up in the conference room and had been going over statements, photos, and case files.

Jack was a little surprised, he'd expected that Dikes had gone home for at least a few hours of sleep, but the pile of evidence and photos scattered across the conference room floor and table told him otherwise.

Dikes was fast asleep on the table, using his rolled-up jacket as a pillow. Jack gave him a gentle nudge, "Morning, sunshine."

Dikes stirred and quickly sat up, at which Jack offered him the coffee.

"Here, try the new morgue free flavoured coffee. I hear it's tasty as hell," he joked as he shot Dikes a wink.

Dikes swung his legs over the table and yawned, rubbing his eyes.

He accepted the coffee with a sleepy "Thanks" and sat up tall, throwing his arms out wide and stretching. He shook his head and said, "I've been over everything six damn

times, but I've come up with nothing new. It's like there's nothing to find."
Jack knelt down and picked up some of the photographs of the scorpion sculpture.

"He's a different kind of killer than we've ever seen before, Jack. None of his killings are spontaneous or motivated by passion or hate, which is why he never loses focus and never leaves behind any evidence or prints. He's also extremely patient and has been killing for so long that he's perfected his own style and method. Which means that when he wants our attention, he knows exactly how to get it."

"Sounds like you respect this guy," Jack snorted.

"No, respect is the wrong word. But I do think we need to change our approach, though. We need to somehow use his own motives against him somehow. Or something." Dikes stifled a yawn.

"His motive?" Jack questioned. "His motive is to make your life as miserable as possible and have us running around in circles. All the while having the world's press televise it."

"Yeah, absolutely!" Dikes nodded emphatically in agreement. "He wants to make me out to be a total failure in the public's eye. He's trying to drag my name through the mud, make me the centre of attention, but in a negative way."

"Alright," Jack said, nodding in agreement. He'd agreed with Dikes so far, but he was unsure where he was going with it all.

Jack sipped his coffee, then slid the envelope and the folded report onto the table beside Dikes. "Here, read this; this might cheer you up," he added before he could attempt to explain the new information he'd just received on his way to the precinct. "It's too full of techno mumbo jumbo for me to explain properly, so it's better if you just read it."

Dikes unfolded the two-page report and read through it.

"I figured your IT background would help you comprehend it far better than I could," Jack stated as he took another sip while waiting for Dikes to finish reading. It took Dikes another two minutes to thoroughly read through the reports, and as he neared the end, he smiled.

"What's the smile for?" Jack asked.

"Our boy made a mistake. It was only for a fraction of a second and..." Dikes re-read a paragraph of the second page. "It might not have been directly his fault, but he made a mistake," Dikes replied with a grin.

"Oh yeah, I got that part. How his VPN thing didn't connect, or it cut out for a second when he called the pub last night."

"Exactly! And great job getting IT onto that so fast, by the way. I never even thought of getting them to trace it. I just assumed it was untraceable. Good detective work Jackson," Dikes said happily while tipping his cup to Jack.

Jack chuckled before saying, "I'll have to start using Bradshaw's cup." The quip escaped his lips before he could contain it. Jack and Dikes looked at each other and smiled, although neither knew what to say next.

"Damn. I'm sorry. But I'm not, you know? It's just..." Jack struggled for the right words. "It feels wrong to be laughing." Jack's expression darkened as he spoke.

"I completely agree," Dikes affirmed.

Jack took a deep breath as if to shake off the sombre mood. "Anyway, understanding the modem part on the report is the best I'm capable of in terms of technology."

"You did great," Dikes said, slapping the paper excitedly. "It looks like Joe's computer, software, or hardware didn't properly conceal his location. We got a partial ping from the tower in the downtown area. And I'm willing to bet that the city cameras in a two-block radius of downtown are all coincidently currently on the fritz."

Jack was already on the phone, waiting for whoever he had rung to pick up. "Yeah, Steve, it's Jack. I need your help, please, mate. Is there any chance you get me some surveillance footage from downtown? I'm specifically looking for cameras between..." Jack was cut off, then turned to Dikes with a knowing smile. "All of downtown is down," he said louder than necessary.

"Okay. Thanks, buddy."

Jack hung up and swung in his chair to face Dikes.

"Well, fancy that!" Dikes exclaimed.

Jack gestured to the envelope he'd placed on the table.

"Let's take a look at what else we have."

Dikes opened the envelope and was surprised to find two sets of grainy photographs of two men. "Who are they?" he asked.

Jack raised an eyebrow as he said, "Smith got them to me early this morning via the tech crew. The techies mentioned that she's got a strange feeling about these two. That she definitely thinks one of them could be our Joseph."

"Are these stills from my walkout videos?" Dikes asked.

"Yep, they're grainy because your phone's shit," Jack said with a smile.

"You mean because it's a phone camera?" Dikes asked.

Jack paused before nodding. "Yeah, that's probably it." Dikes smiled as he looked at the two men's faces.

He tried imagining them with a moustache, beret, and rose-coloured glasses, but to his chagrin, neither of them jumped out at him.

"And why these two in particular?" Dikes asked with a frown.

Jack sighed. "Okay, I'll probably mess this up, but I'll give it a crack. Smith told me that everyone else they could identify in your videos has some kind of digital footprint, you know, an online presence."

Dikes suppressed a smile because he was enjoying Jack's attempt to explain technology, a subject he knew absolutely nothing about.

"So, even if they've tried to delete some of their past face posts." Jack frowned, thinking that that didn't sound right. "Instapost... Argh, whatever they're called."

"A social media post." Dikes threw him a bone. Jack clicked his fingers, pointing at Dikes. "That's them. Anyway, everyone has digital boot prints except these two mugs. They've managed to remain completely anonymous. And that's hard to do, apparently."

"You're right," Dikes said, staring at the pictures. "They've obviously made themselves a little too inconspicuous."

"Okay, this is the part I don't follow," Jack admitted.

"See, Joe's methodical in everything he does, right?" Jack nodded.

"So, if he wanted to be invisible online, I'm sure he could be. However, as these two have proven," Dikes held up the picture of the two men, "having a complete absence from the digital world might suggest that you're hiding something because being this invisible is not normal. It's nearly impossible these days to be digitally invisible, and that's why Smith and I are on the same page with this. We both believe that if one of these two is Joe, and because he has gone to all this trouble making himself impossible to find online, it's actually made him stand out more rather than blend in with the crowd. Thus, him trying to be a smart ass and stay off the radar could very well end up putting him on it."

Jack nodded slowly, comprehension dawning on his face.

"If neither of these two ends up being Joe, I'm willing to bet they're involved in something sketchy, and we should probably keep an eye on them anyway." Clapping Jack on the back, Dikes exclaimed enthusiastically, "We're actually getting somewhere today buddy,"

Dikes was about to continue speaking when he suddenly froze and frowned as he recalled the dead girl's white lotus hand tattoo and where he'd seen it.

"What is it?" Jack asked after noticing Dikes' frightful look.

"I just remembered where I'd seen that lotus tattoo." Jack leaned back in his chair, sipping his coffee as he waited for Dikes to explain.

"She mocked serial killers with a tirade during one of my question times. She suggested that there had to be a connection between serial killers and brain injuries or something to that effect. I remember the tattoo because, instead of just asking a question or, in her case, informing us all about the psychological state of killers' minds, she clutched the microphone stand like she was preparing to perform a song. The tattoo was facing me."

The knowing stare between Dikes and Jack, as they realized this was the reason Joe had chosen her, conveyed how significant this piece of the puzzle was.

"He killed this girl because she inadvertently mocked him," Jack said aloud as he sat forward. "Which means the other two, our male victim, they must have said something equally as offensive, hey? Do you remember any guys bad-mouthing killers?" Jack asked, his eyes lit up with hope, eager for a breakthrough in the investigation. They were finally getting somewhere.

"I don't know," Dikes admitted, staring at the floor in deep contemplation

"It's possible, but nothing stands out. A lot of people say a lot of things at the end of those lectures. Maybe Joe was sitting beside one of them, and he was badmouthing serial killers to his friend."

"Good morning, gentlemen!" Chief Bryant declared as he entered the conference room, a printout in hand.

"Yes, it is, boss," Dikes responded.
Chief Bryant glanced around the room, his face a mixture of surprise and worry. "Oh, goodness, I knew you left your party early, Dikes, but... did you actually sleep here last night?"

"Actually, yes," Dikes conceded.

"You look like hell, son," he said, smiling with one side of his mouth. "Anyway, I was looking for you two because the lab just sent this over. They were able to obtain a partial fingerprint from the remaining coffin," Chief Bryant announced, eliciting a spark of excitement in Dikes and Jack's faces.

"Have you run it through yet?" Jack asked eagerly.

"It's in progress as we speak. We should have a result either way in a few hours."
Dikes exhaled a sigh of relief. "That's great. That's really great," he said, nodding along with Jack.

Jack then glanced at Chief Bryant before jerking his chin at Dikes.

The chief looked at Dikes' puffy, unshaven face, evidence of his sleep deprivation. "Nick, go home."

"No, sir, we're really making progress today. I'm-"

"Fine?" Bryant interjected. "That is what you were going to say, wasn't it? That you're fine?" Bryant placed a compassionate hand on his shoulder. "Go home, Nick. Have a shower, eat some breakfast, get an hour or two of rest, and I'll call you the second we get any news, alright. You won't be any help to us if you're out on your feet." Dikes nodded meekly, then returned the photos and reports to the envelope. "It's been a productive morning, Jack." He smiled and tapped the envelope against Jack's chest as he took his keys out.

"Put them away; I'll drive you." Jack offered. "Don't want you falling asleep at the wheel before we catch Joe. If you died, he'd probably turn all of his attention on me, and we do not want that." Jack flashed the chief a wink as he walked Dikes out.

CHAPTER SEVENTEEN

When Jack's gold sedan arrived at Dikes' apartment building, Dikes hopped out and then stooped to the window.

"I'll come back for you when we have a definite ID. Just take it easy until then," Jack said.
Dikes gave a slight nod, then tapped the car's roof. "See you soon."
Jack gave Dikes a somewhat worried glance as he watched him walk inside.

* * *

Dikes entered his lavish apartment, tossing his keys onto the hall table.
Having decided to settle in the area, he and Sarah had purchased this penthouse three years ago. It was an absolutely stunning place, boasting breathtaking views of the entire city from the lounge and dining area.

"Sarah, you here?" he called out, checking the bedroom and ensuite while waiting for a response.
It wasn't until he was on his way to the kitchen that a note on the dining room table caught his attention.
'If you're home before me, I'm heading to the gym and then shopping with Marilyn. See you soon. Love, Sarah.'
Dikes tossed the note back onto the table, then went to the kitchen and grabbed a crumpet from the fridge,

slathered some jam over it, and then slumped on the lounge. He turned on the TV only to find himself and his squad featured on the morning news. Annoyed, he switched it off, took the phone from his pocket, and was about to place it on the coffee table when it rang. Seeing the name, JOE written across the screen immediately made Dikes' blood turn cold. Wanting to get the call over with, Dikes answered.

"That was no way to conclude our conversation last night, Nicholas," Joe said coldly.
Hearing his slight change of tone, Dikes' mood shifted to one of apprehension. His first thought was that Joe may have already murdered his next victim. "I don't give a damn, Joe," Dikes retorted.

"Perhaps you should," Joe said sternly. "Because it appears your morgue is quickly filling up. And the less attention you pay, the more people you're liable to get killed, Detective." Joe now spoke with his usual calm composure.

"When I catch you, and trust me, I will catch you; I'm going to give you my full attention." Dikes bristled.

"Are you hard of hearing, Detective Dikes? I distinctly recall explaining the rules to you a week ago, and yet here we are with you already having broken them. Did I hear you correctly when you asked to be taken off this case?" Joe waited for a response this time, but none came.

"The next time you make such a monumental miscalculation, just know that the repercussions will haunt your every waking moment for the remainder of your very numbered days. Have I made myself clear, Detective?"

Dikes gritted his teeth; his anger was palpable. He moved the phone away from his ear, ready to hurl it across the room, but refrained. "What do you want?" he asked as calmly as he could. "Seriously, what the hell do you want?"

"From our discussion last night, I deduced that you have already begun to lose your focus and drive; your emotions have weakened you to the point that your desire to catch me and hand me over to your bulletproof legal system has waned," Joe mocked. "My hope is that, through your punishment, you will be able to regain your lost motivation. Then maybe we can get you back to full solidity."

"Like I said last night, meet me man-to-man, and we'll see if I've got the motivation to finish you," Dikes replied angrily.

"Well, well... such bravado!" Joe remarked.

"What do you want?" Dikes asked. He was exhausted and was running on fumes.

"Do you truly love Sarah? I know she loves you; it's in the eyes, you see." Joe whispered as he traced his finger across a photograph of Dikes and Sarah on the red carpet at the art exhibition.

"You keep your mouth shut about her; you don't talk about her, you hear me? She's none of your business; she has nothing to do with... with whatever this is!" Dikes snapped, his temper quickly rising. "If you ever mention her again, I'll tear you apart with my bare hands!"

"You really must control that temper, Nicholas; it could get–" before Joe could finish, Dikes interjected,

"Hey! You fuckin' freak, I know you think you're special and different from everyone else, but you're not. You're no different from the common cold. You're a pain in the arse for a week, and then you're gone. You're exactly the same as every other psychotic prick I've put away - you're nothing special, Joe. You're average." Dikes was enraged, scolding Joe into silence.
There was silence on the other end of the line for nearly thirty seconds, which almost made Dikes smile.

"I hope I didn't hurt your feelings just now, Joseph," he said in his most sarcastically gentle tone.

"Good luck." And with that, Joe hung up.
Smirking, Dikes hung up the phone, only to be suddenly interrupted by a knock at the door. Suspicious, he sat still for a moment before getting up and crossing the room. His hand instinctively went to his holster to make sure his sidearm was still in place. "Who is it?" he called out, peering through the peephole to see an empty hall with closed elevators. "Sarah?" he asked quietly, half-expecting her to be playing one of her pranks. But there was no answer.

Dikes opened the door and stepped into the hallway, quickly glancing in both directions. Seeing nothing, he went back into his apartment and closed the door; as soon as he turned, he was punched hard in the face. The attacker's fist split his lip and made his nose bleed with one strike.

The force of the blow threw Dikes back against the door. Before he could recover his balance, his 6'8" attacker side-kicked him in the stomach, lifting him off the ground and dropping him in a curled heap on the floor. The attacker tried to kick Dikes again, but despite the pain he was in, he managed to regain his senses and grabbed the attacker's foot, twisting it and forcing his entire body weight onto the ankle. The attacker growled in protest, dropping to one knee and spinning around to dislodge his foot.

The attacker then connected a second kick to the side of Dikes' head, throwing him back onto the carpet. The attacker jumped to his feet with lightning speed, only slightly favouring the uninjured ankle, while Dikes was still only stumbling to his feet, rocking back as if drunk. The attacker charged, and the two wrestled through the apartment until the giant of a man grabbed Dikes around the neck and slammed him hard against the wall.

With the attacker pinning him to the wall by the neck, Dikes was lifted until his feet were almost a foot off the floor. Struggling to break his attacker's grip, Dikes managed to land a few desperate punches on the man's face, giving him nothing but a bloodied nose. Then, realising his boots were level with his attacker's groin, Dikes wasted no time in driving his leg forward and up as hard as he could. With a satisfying 'oompf,' both Dikes and the attacker crashed to the floor, Dikes gasping for air and his attacker groaning in agony while desperately clutching at his groin.

After a brief moment of both men trying to recover from their injuries, the larger man was the first to stand and pulled a knife from behind his back. Dikes, still struggling for breath, asked in disbelief, "What are you?" The man smiled, revealing his blood-covered teeth and then spat a large globule of blood onto the floor, which prompted a disgusted response from Dikes.

"Oh, c'mon! That's disgusting. Who spits on someone else's carpet like that?"
Dikes shook his head, trying to clear his vision as he only now remembered he had his sidearm. Reaching for his Glock, Dikes was just in time to see the attacker lunge forward faster than he thought possible. The attacker slashed at Dikes' hand that was reaching for his pistol, causing him to jump back and shake his hand in pain. Despite the bleeding cut, Dikes drew his pistol, but before he could fully raise it, the attacker lunged again, grabbing the pistol with his free hand and thrusting his knife in a stabbing motion with the other. Dikes had just enough time to stop the blow and turn his body so that he was able to keep the tip of the blade mere centimetres from his chest.

The attacker then tried bending Dikes' weapon hand back towards his chest.

Dikes quickly realised his intention and dropped to one knee while spinning away. This allowed him to spin the now bloodied pistol out of his attacker's grip while managing to evade the knife.

Before he could level his pistol at the attacker's chest, the assailant had already moved away with an agility that belied his size.

Dikes tried to aim his pistol at the attacker, but once again, his attacker grabbed the weapon with his large hand and held it out to the side.

Dikes instinctively let off two shots, one of which hit the lounge room window, shattering it with explosive force, reducing it to thousands of tiny diamond-like cubes of glass that rained down onto the street below.

The two men grappled fiercely, struggling to gain control of one another's weapons. They threw each other left and right, and then, feigning movement in the same direction, they tumbled into the kitchen.

As they landed with a heavy thud, Dike's pistol slipped from his hand and fell into the living room while the assassin's knife clattered onto the kitchen floor.

Battling through the pain that was coming from multiple parts of his body, Dikes still shaped up and fought tenaciously until, with a bit of luck, he managed to land an elbow to the side of the attacker's head, sending him crashing to the floor.

Wasting no time, Dikes aimed a flurry of kicks at the floored attacker with all his might, but the stronger man blocked each one with skilled accuracy.

Dikes then spotted the hanging pots, grabbed one and hurled it at his attacker's head, but again, the big man was too quick. The pot collided with his forearm with a dull thud as he stood back up to his full height. Desperate, Dikes grabbed a frying pan and swung it like a bat, attempting to keep his attacker at bay, but on one of the swings, his attacker managed to catch Dikes' arm, twist it, forcing him to drop the pan, and then slammed Dikes' head first into the cupboards. He then spun Dikes around and rained punches down on his face. He then picked Dikes up and threw him against the shelves above the benchtops, breaking them and the dishes inside.

With Dikes now lying on the benchtop amongst broken cupboards and dishes, his attacker then yanked him off the bench, swung him around and slammed him into the refrigerator.

As he was slammed into the refrigerator, Dikes managed to grab the handle of a draw, attempting to use it as a weapon, but it locked in place when he pulled it out.

"Argh," Dikes grumbled.

The attacker grabbed the back of Dikes' head, smashing it down into the open drawer, then let Dikes fall to the floor, along with the draw contents and some of the smashed dishes.

Exhausted, bleeding from multiple cuts and gashes and panting heavily, Dikes struggled to remain conscious as the large man knelt behind him, trapping him in a chokehold. Unable to loosen the arm around his neck, Dikes' hand scoured the floor desperately for anything he could use as a weapon.

Suddenly, his fingers closed around a fork. Without hesitation, he gripped it by the handle and thrust it backward, stabbing the large man in the eye.

The large man released Dikes and screamed in agony, clutching his injured eye.

Seizing his chance, Dikes fell forward and mustered the last of his strength to crawl back to the living room and his blood-covered Glock. As the large man desperately attempted to remove the fork, Dikes was slowly inching closer to his weapon. Finally, with one last effort, he reached it and almost grabbed it when he was suddenly lifted off the floor and slammed head-first into the lounge room wall.

Dikes collapsed onto his stomach as his attacker knelt beside him. Thinking Dikes was unconscious, the man assumed he had a brief moment to try and remove the embedded fork, so he set out gingerly prodding around the skewered eyeball.

Dikes seized his chance, rolling onto his side and delivering a powerful kick, forcing the fork deep into the man's skull. The blow elicited a strange-sounding, deep-throated moan. The man then swayed slightly as one hand flailed uselessly at the fork like he was drunkenly attempting to swat a fly.

Dikes lunged for and scooped up his Glock and then, in the same fluid motion, fired four shots at his attacker. All four bullets struck the man in the chest, centre mass. With a sorrowful moan, the big man fell forward, leaving Dikes scrambling back, narrowly avoiding the body as it slammed into the floor.

Just as the attacker hit the floor, Jack's voice rang out as he banged on the door.

"Hey, Nick!" Jack yelled desperately, trying to unlock the door with the spare keycard Dikes had given him. "Hey Nick, you okay?" The card kept buzzing, and Jack's frustration grew. He banged on the door in aggravation and shouted in rage, but the door would not unlock. "Fucking stupid technology! You okay in there, buddy?"

Despite his pain, Dikes couldn't help but smile as he leaned his battered and bleeding head back against the wall. He was going to tell Jack he was okay, but Jack was too busy yelling at the door to hear him.

Jack kept trying the card and then the handle; each unsuccessful attempt was followed by a string of profanities and another kick at the door. Finally, after two more failed buzzers, several frantic rattles of the handle, and another kick, the door beeped and clicked open.

"Nick! Are you okay?" Jack yelled, concern etched on his face as he rushed into the room with his weapon drawn.

Jack quickly took in the destroyed penthouse and then the badly beaten Dikes, who was sitting against the wall with the dead intruder lying face down next to him.

"Holy shit! Is he dead?" Jack exclaimed.

Dikes patted his attacker's head. "I hope so. I don't think I could handle another round with him." Dikes then nodded towards the keycard in Jack's hand. "Took you long enough. Door trouble?" Dikes asked as nonchalantly as possible.

Jack raised an eyebrow, then took a long look at the bent and dented metal room keycard in his hand. "No. Not really," he sniffed.

Staring at the large attacker, Jack re-holstered his weapon.

"Why did you come back?" Dikes asked as he gingerly touched his lip, then sucked in a breath after making it sting.

"Well, I decided to get a breakfast bagel from the Degani café just down the road, and I was driving back to the office when it started to rain."

Dikes was confused by this, so Jack walked over to the smashed window and carefully picked up a handful of fragments of shatterproof glass, then let them fall through his fingers like sand.

Dikes understood now.

"Who is he?" What is he doing here? And why is last year's Christmas present from Mare and I sticking out of his goddamn eye?"

CHAPTER EIGHTEEN

"It's hard to tell who looks worse - you or him," Dr Michael Frampton, the head coroner for the JAPD, said matter-of-factly to Dikes, who was now clean-shaven but still obviously bruised. Dikes managed a forced smile, though he quickly stopped so as not to reopen the split on his lip.

Dr Frampton surveyed the battered Dikes, who had made an effort to appear presentable by showering, shaving and changing into a fresh suit.

With fifty cases under their belt, the two had a long and successful history of working together.

Lying on one of the sliding tables in front of them was Dikes' mystery attacker. He was uncovered from the knees up.

Jack entered the morgue, clutching a hastily compiled printout of the deceased's CV.

Upon seeing the hitman's body, Jack gave the table a wide berth.

"Your boy Joe must have some sort of cash reserves. Old mate, here was an expensive present. Name is Ivan Plankov. He's an ex-Russian military, ex-French Foreign Legion, ex-bounty hunter, ex-anything else you can think of, and most recently, old Ivan has tried his hand at being a hitman. Word is, he was one of the best out there when it came to making it look like a mugging or room ransacking. A cool half a mill per job."

"Jesus," Dikes said as he took the report from Jack and read through it.

While reading, Dikes' mobile phone vibrated in his pocket. His face turned ruddy as he pulled it from his pocket.

"Does this prick ever leave you alone?" Jack asked peevishly.

Dikes shook his head. "No, he doesn't," he replied and then answered the phone.

"Hello, arsehole."

The coroner and Jack smiled, proud of their friend for standing up to Joe.

"Good to hear you are still breathing," Joe sneered on the other end.

"It's a pity I can't say the same for old Ivan here. He's lying on a slab in front of me. Not worth the half a mill you paid if you ask me."

"He was simply a means by which I sought to exact retribution from you. I imagine you feel adequately chastised from where you are sitting, do you not?"

At this, Dikes was rendered speechless. Joe was spot on. He was feeling very chastised.

"And from what I can hear, you definitely sound refocused, Detective."

"Ohh, I'm refocused!"

Jack saw Dikes' jaw muscles clench after he'd finished speaking.

"Good, then he was worth every cent. See how good it feels to have that heightened sense of aggression back?"

Not wanting to hear Joe's voice anymore, Dikes abruptly hung up.

"Going the old mid-sentence hang-up, hey? That'll piss him off," Jack joked.

"Well, not much for me to do with this one, gentlemen. Cause of death, blunt force trauma to the eye and the frontal lobe of the cerebrum," the coroner explained as he covered the body with the white sheet and slid the table back into its frigid drawer. "That or the four point-blank gunshots to the chest. Either would have done the trick."

Hearing this, Jack patted Dikes on the back. Dikes instantly winced from the pain.

"Oh shit! I'm sorry!" Jack said apologetically. "I forgot. Sorry."

Dikes flashed a gritted-toothed smile and waved Jack off.

"All good," he said, still painfully smiling.

"Oh," Dikes suppressed a painful groan as he reached for a catalogue on the table, then tossed it to Jack.

"I found it in my home office before I came in. Page twelve."

Jack flicked through the catalogue until he got to the double-page spread of the sculpture and painting on which the killer had based his scorpion piece.

Jack had no words as he stared at the model made of clay but remembered the life-sized version made of flesh.

The coroner leaned in for a look.

"Well, you must admit, he did a damn good job recreating that sculpture. Considering he was working with real flesh and on a time limit."

Jack wrinkled his brow in confusion as he gazed at the coroner. "No, we don't have to admit that. Doc," he protested.

* * *

Sitting at his desk, Dikes gingerly sat forward to reach for his laptop's mouse.

Jack leaned over his shoulder, intensely focused on the screen, as Dikes began searching through bank records.

"Look at the money old Ivan brings in!" Jack exclaimed, astonished.

"Brought in," Dikes corrected him with a rueful smirk.

Jack smiled, pleased to be corrected on this occasion. "That's right, brought in," he said, rubbing his chin in contemplation. Jack was about to pat Dikes' shoulder again, but Dikes caught him in time. "Uh uh uh," Dikes said mockingly.

"Oh shoot. I almost Britney'd you."

"What's Britney'd?" Tran asked, looking up from his paperwork.

"Yeah, Britney'd. 'Oops! I did it again." Jack sang severely off-key.

Smith and Tran rolled their eyes in response.

Jack took mock offence to this. "Well, bugger, you two, too," he said. "I thought it was a good joke and sung well."

Smiling, Jack grabbed a chair and sat next to Dikes as a beep from the computer caught their attention. "Access Denied" flashed across the screen.

"I've been able to track down the last payment made into Ivan's account, but the system keeps locking me out as soon as I look for the payer," Dikes explained.

"We'll have to get a warrant, then go to the bank to get the remaining records," Jack said, squinting as he noticed something on the screen. He pointed to a figure at the bottom right of the screen. "Jesus! He's cleared over six million this quarter alone," he said in amazement. This got the young guns' attention. "Holy shit!" they exclaimed in unison as they came over to Dikes' table.

"Oh, hey, Jack," Smith remembered she and Tran needed one of the sets of photos the techs had printed off of the two men who had deliberately made themselves invisible to the digital world. "Can you please pass us a set of the photos? We're going to hit the streets uptown in the blackout zone for an hour, then head back to our original crime scene for one last look around before they demolish it."

Dikes and Jack exchanged a knowing glance, both of them eager to take the opportunity to get out of the office for a while. The thought of being back on foot patrol instantly filled them with a sense of nostalgia.

"I hear you have strong suspicions that one of these two is our guy?" Dikes asked Smith.

Smith nodded. "I really do, sir. The time, money, and effort it takes to make yourself invisible in this day and age is actually quite impressive. And I can't see why your average Joe would waste his time doing it. Pardon the pun. I'm willing to bet that they're both hiding something," she explained with a shake of the head.

Dikes flashed her a smile. "Well said Smithy. I literally said the same thing to Jack earlier today. And great idea on going old school door to door!" Dikes praised Smith and Tran. "Jack and I'll do the same thing, but we'll take one of the other streets before we head across to the bank."

"Oh," Tran cut in, clicking his finger. "They ran facial recognition on the two men through the city's new camera system, it picked up a partial on this guy," Tran pointed to one of the men. "He was photographed in the background of a red-light runner just two blocks up from where our blackout begins."

Smith was on her phone looking through maps, then turned it so everyone could see. She ran her finger down a street that led into the city centre. "His direction of travel was down this way," she said. "Which leads directly towards the blackout zone."

Dikes and Jack gave each other the side eye. Jack slapped the table, a determined look in his eye. "Well, that's the street us old fellas will start on. It's the ritzy part of town anyway, so our fearless leader here should be right at home."

Dikes could only shake his head, hiding his amusement as he pretended to ignore the jibe while the young guns failed to hide theirs.

Smith took their set of photographs, and all four set out to pound the pavement for the morning.

CHAPTER NINETEEN

Jack's gold sedan pulled up out front of a 7-Eleven. Dikes handed a set of pictures to Jack, and they climbed out.

"We'll do this for an hour, then head over to the bank. See if we can't get more from them than, 'Access denied' hey?" Dikes said as he glanced around the area.

"Cool. I'll head up the street to the sushi joint, then cross over and meet you back here," Jack said.

"Sounds good."

* * *

Jack and Dikes went their separate ways around the city block, visiting stores, cafes, bars, and restaurants to show photos of the two unidentified men and ask if anyone had seen them. Despite their efforts, though, they had yet to receive any useful information or positive identification.

At one convenience store, Dikes scanned the faces of the three people inside and then went to the counter, pulling out his badge and slid the photographs across the counter.

"Afternoon, sir, I'm Detective Dikes from—"

"You're the TV cop, aren't you?" the store owner cut him off, then excitedly looked at the other people shopping.

"Sir, have you seen either of these gentlemen before?" Dikes asked as he tapped on the photographs sitting on the counter.

The man behind the counter looked at the photos and quickly shook his head. "No, I don't know them. Did one of these two kill all those people?" he asked, then pointed to the man on the left. "He definitely looks like a killer, that one."

Dikes felt his frustration rise. "No, sir, they're just wanted for questioning so they can help us catch the killer," he said, correcting the man.

The man behind the counter gave Dikes an exaggerated wink. "I got you."

Getting nowhere and only getting more frustrated, Dikes smiled and then left the store.

* * *

Jack had just stepped out of the Terminal BarNGrill nightclub across the street from the 7-Eleven, stifling a yawn and squinting. Coming out of an underground bar, club or strip joint in broad daylight was always a strange sensation for Jack. For whatever reason, it always made him feel a little tired.

It had been almost a decade since he'd been on patrol as a beat cop, and he'd forgotten just how much his feet ached and how boring of a job it could be.

He was looking down the street for Dikes when he spotted a young boy, about ten or eleven years old, sneaking out of a dark alleyway. Jack wouldn't have noticed the alley had he not seen the boy lurking around its entrance. Then he noticed the blood on the boy's hands and shirt—quite a lot of blood.

"Shit!" he exclaimed, his voice tinged with concern. The kid was wiping his hands on an old newspaper he had taken from a nearby bin.

Jack jogged across the street when the boy saw him and stopped mid-way through wiping his hands clean, his eyes widened in alarm.

Jack raised his hands as he approached to show the boy that he wasn't a threat.

"Hey, little buddy, are you okay? Are you hurt?" Jack asked with genuine concern.

Jack noticed the boy was a bit skittish and might run away, so he thought quickly.

"Hey, I just won some money in this club here," Jack lied, pointing back at the club he'd just come out of. "And I thought I would do a good deed for the day, and boom, I saw you," he said, clapping one hand against the photos he had in the other. "So, you can be my good deed if you'd like. Did you want some money?" he asked, receiving a mix of scathing and disgusted looks from onlookers as they walked past.

The boy dropped the bloodied newspaper and started walking up the street. Jack jogged up to his side.

"Hey there, kid," Jack said, mustering a warm smile.

"Don't worry; I just want to help you. You're safe here," he reassured him.

A well-to-do lady walking up the street past them, looked down at the dishevelled boy and scowled at him, saying, "Don't give it money; it'll just stay around here longer and cause more trouble!"

Jack was appalled by her horrible words and stopped walking and yelled at her, "Hey! Screw you lady! He's a human being, too and deserves to be here just as much as you or I. You old cow!" he grumbled the last few words under his breath. "And he's a boy, not an 'it'."

By now, the woman had already gone, but Jack's attention was drawn back to the boy now standing two meters away, staring up at him.

He must have appreciated the fact that I stuck up for him, Jack thought.

Jack quickly assessed the situation as he knelt down and tossed the photographs onto the sidewalk. Concerned that the little boy could bleed to death, he gently asked, "Hey, little man, what happened to your hands?"

The boy jerked his hands away, hiding them behind his back. "I'm fine," he said tersely.

"Well, if that's blood coming from your hands, I don't think you're fine," Jack replied. "What happened?"

The boy glanced away, hesitating to answer before finally replying, "It's not mine."

"Not yours? Then whose is it?" Jack asked as he reached for the boy's hands, but the boy stepped back. It's then the boy saw the photographs; his eyes lit up for a moment as he stared down at the top photograph.

Jack noticed this, glanced at the photos, and then back at the boy.

The boy quickly regained his composure and then stepped back.

Jack, not wanting to pressure him about the photos just yet, opted to continue on the line of questioning about the blood.

"If it's not your blood on your hands whose, is it?" The boy stared distrustfully at Jack, his eyes briefly flicking back to the pictures before looking away. Sensing the boy was about to run away, Jack spoke softer, despite his urge to shout and grab the child and make him talk.

"Whose blood is that on your hands?" The kid glanced down at his hands before quickly slipping them into his pockets.

Jack inhaled deeply to quell his growing irritation as he thought of a different tack. Kneeling down and smiling softly, Jack asked, "I just need to ask you two questions, okay? No matter what answer you give me, I promise I'll leave you alone after that. Does that sound fair?" The boy hesitated, but he hadn't run away, so Jack took that as a sign to continue.

"Okay, question one. Where's that blood on your hands come from?" The boy stood motionless for a moment. Jack was about to repeat his question when the boy's small hand emerged from his pocket and pointed to the alley from which Jack had seen him leave just minutes earlier.

In a low voice, he murmured, "It's from a dog." Jack was perplexed; this didn't seem plausible; however, he was relieved that the child wasn't the one who was hurt. He then resumed his final question. To help with it, he took the top photograph and held it up.

"Do you know this man?" he asked.

The boy briefly scrutinised the photo before turning to Jack and shaking his head.

Jack was sceptical of the boy's response; it was obvious he was not being honest. "Look, you won't be in any trouble if you do know him. He's just an old friend that I haven't seen in... oh," Jack struggled to make his lie convincing, "let's say fifteen years. I have his old police badge from when we were in basic together and would love to get it back to him." Jack realized his mistake immediately as the boy's expression changed the instant he heard the part about the police badge. His eyes narrowed, and his face hardened.

Shit! Jack inwardly reproached himself.

"I haven't ever seen him," the boy quickly answered, then turned and walked away.

"Wait!" Jack called after the boy as he stood up.

The boy looked back and saw Jack getting to his feet, so he ran.

"Argh," Jack growled.

* * *

Dikes stepped out of the corner store, whacking the photographs into the palm of his free hand, when Jack's voice crackled over the radio, urgency evident. "Hey, Nick, where are you?"

"I'm about thirty meters from the corner of Bottle Tree and Twelfth," Dikes replied.

"Okay, great. There's a kid, he's about ten years old, with blood on his hands and shirt, coming your way. He knows one of the two from the photos but doesn't know you're with me."
Dikes immediately caught on.

"Roger, going silent until I have a positive location." Dikes immediately switched off his radio, tucked it beneath his jacket, removed his badge from his belt, and pocketed it. He then did up the top button of his suit jacket to conceal his gun and holster.
Being that the kid was running from Jack and coming his way, the best chance of not looking like a cop or looking like he was following him, Dikes quickly changed direction so that he'd be walking in the same direction as the kid was running if he came down this street. No sooner had Dikes turned; he heard the pattering of little feet behind him, and without turning his head, he rolled his eyes to his left and watched the boy run past.

Over the next few minutes, Dikes increased his walking speed in order to keep the boy in sight. Whenever the boy ran, Dikes would do the same, but only once the boy had rounded a corner.

While Dikes was off following the boy, Jack paced anxiously in front of the Terminal BarNGrill nightclub. Excitement and frustration coursed through him; they were getting closer to getting a lead on Joe, yet they had to rely on a strange, blood-covered boy who, if they lost, they might never find again.

Jack was certain that this kid knew something; he could feel it in his bones. His body flooded with adrenaline at the thought of chasing the little boy down and shaking the shit out of him until he gave up the information concerning the man in the picture. But, in the end, all he could do was wait and see what Dikes came back with.

Jack was certain that if the boy knew the man in the photograph, he would feel compelled to warn him that the police were out searching for him with his photo. Still pacing, Jack looked down the alley where the boy had come.

His mind replayed the boy's answer in his head, *it's from a dog,* the boy had said.

With this thought, Jack decided he'd investigate to see if there was actually a bleeding dog and if it had been hit by a car or attacked by another dog, perhaps.

* * *

The boy turned into the next street, and just as Dikes was about to start running to catch up, he noticed the boy's shadow creeping back up the concrete sidewalk alongside the building.

He's checking if he's being followed, Dikes thought, quickly slowing his pace and pulling out his phone to pretend he was in the middle of an amusing conversation. "Oh, yeah, it was Jase that fell off it that day," Dikes said into his phone as he saw the boy's head peek around the corner up ahead.

Amidst the hustle and bustle of the busy street, Dikes blended in with the other pedestrians.

The kid's gaze briefly passed over him, as it did with everyone else that passed, but he never suspected him.

Not spotting anyone chasing him, the boy dashed across the street, periodically glancing back before slowing to a brisk walk.

* * *

Jack proceeded cautiously down the dimly lit alley, taking in the littered bins and rusty steam pipes that emitted occasional jets of steam along with a strange odour.

He briefly searched each bin, moving bags with the toe of his shoe as he passed.

Jack's nose wrinkled as he reached the end of the alley, where the pungent odour of a dead animal wafted through the air. To his right, an industrial bin was overflowing with bags, making it impossible for its two large plastic lids to close.

He approached it and immediately smelled the familiar scent of a decaying body. Taking out his hanky and placing it over his mouth, he thought, *Surely the little shit wasn't playing with a corpse.*

Jack walked to the other side of the large bin and found a puddle of blood, with a small black-haired mutt lying at its centre, its stomach cut open and its sides having been peeled open.

"What the hell?" he muttered, his words trailing off as a wave of nausea washed over him.

With a sinking feeling, Jack lifted a bag next to the fresh body with the toe of his shoe and, to his disgust, found the leg of another dog buried beneath a pile of torn and tattered garbage bags. Realizing that this must have been the cause of the smell, Jack searched for something he could use to move the bags with other than his shoe. Eventually, Jack found a broken plastic toy claw with only two and a half fingers left on it. Using the claw, he gingerly moved the other bags away from the body and was horrified to discover another small dog's mutilated remains.

Jack had stumbled upon an open graveyard of dead dogs. With each bag he lifted, there was another corpse, each one cut up in the same manner. The boy was getting better with each attempt, it seemed.

He's another Joe, or Joe's got himself a student, Jack thought as he stared at the line of decaying bodies.

"Fuck!" Jack cursed aloud before quickly leaving the alley due to the pungent smell emanating from the corpses.

* * *

Dikes had followed the boy for another two blocks before he'd snuck under the fencing and into an abandoned car park that had been turned into a dumping ground. It was filled with mounds of landfill, general rubbish and run-down or burnt-out vehicles.
Ducking behind the corner of the building, Dikes kept his eyes fixed on the boy making his way towards an old Ford Falcon wagon, its wheel arches having been overgrown with weeds and long stalks of grass.
After quickly surveying his surroundings, the boy climbed in through the rear window.
Gotcha, kid! Dikes thought before sprinting back up the street and around the corner to contact Jack and explain everything he'd witnessed.

* * *

Jack soon met up with Dikes, and together they jogged back to Jack's car.
They quickly drove back to the abandoned car park and discretely parked out of sight on the opposite side of the street corner.

With their lights off, they stayed hidden, patiently awaiting the boy to run and tell his friend the news of the police officer with his picture.

CHAPTER TWENTY

Sure enough, the detectives didn't have to wait long for the boy to emerge from the abandoned vehicle and sprint back to the street Jack had first encountered him. Dikes and Jack followed, always staying at least half a block behind and ended up parking in the same spot in front of the 7-Eleven they had earlier in the day.

The boy had gone into a blue apartment building that sat above the Terminal BarNGrill nightclub that Jack had been in earlier.

Dikes and Jack crossed the road and peered in through the building's lobby window.

After ensuring the boy wasn't loitering around the lobby, they proceeded inside.

Jack nudged Dikes and nodded toward the elevator. It had stopped on the fourth floor.

"I'll take the elevator while you wait in the staircase," Dikes instructed.

"How are you going to sell it?" Jack asked.

Dikes contemplated for a minute. "I'll call you and pretend I've lost my keys and can't get in."

"Got it," Jack replied as the two men went their separate ways.

Standing in the elevator as it ascended, Dikes phoned Jack, so there wouldn't be any suspicious ringing coming from the stairwell while Dikes was possibly engaging in conversation with the boy.

"Yep, I'm here," Jack answered.

"Okay, good. Here we go." Dikes said excitedly as the elevator doors opened to the fourth-floor hallway. The first thing Dikes saw was the boy standing halfway down the hall, directly in front of an apartment door, staring at him. He had his hand raised as if knocking but paused as soon as he heard the elevator doors open and saw a man on the phone step out.

Furtively, he shifted to the next apartment down and pretended it was the apartment he was knocking on.

"Yeah, well, I'm up here now. And I'm telling you, we need elevators like these for our work; it only took me four seconds to get up here." Dikes said into his phone. "Wait up, there's a kid here; he might know."

Jack, listening intently from the stairwell, waited as Dikes was about to make contact with the boy.

The boy froze as Dikes approached but was in a stance that showed he was ready to run at any moment.

"Yeah, I'll ask him," Dikes said into the phone, then lowered it. "Hey buddy, have you seen a set of keys lying around these halls anywhere? They have Thor's hammer as the keyring."

The boy shook his head as he suspiciously eyed Dikes.

"Ugh, bugger," Dikes said and then glanced at the floor as he continued walking towards the boy.

As Dikes approached, he flashed the kid a friendly smile and said, "If you see them, just drop them down at the front desk in the lobby, please, mate."

The boy watched Dikes carefully as he passed.

"Nah, nothing in your hallway either. I'll head back and check out the car park again," Dikes said as he walked towards the door that led to the staircase at the other end of the hall. Once he pushed the door open, he turned to the boy. "See ya, kid," Dikes said in a disinterested manner as he let the door go and disappeared down the staircase.

* * *

Dikes and Jack met up in the 7-Eleven across the street.

"Yeah, he definitely went up there to warn someone," Dikes explained. "He even moved down to the next apartment to try and throw me off."

"Little turd," Jack said. "So, how do you want to handle it from here?"
Dikes paid for a Pepsi for them both and took a sip of his.

"I think it'd be best if we wait until the kid leaves, then we can go knock on the door ourselves," he suggested.
Jack nodded in agreement.

Dikes and Jack had been sitting low in Jack's car for only eight minutes when Jack backhanded Dikes on the chest and nodded across the street.
The boy walked out of the building and ran across the street, disappearing into the alley.

"Creepy little shit is probably going to kill some more dogs," Jack said with a shake of the head. "Once we've finished with Joe, I honestly think we need to go and put this kid in a mental hospital. He's one step away from being the next Joe."

"If what you saw in the alley is what he did, yeah, we should," Dikes agreed.

As they headed into the blue apartment building, Dikes asked in a serious tone, "You and Marilyn want to have one of those?"

"Yes, but not like him. If it came out like him, I'd send the little shit straight back up there."

Dikes laughed as they headed to the building, continuing the discussion on whether or not they should have one of 'those things.'

When they reached the door of Apartment 8a, Dikes pointed out that the kid had been knocking on this door.

"Then he went and stood at that door," Dikes said as he pointed to apartment 9.

"He's got smarts." Jack said as he knocked on the door of 8a. They waited patiently but got no response.

"Try again, only harder," Dikes jibed.

"Oh, really? What a great idea, boss."

When that didn't work, and they still got no answer, Dikes remarked that maybe he needed to work on his door-knocking skills, to which Jack replied with a middle finger.

As they waited for an answer on the third try, Jack had an idea. "Reckon we should go in?" he asked. "I'm only suggesting we go in because it just so happens that I have my trusty lock-pick with me."

Without giving an answer, Dikes took out his phone.

"Give me a minute," he said as he walked down the hall, dialling a number.

Jack couldn't hear what he was talking about or who it was to but noticed Dikes glancing at his watch.

After a minute, Dikes returned, slipping his phone into his pocket. "Let's do it," he said.

Jack donned his rubber gloves and gave Dikes a mischievous smile. "You ever going to tell me his or her name? I mean, it's obviously a judge, right?" Jack asked and stared at Dikes for confirmation.

Dikes shook his head. "Just an insurance policy in case we mess this up."

Jack understood and, without pressing further, took out his pocket lock pick set and began working on the lock.

"So, we're the cops, and we're picking locks," Jack said as he glanced up and down the hallway to make sure they were alone.

"Yeah, I guess so." Dikes said uncertainly.

"Hey, you know we're doing the right thing here. Besides, you're my superior now, and I'm just following orders, so technically, I can't get into any trouble," Jack said, grinning. An audible click sounded, and with one last click of the lock, Jack opened the door and stepped aside and gestured for Dikes to head in.

"Well, let's see if this is worth you being demoted to patrolman," Jack said with a grin.

Dikes and Jack drew their weapons.

"Moment of truth... or idiocy," Dikes muttered as he announced their presence as he stepped over the threshold. "Sir, this is Detectives Dikes and Dunn from the JAPD; we're armed for our protection and would like to ask you a few questions. So, please come out with your hands up, and we can talk."

Jack followed close behind as Dikes pushed the door open and then flicked on the light switch. The front room lit up to reveal the wall to their left was completely covered in photos and news articles of Dikes.

"Bingo!" Jack exclaimed with a mix of excitement and apprehension in his voice.

Dikes took in the strange reality of the wall, then noticed clippings of numerous other murder victims and crime scenes in which he had no involvement.

"This is insane," Dikes whispered.

"I've never seen anything like it," Jack admitted as he surveyed the wall. "So, Joe is just a massive fanboy." In the centre of the picture wall, a small three-drawer desk was pushed up against it, with a closed laptop sitting on top.

As Dikes picked a candid photograph of him walking into the precinct from the wall, a wave of uneasiness overcame him.

Even if it was just for a second, Dikes had to look away from the wall, so he glanced down the small hallway that led to other rooms. "Let's clear this place before we keep looking," he whispered.

Jack agreed, and they split up. Dikes took the hallway to the left, and Jack took the kitchen across the hall and the other room.

Dikes cautiously opened the first door to reveal an empty white room. It was completely bare. The next room was just as empty. It was as if the apartment's occupant had moved out.

With the exception of the front room with a table and laptop, the rest of the apartment was deserted.

"It doesn't make sense," he muttered before meeting Jack back in the main room.

"Nothing. And I mean nothing to do with this case makes sense," Jack explained.

"Did you find anything?" Dikes asked.

Jack shook his head, "It's like he's moved out."

"Yeah, I thought the same thing," Dikes said, jerking his thumb at the rooms behind him. "Those rooms are empty."

Holstering his weapon, Dikes moved to the desk and opened the laptop. He slid his finger across the tracking pad to activate it. The screen activated and displayed a wallpaper of a black, hand-painted infinity logo.

Jack looked briefly at the screen and then back at the photos.

"He's clearly not the flowers and fairies type of guy, is he?" Jack kidded. "And he certainly has a hard-on for you."

Dikes stayed silent as he took in the strangeness of the apartment.

Jack kept moving along the wall, looking at the hundreds of newspaper clippings and photographs carefully arranged into god knows what order; he couldn't tell.

"I wonder what this guy does for fun?" Jack wondered.

Dikes mused. "I think we already know the answer to that one."

Jack moved back to the desk and opened the top desk drawer, finding several books and a set of new scalpels still in their sterile packaging. "Maybe you're his work," Jack quipped as he ran his eyes over the book spines.

"Then I guess the next question is, who's paying him?" Dikes asked with raised eyebrows.

Not having an answer, Jack pulled several books with titles such as History of the Carnivore, Handbook of Handheld Weapons, Hunting Your Prey, and Serial Killers of the 20th Century and several medical journals.

"It's not what one considers light reading, is it?" Jack observed with a smirk.

Dikes took a moment to look over the books before turning his attention back to the computer and its lock screen.

Jack grabbed the book 'Hunting Your Prey' and made his way to the white kitchen, flipping through several pages as he went. Once in the kitchen, the first thing he noticed was the steel coroner's table and the two steel buckets on the floor at the head of it. "This is totally normal," Jack said quietly to himself.

Jack looked around the kitchen, stopping at the trays of hospital-grade and homemade medical instruments laid out perfectly on the bench. He then examined them one at a time but wasn't inclined to pick any of them up.

"I bet forensics will match our cut victim with these," Jack said as he continued studying the line of instruments.

With his heart racing, Dikes surveyed the bottom two desk drawers and was shocked to discover they also contained newspaper clippings and photographs from his and Sarah's personal and public lives. He was all too familiar with invasions of his privacy, but this blatant display was unsettling. Taking a deep breath to steady himself, he slowly closed the drawer, struggling to comprehend the strange and disquieting situation he was in.

In the sterile, bright white kitchen, a whistling Jack had finished examining the trays of hospital and homemade medical instruments and spotted the refrigerator. The tune he had been whistling softly came to an abrupt end as he opened the refrigerator's double doors.

"Why did I think it was going to be a normal fridge?" Jack questioned himself softly.

Inside, he had stumbled upon a collection of human body parts in an array of glass bowls, jars and plates.

Jack's stomach churned as he took in the sight before him. A chill ran down his spine, and the air felt thick with a suffocating dread as he reached out with trembling hands and pinched the top corner of the bag between his thumb and index finger. When Jack looked down and saw he was holding a bag containing a human brain, his feet became rooted to the floor, and his jaw clenched tightly as he struggled to breathe. Then, blinking slowly, he gently placed the bag back into the refrigerator and stood still, staring at its disgusting contents.

Dikes withdrew a special card from his wallet, a card issued to him by the cyber security team after he completed their most intense IT degree three years prior. Concealed inside the mock credit card was a USB arm containing high-level encryption and hacking software not available to the public. He inserted the USB into the computer and prepared to type in the necessary commands.
After a few seconds, the card flashed blue, indicating that it was ready. Dikes was about to type in a set of commands when a loud whack! grabbed his attention. Jack had slammed the refrigerator closed. "Sorry," Jack said as he turned and stared vacantly into the space between them while exhaling.

"Are you okay?" Dikes asked, noting that Jack had gone a bit pale.

Jack swallowed dryly as if trying not to vomit, then pointed to the refrigerator.

"Don't look in there – not until I'm out, out there somewhere," he said, gesturing vaguely towards the front door.

Dikes' eyes were drawn to the refrigerator, and he was about to get up to look when a second round of beeps from his USB brought his attention back to the computer. Drawing deep breaths, Jack made his way back towards the hall, suddenly furrowing his brows as he asked, "Where does he sleep?"
Dikes paused, mulling the question over as his eyes scanned the hallway ahead.

"I mean, this place has no beds, no couches, no nothing." Jack continued as his gaze shifted to the floor at the end of the hall. He tilted his head, indicating he'd seen something. "Look, there's light coming from just there," he said, pointing at the bottom of the wall.
Dikes leaned back in the chair and craned his neck to get a better view. Sure enough, a thin beam of light shone from beneath a bottom section of the wall, along with a thin black line that marked the location of a hidden door that they'd both missed on their initial search.

"Son of a bitch," Jack muttered.
Jack stepped up to the door, pistol in hand, but then he turned back to Dikes. "I bet it's the freak's bedroom," he said with a nod.
Dikes' USB flashed green, then blue, indicating that a powerful worming program had been activated. This

program bypassed every operating system and would use the computer's time machine function to uncover the last websites and programs that had been used, even if the user had deleted their browser history or deleted their programs entirely. Within ten seconds, the website Joe.com was displayed on the screen via the Tor browser.

"God damn, Joe!" Dikes growled before turning to Jack and half-rising from his seat.

Jack quickly told him to sit, reassuringly adding, "It's okay; you get what you can from that magic box; I'll take care of the mystery room."

Dikes looked up, a glint of uncertainty in his eyes. "You sure?" he asked.

Jack nodded confidently. "Very sure, we need to get as much out of this place as we can without him knowing. We need to be quick, too, I reckon," Jack said and then moved cautiously towards the secret door and placed his open-palmed hand against it. "It's hot," he said, frowning with surprise.

Dikes watched him for a moment before returning his focus to the screen, determined to uncover the mysteries of Joe.com.

Jack searched for a handle, but there was none. Then he remembered the secret doors in movies—how the star or spy had to press their hand against it to open it. So, Jack pressed his hand against the edge of the door where a handle should be, and he was met with a click and saw a small, white circular handle appear. Jack quickly glanced back at Dikes to make sure he was still absorbed in the screen, which he was, so, he cautiously put his hand on the handle and pushed the door open slightly, only to be blinded by a brilliant white light. "What the hell!" he exclaimed, shielding his eyes and pulling the door almost closed again.

"More lights?" Dikes asked, squinting.

Jack paused, shielding his eyes. "Argh crap. It's floodlights again."

Dikes remained silent, his expression growing increasingly foreboding as he split his attention between Jack and the computer. Then he read something that scared him to the core. "Shit. Hey, Jack, you need to see this." His voice was rife with nervousness.

Jack ignored him at first, slowly pushing the door open, unaware that it was about to trigger a tripwire connected to two sets of explosives mounted on either side of the doorframe. Just as the door brushed against the wire, Dikes called out again, his voice urgent. "Jack! You really need to come look at this. There's too much to explain!"

Jack paused, opening the door and turning back to Dikes. "What is it?" he asked.

"It's..." Dikes couldn't explain what he'd read. "You have to see it for yourself," he implored.

Reluctantly, Jack closed the door, which had been perilously close to the tripwire, and returned to the laptop. Dikes stepped aside, allowing Jack to lean in and read the screen.

"What the hell is this?" Jack asked, seeing photos of Dikes and five other detectives from different police departments from around the world, each of whom had attained high-profile celebrity status in their respective cities.

Dikes clicked on the 'Past Games' sub-menu, which opened a new page full of thumbnails of deceased detectives. He selected the first one, which enlarged to a full-screen photo of a detective with a gunshot wound to the side of his head. The caption read 'Winner, Joe.Adamstown'.

Jack swore angrily, his face contorted with rage. "That's Andrews! This prick killed Andrews too?"

"No, no, no, Jack, he wasn't killed by our Joe; that was from the Joe in Adamstown"

"So, there's more than one of these fuckers out there?" Jack asked incredulously?

"According to this, there's five of them, operating in different cities all around the world," Dikes explained. "And there's a write-up on how our Joe has been playing and humiliating me," Dikes added, then pointed to the left side of the screen. "But believe it or not, that's not the most interesting part. It's this part here about The Original 8 that is scary." He glanced at Jack before continuing. "Before we do anything, we need to let the other detectives involved in these games know. If we can let them know what's happening ahead of time, we might be able to save some lives."

"I agree; that means we have to photograph all this but not touch a thing. He can't know we know! We have to be out of here sooner rather than later." Jack said with urgency.

Dikes agreed as he reached for his phone and began taking pictures of the various JOE.COM screens.

Jack set about taking photos of the wall of clippings.

"We should shoot these through to the techs, so they can get a head start," Dikes suggested while scrolling to the page that explained The Original 8 and photographed it.

Meanwhile, Jack ran to the kitchen and snapped photos of the medical instruments before reluctantly opening the refrigerator again and photographing its contents.

Once Jack had finished with the contents of the refrigerator, he hurried back to the desk and knelt beside Dikes.

As he began capturing photos of the books, clippings, and photographs in the drawers, the room gradually brightened. "I thought I," Jack began, looking back at the door as it slowly opened. Suddenly, they heard a click and a loud pinging sound from behind the door.

They had just enough time to exchange an uneasy glance when......

CHAPTER TWENTY ONE

A deafening explosion reverberated through the building, shattering windows and sending shards of glass and shrapnel cascading onto the streets below.

Dikes and Jack were thrown through Joe's door and wall, crashing heavily into the hallway and collapsing onto the floor, shrouded in a blanket of dust and debris.

With the building groaning and creaking, large parts of the apartment were still crumbling and burning when Dikes gradually regained consciousness.

Coughing, he attempted to stand, only to realise he was pinned beneath a large wooden beam. With his vision swimming, he strained to look ahead to where Joe's apartment used to be, but all he could see were plumes of grey ash, smoke, electrical sparks shooting out of nearby walls like tiny fireworks and, strangely, the blue sky.

After a few moments of regaining his self-awareness, Dikes struggled but managed to push the beam off himself and got to his knees.

Confused and aching, he surveyed the destruction for any sign of Jack. His head throbbed like he had a massive hangover.

Dikes' ears were ringing terribly, and everything sounded muffled. Attempting to breathe deeply, he coughed up more dust around him. He blinked several times, trying to make out his surroundings through the smoke-filled building. The gaping hole in the side of the building allowed the dust and smoke to escape, making it easier for him to look around the hallway for Jack. At least he thought he was in the hall.

Nothing looked the same as it did just sixty seconds ago. Then he spied it; Jack's arm, poking out from under a large piece of the wall. Dikes quickly scrambled forward to grab it. Thankfully, it grabbed him back.

"Hey! Hey, Jack, are you okay?" he asked worryingly, unable to hear his own voice properly. Semi-conscious, Jack slowly raised his head from the floor, dust and pieces of plasterboard falling from his hair.

"What?" he yelled, spitting out dust. A cut on the top of his head had started to bleed, creating a stark contrast against the white and grey powder that he was covered in.

"I said, are you okay?" Dikes yelled again, louder this time.

"What? I can't hear you!" Jack shouted back as he painfully got onto his knees.

Getting to his feet, Dikes said looked down at him, "I think your hearing is affected." Jack held out his hand, and Dikes helped him to his feet. "No... but I think my hearing might be affected," Jack replied with a shake of the head.

"I'm so sick of being beaten, shot at and blown up," Dikes groaned as he and Jack looked around at what was left of Joe's apartment.

Jack and Dikes were slowly brushing themselves off when a bullet ripped through Jack's left shoulder, sending him crashing to the floor.

As Dikes dived for cover, he saw Joe, at the far end of the hallway, firing a pistol at them, sending splinters of wood and plasterboard flying in all directions before he disappeared down the nearby stairs.

"Jesus Christ! Jack, are you alright?" Dikes cried out, reaching for his gun as he stepped back to check on Jack.

"Damn it!" Jack groaned painfully. "I'm fine; just get that bastard!" Jack yelled, his teeth clenched in pain. Dikes gave Jack's leg a pat before sprinting for the stairwell.

Edging cautiously to the lip of the stairwell, Dikes peered into its centre, listening intently for Joe's retreating footsteps. Suddenly, before he knew it, Joe had fired three shots, showering him in chunks of the ceiling plaster.

Ducking hastily for cover, Dikes continued his pursuit, taking two and three steps at a time as he scrambled down the stairwell. Pausing on the landing of the next floor, he strained to listen, the sound of Joe still running filling the air. With renewed intensity, Dikes rushed down the remaining stairs, jumping the rest of the way. He looked over the railing into the stairwell's centre just as two more shots rang out from the ground floor, obliterating the section of the handrail in front of him into fragments. Instinctively, Dikes dove for cover once more while muttering a curse under his breath.

Fuming with anger, Dikes rolled over and unleashed three shots down the stairwell, aiming in Joe's direction.

It feels good to be shooting at the son of a bitch! Dikes thought.

The bullets only narrowly missed their target as Joe dashed out of the stairwell and around the corner.

Dikes heard Joe's hurried footsteps racing down another set of stairs, and he quickly gave chase.

The building's door was thrown open, and Joe shot out into the street. Ten seconds later, Dikes cautiously opened the door, his pistol at the ready. He caught sight of Joe sprinting away whilst reloading his pistol. Taking aim, Dikes was about to squeeze the trigger when two drunks stumbled out of a bar, obstructing his line of fire.

"Move, goddamn it! Get out of the way!" he yelled. The drunks stared at Dikes, perplexed. One of them then began to mock him, raising his hands as if they were a gun.

"Get down. Quick, Jimmy, get down!" he drunkenly teased. "Pew pew, pew."

Pushing past the two intoxicated men, Dikes searched the bustling street ahead for Joe. His eyes soon landed on a door being shut at the mouth of an alley. He rushed over and pulled it open, scanning the hallway ahead with his pistol.

There was nothing there, so he cautiously stepped inside and jogged to the only other door in the corridor, bracing himself for the possibility that Joe would open it and start shooting at any second. As he reached the door, he placed his hand on the handle, pausing for a moment before slowly turning it and peeking inside.

On the other side of the door was the foyer of an upmarket hotel filled with people cowering against the walls and shielding their children.

At the far end of the foyer, two elevators were waiting, and inside one of them, Joe stood with a smirk on his face as the doors closed.

Dikes burst through the door with a snarl, racing towards the elevator and firing his weapon.

Joe casually stepped back against the side of the elevator, as cool as ever, allowing the bullets to plough into the back wall and the closing doors.

"Damn it!" Dikes yelled in frustration, looking at some of the frightened people.

His brain quickly thought to assure them that they were safe, but he knew Joe well enough not to lie to them.

Dikes impatiently watched and waited for the elevator to come to a stop. When it stopped on the second floor, he sprinted to the stairs and bounded up them two at a time. He entered the second floor, pistol at the ready, but the hallways were deserted.

"Shit!" Dikes cursed quietly. He was about to race back into the stairwell to the next level when he noticed the window at the end of the hall was slightly ajar. Puffing and holding his ribs, which had started to really hurt, Dikes made it to the window and peered through it.

Bang! The window and the top of its frame exploded, showering him with glass and splinters of wood. He dropped to the floor and scrambled back against the wall. After waiting a few seconds, Dikes stretched up and looked out over the lip of the window.

Dikes could see Joe running from the alley and into the main street.

"Argh," Dikes growled; then, with a painful moan, he got to his feet and clumsily climbed out of the window, hurting his ribs on the way out. In the last minute or so, Dikes had begun to notice all his sore spots were aching. Scrambling down the fire escape, Dikes hit the ground and sprinted after Joe.

He quickly gained ground on him by using the street instead of the crowded sidewalk. Within a block, Dikes had almost caught up with him. Suddenly a car screeched to a stop in his path, forcing him to leap over the hood. He landed on the bonnet and slid off, still running.

That was cool! he thought.

* * *

Jack, wincing from his injuries, stepped out of the building and saw Joe and Dikes racing up the street.

'Damn it," he muttered through gritted teeth. Without breaking stride, he dashed after them as best he could.

* * *

Joe left the street and darted into a movie theatre with his pistol still in hand. He pushed past the usher who'd tried to stop him at the door.

"Hey, come back here!" the usher yelled and ran after Joe.

Joe spun around and shot the usher in the head before disappearing into theatre 8.

People within the theatre lobby who had witnessed the usher's murder ran screaming from the theatre as Dikes raced in.

Dikes paused near the usher's body, a feeling of sadness washing over him as he saw the young man's lifeless body. His forlorn expression quickly hardened as he gritted his teeth and ran ahead.

Uncertain which theatre Joe had entered, Dikes had to proceed with caution, his steps weighed down by a mounting fear and annoyance. He was haunted by the thought that Joe could emerge from any of the doors at any moment, firing at him.

With his heart pounding, Dikes stopped briefly at each theatre door to listen for any sign of a disturbance. Hearing nothing out of the ordinary after checking all ten theatres, a frustrated Dikes slapped his pistol against his thigh. "Damn it!" he muttered to himself as he headed back down the main hall.

Dikes was walking back past theatre 5 when he heard a door click open behind him. Spinning around while half raising his pistol, he spotted a mother quickly ushering her two small children out of the theatre 8.

"Mum, look, another one," the little girl said, pointing at Dikes.

Seeing the bleeding, dirty and armed figure, the mother looked horrified as she scooped up her two children and ushered them behind one of the large three-dimensional movie standees. Coincidently, it happened to be advertising the rerun of Metal Universe II. On the standee, Dikes was one of the main characters.

"Oh god, please don't hurt my babies. Please don-"

"I'm with the police, mam," Dikes said in a loud whisper. "I'm Detective Dikes. I'm not going to hurt you." He flashed the two small children a smile, then looked back at the mother. "Did you see a gunman in that theatre?" Dikes asked, nodding in the direction of theatre 8.

The mother nervously nodded. "He rushed in and hid it under his coat, but we saw it; that's why I rushed the children out of there."

"Good call, now go," said Dikes, heading towards the door to theatre 8. "Oh, and please cover their eyes in the foyer, mam. Trust me." He nodded gently and then looked down at the two children.

"When your mummy tells you to close your eyes, keep them closed until she says to open them again; okay? If you do this properly, she'll buy you a chocolate or a toy or something." He wasn't sure what children of this age liked or didn't like.

The children looked wide-eyed at each other, then up at their mother for confirmation.

The mother put on a brave face and nodded. "I sure will," she said quickly, then took them by the hands and whisked them down the hall to the foyer area. She glanced back and mouthed 'Thank you' to Dikes.

Dikes flashed her a smile, then rushed to theatre 8, entering and quickly closing it with a soft click.

With the scene on the screen changing, some light filtered back to Dikes, which lit up a short, right-handed dogleg hallway.

Once he rounded the right-hand corner, Dikes found himself on a gently sloping ramp that ran along the left side of the theatre's seats.

Dikes slowly crawled to the end of the ramp, carefully keeping himself hidden from the moviegoers. When he reached the end, where he had half a meter of the wall to hide behind, he stopped.

Trying to use the flashing scenes on the screen as cover, Dikes cautiously peeked his head around the edge of the wall. Unfortunately, the screen changed to black, and he couldn't make out anyone's face. Suddenly, gunshots echoed throughout the theatre, and Dikes quickly ducked back behind the wall. It didn't take him long before he realised that the shots were coming from the movie.

"Shit!" Dikes felt a twinge of embarrassment, having mistaken the on-screen shots for real ones. Dikes then lifted his head and spotted Joe sitting four rows up and towards the middle of the theatre, aiming a pistol at him. Alarmed, Dikes dropped back behind the small wall as Joe leapt over the seats and sprinted down the aisle, shooting. The theatre patrons screamed as they realized this was an actual shootout.

Some people ducked for cover, others climbed over the seats, and the rest ran for the exit.

"Everybody down! Stay down!" Dikes shouted as he got to one knee while motioning for them to stay low while also keeping low himself.

Joe made his way to the exit door by the movie screen and looked back for Dikes.

Dikes popped his head up and saw Joe pause at the open fire exit. He dropped to one knee and took aim, but there were too many people running in front of him to fire.

Joe had no qualms with collateral damage and opened fire, wounding two moviegoers directly in front of Dikes. The theatre lights came on just as Joe slipped out of the exit door.

Dikes quickly checked the injured patrons and ordered others to help them, then raced for the exit door.

Without hesitation, Dikes burst into the hallway, pistol drawn, only to find it empty. A door halfway down creaked, so he dashed to it and threw it open. To his dismay, he found himself in another empty alleyway.

"Another damn alley," he grumbled.

The sound of shuffling feet from somewhere just ahead and around the corner got his attention, and with a yell of frustration, Dikes continued his pursuit.

* * *

Gripping his shoulder tightly to try and stem the bleeding, Jack entered the movie theatre as chaos unfolded around him. He checked the usher's body for a pulse, then spotted one of the employees peeking from behind the candy counter.

"Hey, kid, I'm a cop," he called out.
A terrified-looking teenage boy slowly stood and put his hands up.

"Put your damn hands down, son. Do you have any large sheets or posters out back anywhere?"
The teenager nodded, and Jack continued, "Okay, good. Go get something to cover him up."
The teenager nodded and then ran to the storage room when Jack called after him. "Hey, kid, which way did they go?"

"Number eight," the teenager yelled, shakily pointing towards the main hall as a woman rushed past with her two children.
Suddenly, theatre 8's doors burst open, and people ran out, pushing and screaming.
Jack groaned in pain as he stumbled to his feet, hurrying towards the theatre as a wall of people came screaming towards him.

"Hurry up and cover his body; people are coming," Jack yelled back at the candy bar employee.

* * *

Dikes dashed into the narrow alley lined with parked cars. He broke into a sprint whilst keeping an eye on the approaching corner when suddenly, an SUV's front door swung open, slamming into his chest and sending his gun clattering onto the concrete.

Gasping for air, Dikes was desperately trying to pick himself up when he got walloped in the face by the door as it swung open again. The force of the door threw him back, hitting the concrete hard with a broken and bloody nose.

Joe's boots calmly stepped out of the vehicle and walked slowly towards the moaning and winded Dikes, who was still writhing on the ground. Then, in a quick, violent motion, Joe's right boot kicked Dikes across the face. As Jack's voice echoed through the alley, Dikes lay sprawled out on the concrete, barely conscious.

"Dikes?" Jack's voice called out from the theatre's exit hallway.

Because of his blurred vision, when Dikes heard Jack call out, all he could make out were Joe's legs disappearing behind the SUV.

"Dikes!" Jack called again, only this time it sounded closer.

Weakly, Dikes tried to call out a warning, but all he could manage was a painful groan.

Jack pushed open the door and immediately spotted him lying on the ground, struggling to speak while clutching his face.

Jack's face was a mask of shock and worry as he scanned the empty alley. He swiftly put away his weapon and ran to Dikes.

"Oh shit! You okay, Nick?" Jack shook his head, furious at himself for asking such a stupid question. "Of course, you're fucking not okay," he berated himself. "Just stay down," he said as he knelt beside Dikes, assessing his injuries.

Dikes tried to get his breath back and warn Jack as he rolled over, but his attempt to speak went unheard.

"Sorry, buddy, I couldn't understand that," Jack said, trying to gently sit Dikes up. But his injured shoulder caused him to cry out in pain.

As Joe rose up behind Jack, Dikes' eyes fluttered open for a second.

Seeing his best friend's eyes fluttering open brought a smile to Jack's face.

"Hey there, bud, we're going-" Jack's words trailed off as he felt a presence behind him. In an instant, he slid his pistol out from under his jacket, but before he could spin around, he was struck across the face by a tire iron and knocked unconscious.

Suddenly, a midday sun shower began to pour down—a common occurrence at that time of year.

Joe casually walked over to Dikes, knelt in front of him then pressed the cold barrel of the detective's own pistol firmly against his head.

Dikes was regaining his breath when he felt the cold steel; his eyes widened in fear as he froze, blinking slowly as blood trickled from his head into his eyes.

"Through your brain... or his?" Joe whispered, pure malevolence dripping from every word. "Or through the head of that pretty wife of yours?"

"No..." That was all Dikes could manage.
Dikes could feel anger building up inside him, but it fizzled away just as quick as it came due to his barely conscious body being paralysed by pain.
After a moment, the barrel slid away from Dikes' head. Joe stepped across to Jack, knelt beside him, and pressed the barrel of the pistol firmly against Jack's temple. The hammer was cocked and the tyre iron laid down casually. Dazed and blinking slowly, Dikes tried to open his eyes, but the blood and rain trickling from his head blinded him.
Joe flashed a sinister grin and asked, "Shall Jack and I paint the town red, as they say?"
Through his blurred, blood-filled vision, Dikes saw Joe lean back and turn his head slightly, readying to fire and blow Jack's brains across the brick wall behind him.
Then, after a drawn-out moment, the weapon was slowly withdrawn.
With a temporary sense of relief, Dikes rested his spinning head against the hard concrete.
As soon as he did, the rain washed the blood down into his eyes and mouth.

"How about I give you a fighting chance." Joe said as he released the magazine then using his thumb, flicked bullet after bullet onto the ground.

Dikes heard bullets pinging off the concrete, followed by the clattering of the empty magazine and then the pistol body.

"Jack!" Dikes let out a cry as crawled then stumbled forward. He felt dizzy and disoriented, like the feeling you get when you first lay down after a heavy night of drinking. His heart was racing as his stomach churned, and his chest hurt to breathe.

Jack groggily stirred, but before he could fully wake up, Joe landed a sucker punch to the side of his head, knocking him out again. Joe then slid his hands under Jack's armpits and dragged him back to the SUV.

Dikes heard groans of exertion as Joe struggled to lift Jack's unconscious body into the back of the SUV.

Dikes snarled angrily as he struggled to crawl forward, attempting to rub the blood from his eyes. He frantically searched the ground for the pistol body, then the magazine, when he heard Joe trying to hotwire the SUV. Dikes was determined not to let him take Jack, and miraculously, his shaking fingers stumbled across a bullet which he managed to load into the magazine.

From inside the car, Joe looked down at Dikes, flashing him a wicked grin and warning him, "Prepare yourself, Detective. You've brought this penalty round on yourself."

Dikes then heard the engine of the SUV roar twice and then speed away down the alley, leaving him behind, still trying to load the magazine into his pistol.

Dikes eventually tipped forwards and fell unconscious onto the hard concrete; his last vision was of the rain obscured vehicle, retreating down the alley.

* * *

The general sounds of the city stirred Dikes from his fitful slumber. He awoke still sprawled out on the concrete, his pistol and magazine lying next to his hand. The rain had stopped, and his head and entire body pounded with aches and pains, his vision blurring as he strained to lift himself onto his right elbow. As he slowly regained focus, Dikes felt a throbbing pain surge to both temples like sledgehammers, making him feel nauseous all over again. He was able to get onto all fours within a minute, then sat back on his heels.

When he gingerly touched his nose, a stinging pain shot through him, forcing him to quickly withdraw his hand. After several more attempts to evaluate the injury, he gave up. Struggling to stand, he eventually managed to do so, albeit on unsteady legs and he had to lean against the wall for support.

Licking his sleeve and then using it to try and clean the dried blood from his eyes and lashes, Dikes stumbled around the alley, collecting the scattered bullets, pistol, and magazine before returning to the wall to lean against while he reloaded the magazine.

Once he'd managed that and was confident he could walk the distance back to the car, he ventured into the bustling city street, where onlookers gasped in shock, quickly reaching for their phones to capture the moment.

On his way back to Jack's car, Dikes noticed the area around Joe's building had been cordoned off by first response units, and the fire had already been extinguished. He wondered how much of the apartment had been destroyed and how much evidence remained for them to collect. The amount of thick, grey smoke still billowing from the gaping hole in the wall pretty much answered his question: not much.

Between Jack's car and the fire trucks, two ambulance units were parked. Four paramedics were chatting among themselves when one of them noticed Dikes limping up the street, heading towards the scene.

"Holy shit! That's Dikes!" the female medic exclaimed.

Everyone turned to see the detective, looking pained, battered and blood-covered as he limped to Jack's car and slumped onto its roof, his head in his hands.

The paramedic reached for her emergency kit and ran it to Dikes. Upon reaching him, she quickly introduced herself and placed a hand firmly on his bicep, ready to guide him should he fall or pass out. Judging by his external appearance, the latter was a strong possibility.

"Sir, you need to sit down. I need to take a look at that head."

Dikes complied without argument, retrieving his keys and unlocking the car before collapsing into the driver's seat. As he settled in, Dikes' mind raced to Jack and the arse-kicking they'd both suffered at the hands of Joe. He was particularly pissed off that Joe had taken Jack hostage, and he was unable to stop him.

The paramedic, seeing his distress, acted quickly. She unzipped her first-aid kit and took out several pieces of gauze to wipe away the dried blood from the deeper cuts and abrasions on Dikes' face.

"Where's Chief Bryant? Is he inside? I have to tell him about Jack!" Dikes asked, his croaky voice cracking with emotion.

His throat had been sore since he'd regained consciousness in the alley, but this was the first time he'd spoken.

"Um, no. He's not here, sir," the paramedic replied, replacing the already bloodied gauze.

"What do you mean?" Dikes asked as he frowned, which also hurt to do. "You mean no, he's not here yet or?"

"No, I mean, this isn't his crime scene. We're under Chief Graham from the forty-third on this one," she explained.

"What?" Dikes exclaimed, unable to make sense of the information.

Dikes sat forward to get a better view of the crime scene, but the sudden movement caused immense pain in his left ribcage. Reaching to hold his ribs, Dikes winced and had to lean back slowly into his seat, exhaling heavily.

"Jesus, that hurt," he muttered.

"By the looks of it, you might have a few broken ribs, sir," the medic said.

Just as Dikes was about to ask why Chief Bryant wasn't taking control of the scene, the car radio crackled to life.

"8-11, this is Chief Bryant; come in, damn it, 8-11, this is Chief Bryant; come in," the chief's voice barked. Moaning, Dikes gingerly reached forward and grabbed the hand piece.

"Dikes, come in!" the chief said sternly.

Dikes was surprised at the distress in the chief's voice.

"Excuse me for a second," he said to the medic, who had just finished cleaning the blood from the cuts on the side of his face and nose. The medic leaned back to replace the second blood-soaked gauze with a fresh one, then politely waited for Dikes to finish his conversation.

"Chief, come in," he said in a raspy voice.

"Dikes!" the chief exclaimed in surprise. "He's here; I've got Dikes on the other end," Dikes heard the chief say to someone in the background.

"He's got him, Chief!" Dikes affirmed.

"What? No, we have him, Nick," the chief corrected him.

Confusion swept over Dikes as he wondered what he had missed while unconscious in the alley.

"Who? I'm talking about Jack," Dikes explained.

"Oh… No, we don't, well...yes." The chief was silent for a moment, leaving Dikes even more confused as to what was going on.

"We have Joe, Nick," the chief said, his tone not quite matching the urgency of the situation. "We have him pinned down in an abandoned warehouse on Sodium Drive. You need to get here now!"

A shot of adrenaline surged through Dikes' veins as he turned to the paramedic, "Excuse me, I really have to go!" Dikes exclaimed as he grabbed a handful of gauze and hastily slammed the door closed, put Jack's car into gear and then sped away at breakneck speed.

CHAPTER TWENTY TWO

Crying, Dikes turned to Marilyn, "I'm so sorry, Mare," he apologised. His words sounded hollow in his ears, and he could only imagine how empty they sounded to Marilyn.

Despite the gag, she still tried desperately to communicate with him, tears streaming down her cheeks.

If I'm going to do this, I have to make it quick for him, Dikes thought to himself as he closed his eyes and turned back to Jack.

Drawing a deep breath, he opened them again and tightened his grip on the sword's hilt.

* * *

Tran rushed up the stairs, his pistol drawn. "Dikes, stop! Don't do it!" he yelled.

* * *

"I'm sorry, my friend," Dikes said, barely above a whisper, his tears flowing freely. Then, drawing one long breath, he closed his eyes.

Dikes exhaled and, without overthinking, plunged the sword deep into Jack's chest, letting out wails of agony and horror as he did.

Marilyn screamed until her voice broke.

Crying, Sarah hung her head.

Tran reached the top of the stairs, briefly pausing when he heard everybody's tormented screams.

With the blade embedded in his chest, Jack convulsed, and a guttural gargle escaped his lips beneath the bloodied pillowcase.
Hearing this, Marilyn's muffled screams grew louder until her voice gave out again.

"Goddamn, you!" Dikes roared, his arms falling to his sides in a moment of utter helplessness. He bent forward, coughing and dry-heaving in revulsion at his own actions.

"Stay where you are, Detective Tran!" Joe bellowed. "If I so much as catch a glimpse of you coming through this door, I will drive this blade right through Sarah's chest!"
Panting, Tran skidded to a stop two metres from the door. He swallowed hard and clenched his jaw but stayed put.

"Do I have your word, Detective Tran?" Joe asked calmly.

"Yes," Tran yelled bitterly, having no other choice but to comply.

"There's a good, brave boy," Joe drawled with a mocking edge.
Marilyn wept loudly as Joe removed the knife from Sarah's chin, and Jack's body twitched one final time.

"I commend you on a job well done, Detective Dikes," Joe began. "It was a hard assignment to complete, and it took a great deal of courage—"

"Shut your goddamn mouth!" Dikes yelled, cutting Joe off as his emotions got the better of him.

Joe calmly responded, "You are going to tear off my what, Detective? No please, I am all ears. So, tell me what you are going to tear off and how you are going to do it from over there?" His words were laced with vexation as he glared at Dikes through the fleshy mask. Dikes' eyes instinctively flicked to his gun as Joe spoke. Then, abruptly, the digital clock mounted to the front of Sarah's vest buzzed loudly, breaking the tension.

All eyes were drawn to the clock and the explosives it was attached to.

Dikes, wide-eyed, was transfixed.

Joe made a mock laugh, then spoke up reassuringly, "Do not worry about the clock, Nicholas. It is all for show; it was just a device to help keep you on track."

Joe took a long pause as he glared at Dikes.

"You should not be angry with me," Joe said solemnly. "In fact, I believe you should be thanking me. I gave you the opportunity to save your friend from a life of unbearable pain and humiliation. Not to mention the countless times he would have been publicly shamed. He would have had to live out the rest of his life without a face; I mean, people would have crossed the street to avoid looking at him. And in the end, he probably would have killed himself anyway. So, you may have just saved his soul from eternal damnation, Nicholas."

Marilyn, who hadn't looked up since her voice had cracked, was shaking her head while crying uncontrollably.

Sarah, who was also crying, watched as a teary-eyed Dikes considered Joe's words.

Joe then posed a sobering question: "Or did you?"

Dikes felt his heart stop, and the world fell silent around him as he gazed between Sarah and Marilyn.

Outside the room, Tran frowned deeply as he wiped tears from his eyes.

Dikes' tears continued to flow, his heart aching as the realisation of his actions smashed into him.

"Or did you just murder your best friend and fellow detective in cold blood?"

Joe let his words marinate for a while as he watched Dikes stare at Jack.

"Remove his cover," Joe commanded coldly, a sinister smile playing on his lips below his Jack mask. "I have played you, I have bent you, I have beat you, and I have broken you, Detective," Joe crowed.

"You're full of shit," Dikes spat.

"Am I?" Joe replied, grabbing Marilyn's head and reefing it back. "Does it look like she's grateful to you for ending her husband's suffering? Or has she just seen you run a sword through a man she loves who was in need of nothing more than a thousand-dollar skin graft?"

Horrified, Dikes turned to Jack, then down at the sword buried deep in his chest.

Joe removed the mask and threw it at Dikes, who caught it before it could hit him. "It's very realistic, isn't it? But it is made of silicon, not skin, you simple-minded pig." Joe spat. "Predictability, Nicholas. That is your weakness. That is how I beat you!"

Dikes felt the texture of the mask between his fingers and then looked at Marilyn, who still wouldn't meet his gaze.

"Mare?" he whimpered.

Joe then thrust Marilyn's head forward before pulling Sarah's head back.

Joe shuddered as if feeling the sensation of the last breath. "I am curious. Could you taste his soul as it left his body, Nicholas?" he asked seriously.

Dikes had had enough. He lunged for his gun, grabbed it and raised it, pointing it at Joe.

"Let her go! Let her go, now!" he demanded.

"What did I tell you about having a weapon in here?" Joe replied coolly. "Fuck your rules! Let her go!" Dikes barked back.

"We need rules in here, Nicholas, just as we need them in life. Otherwise, people could go around stabbing others in the chest with swords willy-nilly," Joe replied snarkily, tilting his head to briefly catch a glimpse of Dikes' expression.

Dikes ignored Joe's jibe.

"You know I'm going to hunt down those other sick arseholes from your website," Dikes growled.

Joe was momentarily taken aback.

He knows, Joe thought.

"Is that, right?" Joe said after a noticeable pause.

"We've already forwarded the information," Dikes retorted.

Joe blinked slowly.

"Go to hell!" Dikes hissed as he took careful aim and readied himself to dive to the right and attempt to shoot Joe by shooting around Sarah.

"Maybe later," Joe replied, then pulled a lever to his right, one that was hidden and Dikes hadn't seen.

Pulling the lever opened a trapdoor beneath him, and suddenly Joe was falling. But two things happened in the split second before he disappeared beneath the floor.

The first was, as Joe fell, the pins to the grenades attached to Marilyn and Sarah were pulled.

And the second, Dikes had fired a shot, blowing away Joe's left ring finger.

With all the pins pulled, the women desperately tried to remove the grenades from their vests.

Hearing what had happened, Tran rushed into the room, quickly took in the chaotic scene and grabbed ahold of Dikes.

Joe's fall was abruptly halted when the trench coat he was wearing snagged on the sharp edge of the chute he was supposed to drop down, suspending him in mid-air with his arms stuck in the trench coat's sleeves above his head. Underneath the long trench coat, Joe was wearing a JAPD police uniform.

"Run!" Dikes heard Sarah desperately scream from beneath her gag.

Tran had hooked an arm under Dikes' armpit and yanked him back towards the door.

Screaming for Sarah, Dikes desperately struggled to free himself from Tran's grip. "No! I won't leave her!" he yelled.

Despite his protests, Tran forcibly dragged him out of the room and several steps down the hall.

Marilyn continued to scream and fight against her vest while Sarah exhaled calmly and slowly closed her eyes. Then, a deafening explosion rocked the entire building.

The ground shook, and the air was filled with the thunderous, concussive thud of the explosion that ripped through the upper level of the warehouse. Shards of metal flew in all directions, sending a shower of deadly debris for fifty metres, smashing every window in the warehouse and many of the buildings nearby.

A large piece of steel girder flew through the air and had speared itself through Officer Peck's cruiser.

Dikes and Tran had been partially protected by a metal door they had just passed, which partly shielded them from the blast. The force of the explosion had still thrown them both through several plasterboard walls before violently rag-dolling them into a brick wall two rooms away from the initial explosion.

Because Dikes was still trying to get back into the room to save Sarah at the time of the explosion, he had inadvertently positioned himself in front of Tran and had absorbed the brunt of the blast.

As the rumble of the explosion died down, it was replaced with the loud cracking and groaning of the collapsing interior walls and ceiling sections as they began to crumble inwards.

CHAPTER TWENTY THREE

Dust flew, and debris continued to rain down as Captain Hale, and two SWAT officers forced their way through the holes in the walls made by Tran and Dikes. Careful to avoid any further destruction, Hale cautiously led his team through the debris-covered room, where he heard a groan.

"In here!" he shouted. The officers swiftly slung their weapons and began to shift the rubble, eventually uncovering Dikes and Tran.

Dikes was severely injured, and his clothes were badly burnt; the left side of his body was cut and charred, with some of his clothing having melted onto his forearms. The rest of him was covered in dust and blood, and Hale wasn't able to properly assess his injuries. Thankfully, Tran was in better condition and quickly regained consciousness.

"Akeno, it's okay; I got you - we've got you," Hale said, helping Tran gently to his feet. "You look damn good for a man that just got blown up."

Tran didn't hear the comment because his ears were still ringing. Wincing at the cut on his head and then the one across his ear, Tran replied loudly, "No, it's okay, I'm okay, Captain. Just get Dikes."

The SWAT team carefully lifted Dikes and rushed him out of the room, pausing only to glance at the fifteen-meter hole in the side of the building.

"You sure you're alright, kid?" Hale asked, making sure Tran understood him this time. "That's one hell of a thing to survive." He gestured with a nod at the gaping hole.

Tears pricked at Tran's eyes, so he bit his bottom lip and gave Captain Hale a nod. With Hale's help, he followed the SWAT officers as they carried Dikes along what was left of the hall and down the stairs to a waiting stretcher. As they wheeled Dikes towards the ambulance, someone shouted, "Wait! We have another officer down here. Wait!"

Two officers rounded the corner of the warehouse, carrying an unconscious Joe. His police uniform was singed and tattered, and the severity of his injuries almost mirrored Dikes'.

Medics ran up with a gurney, quickly placing Joe onto it. He was bleeding badly from his finger stump, and his face and his left shoulder were severely burned. A medic checked Joe's vitals and then applied a wad of gauze to his gushing finger wound.

An unconscious Joe and Dikes were both placed in the same ambulance, side by side, as the medics attended to their respective wounds.

With a loud chirp of its siren, the ambulance flashed its lights and sped away.

Tran, limping and with Smith and Hale's support, watched in silence as the ambulance raced away with lights flashing and sirens blaring.

Chief Bryant moved out and joined them. "I cannot believe you're still alive, son," he said to Tran as he placed a caring hand gently on his shoulder.

"Honestly, neither can I," Hale said, awestruck. "You should have seen it up there! The fact that they were passing that metal sliding door when they were-" he shook his head. "Incredible."

Tran turned to gaze up at the smouldering warehouse as he massaged the back of his head, wincing.

The chief's eyes followed Tran's up to the smoking warehouse.

"At least he got his," the chief said sternly.

* * *

At the Jadestown City Hospital, the ambulance carrying Dikes and Joe came to a sharp but controlled stop in the emergency stopping bay. A medical team was ready and waiting as the doors were flung open.

Dikes was wheeled out first, and the team of doctors and nurses immediately began examining his many injuries as he was pushed into the hospital.

Doctor Johns, the principal doctor, took a close look at Dikes' arm and then started shouting instructions.

"If we're going to save that arm, we need to get him into the theatre now. Don't hold him in triage. Margret, what's the wait time?" he asked the nurse at the red emergency phone mounted on the wall.

Pulling the phone away from her ear, she slammed it down and exclaimed, "No answer from either theatre one or two, doctor! I'm going to run up and find out." With that, she was already running for the elevators.

Dikes' eyes fluttered, and he managed to stay conscious for a few seconds.

As they waited for the elevator doors to open, Doctor Johns injected Dikes in his severely injured shoulder, which, even in his current state, made him flinch.

"I apologise, sir," Doctor Johns said in a soothing voice. "I needed to numb you quickly so that we can attend to your arm and leg."

One nurse was inserting Dikes' cannula while another two were carefully cutting away the burned and melted fabric from his right shoulder and arm, while Doctor Johns and another nurse attended to his severely damaged right leg.

With great effort, Dikes managed to open his one good eye, the world in front of him swaying and blurring in and out of focus as his damaged brain slowly rebooted. He could not remember where he was or why he couldn't move, yet one face and the name were etched into his mind: Joe.

Desperately, Dikes tried to make his body obey his mental commands, to form words and communicate his questions, yet the head injuries he had sustained over the past two days left him unable to do so.

Just then, Joe's gurney was wheeled in and placed right beside him, directly in Dikes' eye line.

At the sight of the killer being so close, Dikes' eye flared with rage. Despite the oxygen mask covering his face, Dikes could detect the smug expression on Joe's face as he stared unashamedly at him.

Suddenly, another doctor burst in, inquiring, "Johns, where do you want me?"

"This one!" Doctor Johns replied as he pointed at Joe, "he's suffered a partial amputation of the left index finger, third-degree burns, lacerations to the upper body, and a possible broken collarbone, and we think he also has a severe concussion. Which is why we think he's being so calm," Doctor Johns responded.

Dikes, groggy from the drugs that had just been administered to him, struggled to keep Joe's face in focus. With an outstretched arm, he attempted to reach for Joe before his vision and mind began to inevitably betray him and allow him to slip into unconsciousness. All Dikes wanted to do before then was to grab Joe and tear his head from his shoulders.

One of the nurses kindly took Dikes' arm and placed it back by his side. "Your partner's going to be fine, darling. He'll be going into theatre at the same time as you." She gave him a warm smile, indicating her reassurance.

Dikes gritted his teeth and, despite his inability to properly control his body, still tried to speak to warn everyone of Joe. Unfortunately, his effort was futile and only made him feel more nauseous.

As he glared at Joe, a single tear rolled from his only open eye.

Joe remained silent and composed, his blinks slow and measured.

To Dikes' spinning head, it felt as if Joe was somehow in control of the entire situation and everyone here was just part of another one of his schemes.

I need to stop him! Dikes thought.

With his last ounce of strength, Dikes painfully reached out and grasped Joe's oxygen mask. He let out a groan of agony as he pulled the mask from Joe's smug face.

The nurse quickly intervened, taking Dikes' hand away and gently placing it by his side. "Let's try to keep your heart rate down, okay?" she said in a soothing tone. All the while, Joe stared at him with a cold, calculating expression.

Dikes grumbled indignantly and incomprehensibly under his breath as he glared menacingly at Joe.

"He'll be just fine," the nurse said reassuringly as she injected Midazolam into Dikes' IV.

Dikes' eyelids fluttered as he felt himself growing drowsy; it felt as if he had been enveloped in a warm, comforting blanket as he felt himself drifting into unconsciousness.

Suddenly, a voice cut through the silence. "Sir, can you hear me? Damn it, he's going into hemorrhagic shock!" Doctor Johns yelled.

Joe observed the scene unravelling beside him with a feeling of serenity as Dikes' body began to shake and tremble. Finally, with a look of contentment, Joe's gaze slowly shifted away from the spectacle, and his head tilted back towards the ceiling.

CHAPTER TWENTY FOUR

<u>18 HOURS LATER.</u>

Fully bandaged and connected to various machines, Dikes lay motionless, surrounded by Doctor Johns, the commissioner, Chief Bryant, Tran, Smith, Hale, and the mayor.

It was a terrible sight, seeing Dikes with tubes running from his body to the machines, pumping necessary fluids in and out and breathing for him.

Doctor Johns pushed several buttons to check particular vitals before addressing the group.

"We had to put him in a medically induced coma to help his body heal from the extensive wounds and burns he'd sustained. It should only be for the next twenty-four to forty-eight hours. We're giving his body a chance, especially his brain, to recover without having to perform invasive surgery. But there's no guarantee," the doctor warned grimly. "We just have to wait and see."

The commissioner inquired, "What about his arm and leg?"

"We've done all we can for him, for now. But honestly, what lies ahead is a long and painful journey of skin graphs and operations. I'm not going to lie to you; like all burn victims, his immediate future will be filled with a lot of pain and suffering, both mental and physical. Now, I know that he lost everyone in the explosion, so it's going to fall to you all to be there for him every step of the way. Give him time, give him support, and most of all, give him hope. Just be there for him, or no amount of our medical intervention will be enough."

Chief Bryant's jaw tightened as he gazed down at the heavily bandaged Dikes. "We will do whatever it takes to make sure you recover," he vowed.

"What about the sergeant?" the mayor asked.

"Fortunately, the other officer is faring better; while he did lose a finger, a lot of blood, and skin from his back and shoulder, he'll be making a strong recovery," the doctor replied, glancing at the police officers.

"Have we found out which precinct the Sergeant is from yet?" the commissioner asked Chief Bryant. "I'm sure his family is anxiously awaiting any news of his recovery."

"Not yet, sir," Bryant replied, his gaze fixed on Dikes, his best detective and close friend. "We had a lot of people out there; we're just waiting for a roll call from Central."

"Alright, I want armed units to guard these two until they're discharged," the commissioner ordered. "If that murderer somehow survived the explosion," he raised his hands before anyone could interject. "I know, I know, as unlikely as that scenario is, I want these boys looked after. I don't want him getting within a block of here if he gets the idea to finish the job. And this goes without saying, but no press either; I don't want a single picture taken of either of them while they're in here. And all visitors must be approved by me," he said sternly.

"Yes, sir," Chief Bryant said, then looked back at Dikes.

"You give him whatever he needs, Chief. I mean it, whatever he needs," the commissioner commanded. Chief Bryant nodded, still not taking his eyes off Dikes.

Down the hall from Detective Dikes' room, through a set of double doors, sat an empty chair in front of a closed door. Behind the closed door was an empty room, the curtains of which flapped gently in the morning breeze. On the floor of the room's running shower, stripped down to his underwear, was the body of the policeman who had been assigned to guard the room. His throat had been cut. The water was running red with his blood as it swirled and circled the drain.

TO BE CONCLUDED

www.ingramcontent.com/pod-product-compliance
Lightning Source LLC
Chambersburg PA
CBHW020123180626
46810CB00014B/2109